MISS CALCULATION

ANNIE HOLDER

www.annieholder.com

Proverbs 7:5;

That they may keep thee from the strange woman,

from the stranger which flattereth with her words…

ONE

At the Blackjack table, an elegant, middle-aged woman curls a ringlet of hair around one manicured fingertip and flirts shamelessly with the dealer. He doesn't know if she means it, or whether she's teasing him for her own amusement. She's good-looking, obviously rich; it's nice to be flattered – but there's something in her eyes he finds unsettling, as if they are a curtained window behind which quite another character secretly flits. Across the room, at the bar, an urbane, silver-haired man watches the woman unblinkingly.

"Faites vos jeux, Messieurs-Dames; faites vos jeux…"

Lurking on the fringe of the gaggle around the adjacent Roulette Wheel, a nondescript figure observes them both. He is known to one, but not the other. He is a friend of neither. He has waited a long time for an opportunity as propitious as this.

****

Stupid tourists, or bloody kids! Pompier Gregoire Laçon irritably shifts the small extinguisher he carries from one hand to the other and shuffles wearily, his heavy boots leaving deep imprints in the sandy pink soil. The heat rising from the sun-baked ground lifts the hairs on the back of his neck, making the skin tingle. The chirruping cicadas sound like a million carnival maracas all shaking at once. Gregoire drops moodily into a gully, the land rippled like a fold in a tablecloth, from where the barely-discernible trail of smoke curls lazily into the cloudless summer sky. A scent tantalises. His brain tells him it's barbecue, insides gurgling at the thought of spit-roasted pork dripping fat onto glowing embers. All thoughts of hastily-abandoned luncheon vanish as he crests a gentle rise. There's a fire all right, but not of the kind Gregoire's been expecting.

Horrifically burned down to tendon and sinew – faceless and unidentifiable – the barbecue smell is explained; incinerated flesh competes for supremacy in his revolved nostrils with the astringent, cleansing perfume of pine. Gregoire's empty stomach rolls and he belches bile, swallowing rapidly and instinctively taking several steps away from the sight. He can only tell that the figure lies on its back because what's left of the arms are drawn up in front of the remains of the face as if attempting a fruitless defence. Hiccupping with shock, Gregoire fumbles his mobile 'phone from his pocket, and rings for help.

****

Marc Pickford lurches to a sitting position, the urge to vomit uncontrollable. He's tethered – handcuffed – by the left wrist. He can only get away as far as his stretching arm will allow, so that is where he's forced to kneel, a pool of acidic liquid spreading back across the flagstone floor towards him. Eventually, the heaving stops and he slumps back against the wall, swimming head throbbing. It's dark, but there's enough light for him to see the glint of the metal cuff fastened around what might be a water pipe, running vertically from floor to ceiling. He tugs with all his might, but there's no loosening either the cuff or the plumbing. To the right of him is a bowl, the surface of which glistens in the dimness. He dips in a tentative fingertip, touching it to his lips. It's water – thank God! He shuffles across, takes a generous scoop, swills it around his stale mouth, and again spits it as far away from himself as he can manage.

You hear about this stuff all the time; valuable members of influential families being kidnapped for ransom – but who is he trying to kid? If he's been snatched for profit, then they've picked the wrong son. His elder brother Geoffrey is the prized heir. He's just the inconvenient spare. Dad'll never pay to get him back! He does remember the chap in Antigua, but can't recall a name, a face; only recollecting his unconfined joy on being told he's to be returned to England with immediate effect! Walking to the man's official-looking car, appreciating the cool of the air conditioning after nearly four years in a sweatbox Caribbean jail, gratefully accepting the proffered bottle of drink, and...?

Disorientated, body sore and aching, he has no idea how much time has passed, and no sense of where he might be. He's not in England, that much is obvious. The air doesn't smell right, and it's stuffy and oppressively hot. Cicadas hum outside, but there's no traffic, and no voices.

Wherever in the world he is, but for a bunch of noisy insects, it seems Marc Pickford is utterly alone.

****

Tammi Rivers chooses a table in the dappled shade of a potted fig, settles in the plumply-cushioned wicker chair, and yawns discreetly behind her paperback. Monaco's all very well for a week or two, but eventually its relentlessness becomes wearing. Further around the coast here, the pace of life seems less frenetic. She can breathe, take stock, bring herself back under control; get a handle on what's real, and what elaborate fiction. Her chosen resort is expensive enough to discourage the hordes, but not sufficiently exclusive to draw unnecessary attention. Amongst the smattering of German, Italian, and English visitors, she can take a little holiday from the neverending psychological pressure of remaining alive and at liberty. Deep in thought, not taking in a syllable of the print over which her glazing eyes swim, the sudden appearance of a waiter makes her jump.

"Pardon, Madame. 'Cosmopolitan', Madame."

He places the distinctive pink cocktail on the table before her, and wipes up a ring of liquid left by a previous glass with an efficient sweep of the napkin draped over his forearm. Confused, Tammi raises a hand to detain him, "Um…wait. I didn't order this drink."

The waiter leans forward and murmurs in conspiratorial tone and halting English, "From Monsieur, Madame. You want I take it away?"

Tammi eases to the right to peer around the young man. On a stool at the bar, body already half-turned towards them – obviously keen to gauge the impact of his overture – is a tall, slim man; deep suntan contrasting with a fashionably-styled upswept quiff of grey hair. He makes expectant eye contact. Expression neutral, Tammi raises one questioning eyebrow, which makes him grin with endearing shyness, and swiftly drop his gaze.

More intrigued than she can rationally credit, and suppressing an immediate, spontaneous smile of her own, Tammi extends a hesitant hand, lifts the cocktail to her nose, and sniffs experimentally. She looks up at the waiter, assuming his comprehension, and hisses, "This is all right, yes? There's nothing funny going on here?"

The waiter beams reassuringly, "Non, Madame; it is ok! Only a…flirtation…you know?"

Tammi doesn't allow her expression to alter, merely muttering, "I see."

"You want I take it away?"

"Non, merci. You can leave it."

"Bien!" The waiter nods in satisfaction, boyish dimples deepening like Cupid himself, and sashays off surefootedly between the tables to serve the terrace's only other occupant – a nondescript individual in a baseball cap, buried in an English broadsheet with a week-old headline.

She turns back to the bar. The silver-haired man still regards her keenly, a look of cautious anticipation on his face. Tammi decides it's most sensible to frighten him off before he gets his hopes up. She lifts the drink illustratively, and challenges witheringly, "Did you see that in a film?"

Unfazed, the target of her sarcasm smiles broadly, and replies in smooth, barely-accented English, "It always works for James Bond."

A snigger bubbles out of her before she can stop it, "Ah, James Bond, that famous feminist. Perhaps not the best role model for the modern man?"

Still grinning engagingly, he stands and walks unhurriedly across to her table with a lithe grace that puts Tammi in mind of a prowling panther, "I disagree. Monsieur Bond always gets his girl, no?"

Tammi chuckles despite herself, dismayed by the rashness of her own behaviour – she's meant to be getting rid of him, not encouraging him! She hears her own voice admit, "I suppose he does…whether she wants him to or not."

He indicates the chair opposite hers, "May I?"

"Be my guest." *What?!*

"Merci."

He sits. His attitude is relaxed, as if she's been placed here purely for his amusement. Tammi isn't sure how this makes her feel. No one spontaneously tries to pick her up – *ever*. She's so good at being invisible until she chooses otherwise, switching the charm on and off at will as anyone else might operate a light. She's grown accustomed to dictating the pace of every encounter, and the reason for it. An excruciatingly-long silence therefore extends until Tammi feels so uncharacteristically awkward she's forced to fill the void, stammering, "Thank you…for my drink…"

"My pleasure. I saw you sitting alone, and I wanted an excuse to talk to you."

Stunned, Tammi blurts, "You *saw* me?" She's supposed to be on holiday…unremarkable, anonymous; certainly not prey for bored men in bars! Perhaps this bland little Mediterranean resort is the wrong place to be after all? Should she just have stayed in Monte Carlo, counting cards and picking pockets?

"Naturally I saw you."

"But no one ever sees me!"

"I do not believe that for one moment. Personally, I consider you very noticeable."

Tammi massages a sudden, sharp headache pulsing along her right eyebrow. *Noticeable?*

Perhaps inferring he's overstepped the bounds of politeness, the man swiftly clarifies, "I am sorry. It is the wrong word, I think. My colloquial English needs much practice. What I mean is that I noticed you as soon as I arrived, and I wanted an excuse to talk to you...and so I sent the drink. I hope I haven't insulted you. I just wanted a reason to make your acquaintance..."

Tammi is washed over with weariness, the thrust and parry of conversation suddenly too tiring to contemplate. She rubs at her watering eyes. Softly, the man murmurs, "I desire to talk, only to talk...but I have offended you."

"No, no..." Why so anxious to spare this stranger's feelings? "You haven't offended me – not at all. What you've done is surprised me." She sighs heavily. In a small voice, she volunteers the most truth she's uttered in years, "I'm not accustomed to being noticed."

He fixes his brown eyes on hers, and purrs, "Then clearly all Englishmen are fools."

Tammi blushes – she *never* blushes! – agitatedly crossing and uncrossing her legs, jogging the table, spilling a centimetre from both their drinks, and knocking her paperback to the floor. Reaching down to retrieve it, she bashes her elbow on the table leg. Wincing, she jerks upright, and sits with arms clasped protectively across her chest, cradling the bruising elbow and inwardly cursing her suddenly-graceless vulnerability. She lapses into tongue-tied, flamecheeked silence, from which he rescues her with a gentle, "What is your name?"

Tammi weighs up her options and plumps for the prudence she should have adopted in the first place, utilising the name on the only genuine passport in her considerable collection – that of her long-dead twin, "Annelisse."

He extends a slim, tanned hand, "Enchanté, Annelisse; I am Guy." He pronounces it the French way – Gi – with the swift cutting off of the syllable in the back of his throat.

"Nice to meet you."

The hand is warm, dry; long fingers slide smoothly across her knuckles. She experiences the pressure of his hand on her tingling skin a long time after he's released it. Increasingly tight and tense, as if she's a rag being twisted dry between a window cleaner's massive fists, Tammi squirms like a gawky teenager as Guy casually raises his drink in a teasing toast, "To James Bond. My hero." Chestnut eyes twinkle provocatively, and Tammi's hand stutters on the way to her lips, causing the rim of the cocktail glass to clink on her teeth. She clamps her mouth shut without taking a sip.

"You are here on holiday?"

"Um…yes…"

"Have you visited the Riviera before?"

"A couple of times. And you; are you from around here?"

"No, I am from Bruges…but I come here every year. I sail my yacht. It is the greatest freedom to sail. I can go anywhere. No rules, and no bosses, yes?"

"The master of your fate, the captain of your soul…"

This was easier; less disarmingly direct. She could manage this; even enjoy the diversion of it.

"For sure. The whole world becomes my playground."

Tammi, whose furtive and complicated travel arrangements always depend on someone else conveying her from place to place, murmurs enviously, "I can understand the appeal…"

"Total freedom. Not all places enforce the proper regulations by any means…and you can go wherever, whenever. No timetable, no delays, no strikes, no breakdowns. You must only observe and respect the rhythms of the ocean."

She wonders why he's telling her all this, "Sounds divine."

"But lonely…"

Ah. Off the safe territory of politely-impersonal smalltalk, and back to those unwaveringly soulful brown eyes, like a puppy begging for fuss.

Tammi plays for time while her panicked brain races to manufacture a polite escape, "I'm not sure what you expect me to do about that."

"Have dinner with me tonight."

How had they arrived *here* so quickly? She should just say no. Immediately. Thanks for the offer, but you're not my type, Sonny Jim – too suave and manipulative by half. In fact, you're so slippery you remind me of me, and I know I'm definitely too dangerous to have dinner with. In her head, she rehearses, 'Thank you, but I already have plans for this evening…*with my boyfriend…*'

Instead, what comes out of her treacherous mouth is, "Where? I've only just met you!"

"Here, perhaps? A popular restaurant? A good menu?" His eyes slide up and down her body, once, as if he's taking a mental photocopy for future reference, before murmuring, "Many witnesses."

Tammi jerks, disturbed he's read her thoughts so accurately. She instinctively glances across to Mr-Stereotypical-Englishman-Abroad, the only other patron on the terrace, but he's still safely ensconced behind his newspaper.

Guy leans forward, whispering, "One dinner. Warm summer evening, sea breeze, good food, pleasant conversation…my treat. What harm can it do?"

Tammi's heart beats so fast she's breathless. *Harm?* Her brain rehearses every terrifying outcome on fast-forward. She inhales sharply, and pants, "My head says I should decline."

Exuding disconcerting confidence, he folds his arms, cocks his head, and counters, "Yet you don't. I wonder why?"

TWO

Inspecteur Masson opens the bottom drawer of his filing cabinet. Not to put anything away or extract a vital piece of evidence, but so he's got something to rest his feet on. He crosses his heels, squashing the tops of all the folders in the drawer, leans back in his chair, and flicks casually through the photographs on the tabletop, picking up the occasional one and peering at it more closely.

"Right, what have we got?"

Newly-promoted Détective Xavier Hâche grins to himself. He likes Inspecteur Masson. He's reportedly only about fifteen years' older, but there's something paternal in his manner that Xavier finds reassuring. He reaches across their shared desks to the same open file the Boss is riffling through, and slides out the Pathologist's initial report, reading aloud, "Caucasian male, about 6ft 2inches, no way of determining age at this point – "

Masson grunts, "Given he was mostly burnt to a cinder." He dangles the full-frontal photograph of the corpse in languid fingers, "Reminds me of my mother-in-law's cooking…"

Xavier is appalled, convinced Masson shouldn't be talking this way, even in private. He remonstrates hesitantly, aware of Masson's mercurial moods, "Boss…!?"

"Too near the mark?"

"Maybe a bit…?"

"You haven't had her Boeuf-en-Croute," Masson taps a knuckle on the photograph, "It's not a million miles away, you know…"

"Please, sir – the bloke's dead!"

Masson rolls his eyes, and snaps, "Honestly, Détective Hâche, it's a crime scene photograph! If you want to make a go of this promotion, you've got to get used to looking at grisly pictures! It's going to be half your life!"

"I know, sir…but it's bad, isn't it…all charred, and the skin almost gone, and his hands up like that…?"

Masson swigs his cooling coffee, and mutters, "Boxer grip."

"Huh?"

"It's called a Boxer grip. In severe burns cases, the skin contracts, and the arms cross and raise up."

"Oh. Oh…that's sort of a relief, actually. I thought he was trying to protect himself."

Masson glances at the photo again, "A possibility…but that's not the main reason for the attitude of his arms." His index finger thuds onto the picture like an arrow into a target, "This happened because of the fire, not before it."

Xavier nods, eyes flicking distractedly from the report in front of him to the gruesome image uppermost on the pile. Masson studies him closely, and checks their colleagues are well out of earshot before asking, "Are you all right about doing this, because I can get someone else to help me if you'd rather not work it? You can move across to another case, no problem. Christophe could do with an extra hand on those robberies – "

"No, Boss…no. Thanks, but I'd like to work this case."

"Sure you're not going to wobble your lip constantly…'cos that'll get annoying…?"

"I'm sure, sir."

Masson gives him a lengthy stare, then nods decisively, "Good. Ok…look, none of this is nice – that's the job – but it'll be useful experience for you."

"That's why I want to do it."

"I remember the first bad burns case I did. It was all these kids and their grandma who'd died in a house fire. That turned my stomach a bit, I can tell you. The *smell*…"

Masson shakes his head violently to dispel the memory, and turns back to the folder, sparse but for the crime scene pictures.

"No ID on the body – wallet, 'phone, keys?"

"None, sir."

"Obviously no fingerprints. No DNA matches to the database?"

"No, sir."

"So, not a recent offender."

"Probably not, sir."

"What about his clothing?"

"Oh yeah, this bit's interesting. All the labels were cut out."

"What?"

"You know, cut off with scissors, up tight against the hems on everything he was wearing – shirt, trousers, underpants."

"Well, that's funny in itself, isn't it?"

"Not necessarily, sir. Some people don't like labels. My cousin…when he was little, my auntie used to have to cut all the labels off his clothes because he said they rubbed."

"Really?"

"Yeah."

Masson chuckles, "Now, that *is* eccentric! Ok, well our chap's either a weirdo label-phobe, or they've been deliberately removed to prevent us tracing where they come from."

"Surely that's near-impossible anyway?"

"If you're buying your underpants in the local *Rallye*, then maybe…but if you're buying limited edition designer ones…or your stuff's from a shop with only one branch, or if the labels are a foreign brand – that could tell us quite a lot about our mystery corpse."

"I suppose…"

"We can't rule out the possibility they were removed for a reason connected to his death. Make a note of that."

"Yes, sir."

"Right…that's interesting, but it doesn't get us anywhere with identifying him. Anything else?"

Xavier skims the report again, "Only the stuff about his feet."

"*What* about his feet?"

"He was found barefoot."

"Yes…?"

"But that area up there is sand, rock, stones…there's little cacti and other rough-growing plants. It was very hot, so the earth would have been extremely uncomfortable to walk on barefoot…yet the report says there was no damage to the soles of his feet at all. Nothing. Not a scratch. They even say his feet were in very good condition – no hard skin, nails tidy…like he'd been pedicured, or whatever it's called. His feet were as tanned as his lower legs, so he clearly didn't always wear socks and shoes, but this was a man who took very good care of his feet. The report uses the word 'pristine'…apart, obviously, from what happened to them because of the fire…"

"I don't see what you're getting at Xavier."

Xavier's well into his stride, gaining confidence with every syllable, "You can't get a vehicle all the way up to where he was found. It's at least a five-minute walk from the nearest vehicle access. Even the Fire Department four-wheel-drives can't get up there because it's too narrow and rocky – "

"Get to the point."

"He couldn't have driven right up to where he was found, sir! And the report suggests from the condition of his feet he didn't walk it. There are some footprints close to the body, but we don't know if they're connected. Imprints of the soles of shoes, fairly large, probably men's…so, either someone carried him up there…well, who? And why? Or, he walked there himself wearing the shoes that left the prints. But if he did that, then where are they? They wouldn't have been completely destroyed by the fire, because the intensity of the blaze was at the head end…and if he took the shoes off when he got there – "

"Then why weren't they found at the scene?"

"Exactly! The report even specifically mentions the lack of shoes at the scene, given the 'pristine' condition of the bottoms of his feet!"

Masson cups the back of his head in his clasped palms and rocks in his chair, deep in thought, "That's good, Xavier. That's a good spot. Well done. Make a note of that too."

"Yes, sir!" Détective Xavier Hâche makes his notes with confident pride.

"Witnesses?"

"Some guy in the apartments on the opposite hill came out onto his balcony, saw a trail of smoke, shat himself about forest fires, and called the local Brigade."

"And the person who found the body?"

"The luckless Pompier who got called off his lunch break to go up and put it out."

"And that's it?"

"Yep. No one else in the apartment block said they saw anything until a couple of them noticed the Pompier's four-wheel-drive up there around lunchtime. Most of the residents weren't even there – they were at work. We're verifying statements, but so far no one's flagged up as suspicious. They were all where they said they were, and umpteen other people can alibi them."

"What about CCTV?"

"The only good traffic camera with views in both directions is at the base of the mountain road, where it turns out onto the main route into town."

"And that road doesn't only go straight up the mountain; it follows the coast as well…"

"Yes, sir."

"So we've no way of determining the direction of the vehicle even if it turned up the mountain road."

"Not really, sir. You could look for all vehicles that morning driven by one white male…?"

"Except there's a distinct possibility he didn't drive himself up there, Xavier. There's a hefty chance he might have been a corpse in someone's boot!"

"I didn't think of that. I just assumed the fire killed him."

"It might have done. We don't have enough Forensic Pathology yet to know for sure. We at least have to consider that he could have been killed somewhere else, and only taken up there for disposal…"

Xavier shudders, then glances fearfully at the Boss to make sure he hasn't noticed.

Masson rubs aggressively at his face as if endeavouring to wake from a long snooze, "There's enough about this to make it distinctly fishy. Who goes for a stroll in the countryside at the hottest part of a summer day in trousers and a long-sleeved shirt, without their wallet or 'phone…without their bloody *shoes*, for God's sake?! Who do the footprints belong to if not our man? And then there's the labels cut off his clothes. It's just weird! He might be a barefoot-walking, label-hating oddball…or he might be a murder victim!"

"What now, then?"

"Whether it was suicide or murder, our first job is still to identify our crispy chum. Until Forensics can give us any more than is contained in this dispiritingly-thin report, we need to initiate a very routine and boring missing persons enquiry. Whoever that poor, fried fella is, someone is eventually going to notice he's not where he's supposed to be. Maybe he'll default on a payment, fail to call his dear old Mum when he should, or the Postman won't be able to cram another letter in the box? Let's get the ball rolling with an appeal for information – local radio, regional tv. You can handle that, right?"

"Yes, sir."

Masson glances at his watch, "1.15pm. Hmmm... How are the bottoms of your feet?"

"What?"

"Are they 'pristine'?"

"Oh no...Boss...*please.*"

"We're off up the hill to test your excellent theory, Xavier!"

"Why do I have to do it, sir?"

"Because I'm an Inspecteur, and you're not. Come on, get moving!"

****

"Knock, knock!"

Tammi steps gingerly off the pontoon onto the deck of Guy's yacht with a flutter of girlish excitement. She can't recall feeling such bubbling exhilaration in the presence of a man since the clandestine trysts of late teenage.

Guy's groomed head appears in the cabin doorway, handsome face crinkling into a smile that floods Tammi's insides with giddy warmth. Surely she should be beyond this at her age – but there's something about Guy that appeals to her secret, fairytale fantasy of what a man *should* be. Prince Charming: beautiful to look at, exquisitely-behaved, and just rich enough to make life too beguilingly delightful to resist.

"Good morning."

"Too early?"

"No, of course not. I have been for a run already."

"Show-off."

Guy chuckles indulgently. Tammi indicates the canvas bag over her shoulder, "I've brought breakfast!" Her face falls, "Oh…but you've probably already eaten, right?"

"Before my run. Now, I could certainly enjoy…what do you call it? Brunch?"

Tammi beams.

"Don't you want to check if you like what I've brought…before you agree to eat it?"

Guy shakes his head, and shrugs with characteristic Gallic unconcern, "I am sure it will be delicious. Come inside."

He backs away as she advances down the narrow steps to the cool of the cabin, taking her hand to gallantly assist her, and bending to press a lingering kiss onto her cheek as she draws level with him, "It is so thoughtful of you to bring me something."

Tammi trembles all over, eventually summoning sufficient presence of mind to gush, "Well, I owe you more than one meal already…"

Guy winks, "It's not a competition."

"No…but I don't want to be considered a sponger."

"A what?"

"A sponger. Someone who takes but never gives…who soaks everything up and holds onto it like…um…well…a sponge."

"I see."

Tammi places the bag of ingredients on the galley's small worktop, and fidgets self-consciously under Guy's steady stare.

"Annelisse, if I did not want to spend time with you, surely I wouldn't invite you?"

"I suppose not."

"So stop worrying about being a sponge."

"Er."

"What?"

"Not a sponge; a sponge-er."

"You want to speak the rest of the day in French instead?"

"No, because I'm British, and my French is consequently appalling. Don't be so sensitive! You said yourself you wanted to improve your colloquial English."

Guy acknowledges this with a wry smile. Suddenly, Tammi realises what he's said, "Am I staying the rest of the day, then?"

"Up to you. On current progress, it's going to take the rest of the day for you to make this Brunch you've been promising."

Tammi feigns offence, seizing the opportunity to push playfully at his bare chest, "Cheeky! I bring you a special breakfast, and you just pick on me!"

Guy smirks, lights a fragrant, strong French cigarette, and points out, "But I *am* still waiting…"

Tammi rolls her eyes theatrically, and indicates the kitchen, "Can I get on then?"

"The galley is yours…"

"Why, *thank* you!"

Guy opens the slim fridge to one side of her, "Is it too early for a little something?"

He's popping the cork of an expensive white wine.

Tammi glances at her watch, "It's eleven!"

Guy shrugs again; charmingly, exotically European, "We are on holiday!"

He pushes the cool drink into her far-from-unwilling fingers, and clinks his own glass against hers, "Salut."

"Cheers!"

"To Brunch…that I might get to eat sometime before I die…"

"Oh, get out! Go on!" Tammi is laughingly shoving him across the cabin towards the stairs, "Go and swab the decks or something! Shin up the rigging!"

He catches her hand in his own, lifts it to his lips, and kisses it gently, stilling her as immediately and effectively as encasing her in ice. Softly, he asks, "Shall we eat upstairs on the deck?"

Despite the conviction her body is melting away to nothing, Tammi toughs it out, "Why not? It's going to be another scorcher!"

"I will put up the sunshade."

He slides an arm about her waist, bends his head, and whispers in her ear, his warm breath tickling her neck, "Hurry up, so I can look at you some more."

He leaves her at the bottom of the stairs, mouth and eyes open in amazement, immovable as a mannequin in a department store window. It's *never* been like this before.

THREE

"Boss, a bit of good news!"

"We've both been given the rest of the week off?"

Xavier smirks, "Afraid not, sir…but there has been a response to the tv appeal."

"At last…"

"Yeah – Harbourmaster round at Point Miroir…says a bloke's been suspiciously absent from his yacht for a few days…"

Masson grunts humourlessly, "Probably got lucky. If he can afford to moor at Point Miroir, he'll be beating the chicks off with a stick."

Xavier sniggers, "The 'chicks'? Well, it's a missing person, sir…and the timings tie up."

Masson stands abruptly, and starts shoving wallet, keys, and mobile into his pockets, "As it's the only bloody lead we've got, we'd best go and have a chat with him, eh?"

****

"It's down here."

The Harbourmaster marches them briskly along a concrete promenade edged with immaculately-cut box hedging infilled with bright cistus and bougainvillea.

"He was around, you know? Up and down to the café, the shops, the bars…on deck a lot…and then suddenly, he wasn't. I saw the thing on the tv and I thought…maybe…?"

He stops before a considerable vessel – all smooth curves of shining bodywork and gleaming varnish. Even the determinedly-unimpressed Masson can't disguise his envy, "Blimey – that's a nice bit of kit! What would one of those set you back?"

The Harbourmaster appraises it with a practised eye, "North of two-hundred-thousand euros, I expect."

Masson whistles, "Very nice, too…and who's the owner?"

The Harbourmaster hands over the printout he clutches. It's a colour photocopy of a passport scan. Masson peruses it, then hands it on to Xavier, grunting, "Looks like a rich boy, eh?"

Deep tan, dark eyes, clean-shaven, greying hair, sharply-incising cheekbones prominent in a thin, angular face; full, almost sensual lips: a Renaissance sculpture of a man. Xavier skims the details, "Guy Montparnasse…fifties…Belgian… Address?"

"He didn't give one. It's not our policy to request one if the person is an EU citizen and they're living on their yacht, which he certainly seemed to be…until a few days ago, anyway. We take a copy of the passport and keep it on the computer. He was just another wealthy tourist. It's July – the place is awash with 'em!"

Masson nods, "It's fine. We're not criticising your procedures, sir." He glances sidelong at Xavier, doesn't ask permission, but hooks a long leg over the chain clipped in place to indicate a private pontoon. Xavier gets the hint, and instantly follows his lead. The Harbourmaster starts, "Oh! Strictly speaking – "

Masson holds up a hand to stop him, "Just having a little look, sir. You can't call us down and then expect us not to investigate. All we're doing here is the nautical equivalent of walking up someone's garden path to knock on their front door."

Masson strides up the pontoon, and leaps energetically onto the deck of the boat. The Harbourmaster steps forward, mouth opening to protest again. His shins knock and sway the chain barrier. This is sufficient to stay his advance. Given Masson seems impervious to his objections, he looks plaintively at Xavier instead, "Our guests pay a premium to ensure absolute privacy!"

Xavier shrugs apologetically, as Masson bulldozes onward, "Sir, we're police officers! We are duty-bound to investigate your genuine and well-meaning concern about one of your guests. What if Monsieur Montparnasse has been taken seriously ill and is stuck down there in the cabin praying rescue will arrive as soon as he's missed, and you're all too worried about his platinum-plated privacy to go within thirty feet of him?"

The Harbourmaster scowls and fidgets, clearly regretting his earlier public-spirited 'phone call; evidently more concerned to avoid an ear-bashing from his privileged client for allowing the police to board his yacht without permission. What had he expected them to do – show up, buy an overpriced coffee, stand on the dock and stare in admiration, then simply leave again?

Xavier can feel the irritation washing off Masson and buffeting him like the waves against the hull below. The Inspecteur snaps, "*We* are looking for a missing man, and *you* think you've got one – otherwise we wouldn't be here – so why don't you just shelve the sycophancy and let us make sure they're not the same person, all right?"

The Harbourmaster smooths his shiny moustache, and says nothing, glaring venomously at Xavier the moment Masson's intimidating back is turned. To escape the Harbourmaster's icy stare, Xavier clambers inelegantly onto the deck behind his senior officer, who's already advancing towards the cabin door. Masson edges back an inch or two, just far enough to show Xavier that the door is ajar, before reaching forward and knocking intentionally hard enough on its shiny surface to swing it wide beneath his hammering fist, "Monsieur Montparnasse – it's the police, sir! Is everything all right? Your door is open." Masson bends, and sticks his head down into the cabin, "Monsieur Montparnasse – are you quite well, sir? Can you hear me? There's no need for alarm, but we're coming in, sir!"

Masson indicates that Xavier should wait, and advances several steps into the cabin. It's dark down there, all veneer and velour. Xavier can't see much with Masson's gangly frame blocking his view. There's silence for a heartbeat, then Xavier hears Masson exhale one short, sharp, "Shit!"

"Sir?"

Masson's head pops back out into sunlight, hissing, "Signs of a struggle, smashed glass, stuff knocked over."

He pulls latex gloves from a fat wadge in his jacket pocket.

"Get your gloves on and try not to disturb anything. We need to check the forward cabins."

"My gloves are in the car, sir."

Masson shoves the two he's extracted into Xavier's hands, and teases out another pair, "Lesson learned. Unless someone's actually nicking *your car*, that's never where the crime scene is, so that's never where you need your gloves, is it?"

Xavier blushes, "Right."

Masson jerks a derogatory thumb in the direction of the fretful Harbourmaster, "Don't let our officious friend so much as *breathe* near this boat until we've had Forensics down here."

"Ok." Xavier leans over the side and calls to the Harbourmaster, "The cabin door was open, sir."

The Harbourmaster sticks out his neck like a courting pigeon, then cocks his leg over the chain and scuttles down the pontoon, curiosity triumphing over convention. Xavier stops him before he can climb onto the deck, "There's considerable disarray visible inside. For your safety, you need to remain here, off the vessel, while we check the entire boat, please."

The Harbourmaster gurgles, "Disarray?"

"Wait here please, sir…for your own safety."

The Harbourmaster swallows thickly. Sweat glistens in his neat moustache. Confident the man is sufficiently unnerved to obey, Xavier turns and follows the Boss down the stairs into the cabin.

The interior is luxurious – and a mess. Broken glass crunches under their shoes, and squeaks into the thick pile of the carpeting as they tiptoe towards the sleeping quarters. Red wine stickily stains walls, floors, and upholstery.

"You know what this reminds me of?" whispers Xavier.

"What?"

"One of those boats drug dealers have in films. You know, the ones where there's always a hideous slaughter right at the end? A lot of red blood on white carpet."

Masson stops and gapes at him incredulously, "Now, why would you go and say a thing like that at a time like this?"

Xavier shrugs sheepishly, "It just popped into my head."

"Right, when we get to the bedrooms, we'll swing open the doors and get back against the wall, in case Montparnasse has been watching the same films as you. That way, if he is behind a door with a .44, he'll be shooting it into empty space – all right?"

Masson shakes his head irritably, and starts to creep off again. Xavier catches at his elbow, mouthing, "Boss, should we be calling for some sort of support?"

Masson rolls his eyes, "And look like a right pair of dickheads when there's nothing here but dead wasps and stale baguettes? No, we can deal with this…just *exercise caution*, Détective, that's all."

"Yes, sir."

At the first door, they stand either side, backs pressed to the wall. Masson reaches across, whacks down the handle, shoves the door powerfully inward, and leaps away from the anticipated gunshot. Nothing happens. Hearts thudding, both inch their heads around the open door. An empty cabin, bed made. Masson slips into the room, silently pointing Xavier towards the sliding closets, himself zipping over to the open bathroom door, leaping around it to land in an aggressive squat in the centre of the tiny space like a Maori warrior performing a Haka. Xavier chortles under his breath, quite forgetting he's supposed to be 'exercising caution', and carelessly pushes the closet door. It slides soundlessly on metal runners, the only noise the gentle clack of hanging garments rocking together in the displaced air.

Masson mouths, "Anything?"

"Nothing."

Masson points across to the other cabin, "That one. Same procedure."

"Ok."

A repeat of the pantomime on the opposite side of the boat reveals another well-appointed, empty cabin, identical but for the absence of personal possessions.

Masson exhales lengthily, "Good. That could've been a lot worse."

He lopes back into the main cabin, "One toothbrush. One razor. All men's products in the bathroom, all men's clothing in the wardrobes. One minted Belgian bloke, on his yacht, enjoying the Riviera."

The Inspecteur scowls.

"What's up?"

"Well, you don't smash up your own fancy boat, do you? Especially not if you're living on it! And where *is* he? Look at how tidy everything is – shoes lined up, shirts all pressed…" Masson lifts out a shirt at random, and hooks his finger under the label at the neck, "Hmmm?"

Xavier grins, "*Not* a label-phobe."

"No…and this is expensive stuff. Classy gear, spotless bathroom, pathologically neat…and then *that*, next door – that *chaos*!"

"Do you think he's our fella, sir?"

"It's not for me to say. Let's get the Cavalry down here to pick this place apart. We need to thoroughly interview the very twitchy

Harbourmaster, any other members of his staff, and the people on the boats to either side of this one. If they've got CCTV here that covers the Marina, we want to look at it – from the date this Montparnasse guy arrived until the moment we turned up. We need to get onto the Belgian police and find out if he's got a record there, or if anyone's reported him missing."

Xavier, scribbling notes like a shorthand secretary, waits for the Boss to draw breath, and asks, "Which should I do first?"

"Get the crime scene team down here, and stick someone from Uniform the other side of that seriously-impenetrable three feet of chain to repel all comers. When the scene's secure, get door-knocking. All the boats close-by. How long have they been here? Where have they come from and where are they going? Did they notice our man? Did they speak to him? Did he have visitors? Do they remember hearing any altercations around the date of our hill-fire discovery? Don't steer them – just get 'em talking and see what comes out."

"Ok. What are you going to do, Boss?"

"I'm going to grill the Harbourmaster, and get him to show me every bit of CCTV footage he's got." Masson peels off his gloves and squints into the bright Mediterranean sunlight, "There's a camera…and another over there, see? Let's hope they're working. I want a good look at Monsieur Guy Montparnasse… Something about this shiny setup feels too good to be true. Where are the photographs of his travels? Where are the mementos of the places he's been? Where's his tat? Everyone accumulates a bit of tat, don't they? We've got a whole pile of it in the corner of our kitchen! This place is like a Show Home. It stinks, Xavier…and I can't put my finger on why."

****

"Sir! Sir!" Xavier skids to a halt in front of Masson's desk, panting and red-faced.

"You all right?"

"Yes, sir!"

"You look as if you're about to have a heart-attack."

"Breakthrough, sir! *Massive* one!"

"What?"

Xavier pushes a folder at him, and gabbles, "*Two* clear sets of prints off the boat! All over the deck, the living areas…but not the bedrooms. Just one set in there."

"Ah…good…and?"

"Interviews with other boat-owners at the marina say there's been a woman around regularly for the last couple of weeks or so."

"Oooh…this *is* getting better! Anyone able to ID her?"

"No sir, not of the people we've spoken to so far – but their descriptions match well enough for us to believe they're all talking about the same person – and she seems to have been his only visitor."

"Great, Xavier! That's a step forward. Another player on the stage."

"That's not the breakthrough, sir."

"No?"

"No." Xavier's hands are shaking. He takes a deep breath, and explains, "Both sets of prints were run through the computer, sir. One didn't generate any hits at all. The other threw up a major flag."

"Which is?"

"Highly classified. Immediate call to the National Crime Agency in London."

"Well I never! Our Monsieur Montparnasse *is* a naughty boy, then? I *told* you it stank, Xavier!"

"No, sir; it's not Montparnasse. It's the woman!"

FOUR

"Julian."

"Blair!" Sir Julian Franklin grasps the visitor's hand in both his own as if greeting him fulsomely, instead yanking him sharply across the threshold, and swiftly closing the door behind them, "Should you be here?"

"Are we recorded in here, Julian?" Sir Blair Stocker-Pickford's eyes roam the wood-panelled walls, the deep mahogany bookshelves, the ornately-plastered ceiling.

"No, of course not." Sir Julian steers the unwelcome arrival to sofas placed in a dim corner furthest from the huge windows. "Sit down. What's happened? You look...*troubled.* Drink?"

"Bloody hell, yes!"

Sir Blair snatches the cut-glass tumbler from Sir Julian's grasp and, still standing, polishes off the contents in one gulp, gasping, "Talisker?"

"Of course."

"The good stuff," breathes Sir Blair, flopping onto the indicated sofa as if his thick legs can no longer hold him up. Sir Julian refills the glass with another generous measure, seats himself slowly on the opposite couch, and asks, "What's happened? It's highly unwise for you to be here, like this, unannounced – "

"My son's been moved, Julian, and no one can tell me where, or – more to the point – *why*…"

"Moved…?"

"At your instruction?"

"Blair, how can you ask me such a thing?"

Cold dread drains the colour all the way from Sir Julian's ruddy cheeks to his Savile Row collar, as Sir Blair growls, "Because I've made enquiries of my own, Julian…and one of *your* chaps did it. I'd like to know on whose bloody authority."

Before Sir Julian can respond appropriately, Blair bursts forth again, "Nightingale! You assured me he was working for *us*! He's supposed to be looking for Rivers, not moving my son from his secure location and taking him God-knows-bloody-where! The cocky little bastard didn't even bother to hide his identity. Reportedly, he turned up at that Antiguan prison where Marc's been, well, not comfortable exactly, but at least secure for the last three years – and just removed him! He had all the correct paperwork, Julian! By order of Her Majesty's Government, for God's sake! Is this your doing?"

Sir Julian uses a question as his answer, "If he was doing something covert, your 'enquirers' would never have been able to discover what went on, would they – still less the identity of the agent involved? He must have had a good reason, Blair."

"Well, what reason? You must know, Julian! When did you last make contact with him?"

Sir Julian lies smoothly, "He's in deep out in the field. He makes contact with us, not the other way round."

"I thought you had control over him! How can you be certain he hasn't gone rogue?"

"I've already answered that question, Blair. You'd never have been able to discover Marc had been moved if Nightingale was doing anything less than his job. Rivers must be threateningly close, or he would have left Marc where he was."

"I want to know where my son is, Julian! I don't trust your Agent Nightingale. I want to know if he's still working for The Cabal, or if he's taken it into his head to freelance for the highest bidder!"

"It's Nightingale's job to track Rivers, Blair. That's been his sole remit for nigh-on twenty years – to bring her back in from the cold."

"I take it he doesn't know why?"

"Of course not! He has his orders, and he is duty-bound to obey them."

"I detest this softly-softly rot, Julian! That upstart little bitch needs to be made to *pay*!"

Sir Julian clears his throat and speaks with measured authority, "Blair, you no longer have autonomy here, and you know it. We *all* have significant amounts tied up in those funds. We *all* want our investments back. Rivers is our only route to that money, and we know how volatile she is, how dangerous to *all* of us – not just to you. She won't hesitate to go public again if we attempt to tighten the screws before first safely securing her somewhere she cannot escape. Look what damage she did to your family reputation the last time she was put under pressure! One son disgraced; his political career over just when he was being touted for a promotion to Cabinet! The other imprisoned thousands of miles away from home, awaiting extradition on fraud charges we've only been able to bury in a mire of red tape because we've got the right people on our side – otherwise he'd already be back under oath in an English courtroom, and plenty more of your family's dirty laundry would be getting an airing in the gutter press! She took down both your sons, Blair…and that was just her shot across the bows! You know it! You'll be next! And with you, down falls our *whole* House of Cards!"

Sir Blair's left eyelid twitches spasmodically, and Julian feels spiteful pleasure at his discomfort. The bullying old bastard has to accept The Cabal is no longer a dictatorship.

"Your vote carries no more weight than anyone else's any more. It was you who allowed Rivers so far into the fold. You did nothing to prevent your idiot son dumping her at the altar. If he'd married her, you'd still have the absolute control you so desperately want – "

Sir Blair erupts spectacularly, "God's Blood, man, you were the one who thrust her under my nose in the first place, assuring me she'd be the ideal candidate to manage our little 'experiment'!"

Outwardly unaffected by the Peer's fury, Sir Julian purrs complacently, "And so she has been, Blair. You can't deny her effectiveness. She's managed it all superlatively for over two decades. She's controlled it all *so* well, and kept it *so* secret, not even *we* know where our money is."

"I've had enough! I want her found! I want our funds located! I want control! I want that little bitch destroyed for what she's done to my family! I want *satisfaction*!"

"And you'll get it, Blair. We've held on this long. Our money is safe. Our secret is safe. Let Agent Nightingale do his job."

"It's taking too long, Julian!"

"Seventy-two hours, Blair…that's all she took to destroy the lives and reputations of both your sons. Remember that. Next time, she'll come after all of us. *I'm* not going down simply because *you* can't keep your temper! You weathered the last storm. It tainted your boys and you escaped unscathed. Do you honestly think you'll come back from the next one? They'll toss us in prison and throw away the key – "

"I'd rather die!"

"Let me do my job, Blair, and I can assure you it won't come to that."

"I want to know where my son is, Julian."

"And you will receive that information when the time is right. Just trust me. You *must* hold your nerve! We're playing the long game, here."

"I'm not getting any sodding younger, Julian."

"She cannot get access to any of the money without all our authorisation codes, and without Marc's presence in person. A master-stroke on your part, Blair, and one I cannot praise highly enough."

Sir Blair snorts derisively, and grunts, "It keeps us all honest, eh Julian?"

"That's why we can relax. She can't steal our money! Nightingale must have moved Marc because he was concerned Rivers was close. You know as well as I do that once she has Marc, she has leverage."

"And what's to stop her making a deal with your Nightingale…offering him a third of what should be ours!"

"Blair, you're not thinking straight. She needs our authorisation codes – every one of us – or she can't get a penny. Once Nightingale has her, secret and safe, *then* we can begin to exact the revenge you crave. Until I receive word his mission is complete, you simply have to wait, Blair. We all do. That's all there is to it."

Sir Julian stands, walks to the huge, heavy office door, opens it wide, looks very pointedly at the still-seated figure of Sir Blair Stocker-Pickford, smiles with formal and false politeness for the benefit of his secretary in the ante-room beyond, and says, "I'll be in touch."

Sir Blair absorbs the affront with a straightening of his broad back, and a lofting of his chiselled chin. Placing his glass carefully on the table at his elbow, he takes his time standing up and haughtily crossing the room. Drawing level with Sir Julian, he tries to deliver a menacing stare, but the telling tic still jumps and flutters his left eyelid. Stocker-Pickford is petrified, and Julian privately knows he has every right to be. He watches Blair stalk stiffly down the corridor towards the lift, and directs a question at his secretary, "Jessica, where's Agent Valentine?"

Jessica clicks and scrolls her computer mouse, "Should be in the building, Sir Julian."

"Find him, would you? I need a word."

"Any time more convenient for you, Sir?" She's flicking through the pages of his appointments diary (he's never been persuaded to convert to the electronic version).

"Yes," says Sir Julian Franklin with quiet force, "*Now*, if you would be so kind."

****

Standing before his office window, he does not register the majesty of his city view; body taut as the tightrope he's walked for twenty-five years – between legal and illegal; perception and reality; duty and desire. Originally infiltrating The Cabal as an undercover operative, the deeper he burrowed, the more the boundaries blurred.

What troubles Sir Julian Franklin most is that *he* hasn't told Nightingale to move Marc Pickford from his Antiguan jail cell. He can't be hearing intelligence of this magnitude from the likes of Stocker-Pickford! If Nightingale truly has – how had Blair put it – "taken it into his head to freelance," what then? Where does that leave the unimpeachable reputation of one of Britain's most influential men?

Sir Julian Franklin *needs* Tammi Rivers; either her sworn testimony – the damning evidence in her sole possession – or else the permanent stopping of her toxic mouth.

Under oath, Tammi can prove it all…and Sir Julian's not sure how it'll play in the corridors of power.

An old University friend of Julian's had scouted Rivers from the Cambridge ranks and recommended her to the Service. At twenty-one, she'd met Julian privately in her Tutor's office, stared him down with steely determination, failed to crumble under persistent and concerted pressure, and flatly refused to be directed by anything other than her own judgement. She didn't want to work for the British Government. She didn't want to sign the Official Secrets Act. She didn't mind helping him out now and again…but only if he promised something in return. They came to an arrangement, but plain old Julian Franklin as-was left the hallowed halls red-faced at his ready capitulation. Tammi wanted a leg-up, a means to leapfrog her competitors and kick-start her career. Her strategic placement in the Stocker-Pickford empire had been Julian's idea. If anyone could interpret the data in front of her, it was Tammi Rivers. If identification of anomalies was required, Rivers was your girl. Sir Julian could now see she'd never been 'his girl'. He'd wilfully mislead himself believing he'd ever had control over her. A young man from a comfortable background, he hadn't fully understood the lure of privilege to a girl from straightened social circumstances. Tammi Rivers' innate brilliance opened many doors, but it could never expunge the stain of her class. Only a suitable marriage could do that. Marc Pickford, the youngest son, foolish and easily-manipulated, had proved too tempting a forbidden fruit; too ripe for the plucking…

Julian had viewed even this seismic upset with a degree of optimism. As he cultivated the crooked father, so he hoped Tammi Rivers would work on the suggestible son. Nightingale, one of his most-talented junior operatives, was deputed to handle Rivers, as Sir Julian made all the right contacts and romped up the career ladder with indecent haste (it did one's promotion prospects no harm to be embedded within the British Establishment's most fraudulent secret society). Unfortunately, if the Service had one failing at the time, it was to persistently recruit posh boys from ancient public schools. Women were a mystery to them, for the most part. Nightingale, as pompous and upper-class as all the rest, fatally underestimated Tammi's considerable capabilities. He failed to keep her on a sufficiently-tight rein. It suited Sir Julian to blame Nightingale for this, even though it was highly unlikely he'd have done much better if the job had still been his. When the idiot Pickford son abandoned Rivers at the altar, she vanished, and took with her everything she knew. Not only concerning The Cabal and its high-profile members – the spectacular unmasking of whom was to be the defining triumph of Julian's burgeoning career – but also with categorical and quantitative proof of the questionable depth of his own involvement. There's undercover, and there's rogue. Sir Julian Franklin can't accurately recall which he is any more. Upstanding public servant, scourge of corruption; a tireless, justice-seeking hero across forty years…or, in a court of law – with Rivers on the stand speaking her powerful, evidential truth – a double-dealing villain as vile as those he purports to pursue?

If he can once again lay his hands on the money Rivers secretly manages on behalf of The Cabal, will he realistically turn his back upon a true fortune to bring down all those who have raised him to the exalted heights he occupies today, or is it simply too late for that? How deeply in is too far? When do you cease to be the person you were, and become the fabrication you never intended to be?

FIVE

Sir Julian glances over the top of his glasses at Agent Valentine, who sits calmly before his desk, awaiting instructions. He flicks through Valentine's file, underlines a couple of sentences, pushes the cap onto his expensive fountain pen, places it prissily-perpendicular to his desk blotter, and beams genially, "Agent Valentine. I see from your file you don't get much field work?"

"No Sir. I'm asked to do analysis most of the time."

"Your aptitude tests are off-the-scale, Valentine. The Number One in your department seems extremely satisfied with your performance. He says your interpretation of evidence is, and I quote, "unerringly accurate". You enjoy analysis-work?"

"I do, Sir, yes…I like the challenge of solving a mystery…getting to the truth, Sir."

"The excitement of active service in the field holds no appeal for you, then?"

"I didn't say that, Sir…it's simply the jobs I tend to get given are more theoretical than operational, Sir."

If Valentine is at all perturbed by being summoned at speed from his second-floor cubicle to the Director's palatial office, he's hiding it impressively.

"Do you have a use for me in the field then, Sir?"

"Your very particular skillset is a match to a current requirement we have, Valentine, yes."

"Ah…that's interesting, Sir…"

"Your analytical mind, your fluent French…the Service finds itself in urgent need of this exact combination."

"In what respect, Sir?"

"Have you heard of Nightingale?"

The merest hint of a frown fleetingly darkens Valentine's even features, "Purely through myth and anecdote, Sir. I've never met him."

"He is quite a few years older than you – and he's spent most of his life out in the field. He's one of our most notable deep-cover operatives."

"Do you need me to provide him some sort of functional backup, Sir?"

"In a manner of speaking, Valentine. I regret I can't give you the full s.p. This is highly-classified. It's of interest at the very highest echelons of Government – "

"Extremism, Sir?"

Sir Julian doesn't answer, merely giving Valentine the sort of dirty look that should stop him interrupting again, "Nightingale was tracking a witness who is required to give evidence in the UK against some very dangerous people. At one time, she was willing. Now, she's not so sure she wants to return home, even though she is a British citizen."

"*Was* tracking, Sir?"

"Sorry?"

"You said '*was* tracking', implying he's not doing it any longer."

Sir Julian clears his suddenly-gravelly throat, "Recently, Nightingale's been in Monte Carlo. This suggests his quarry is close by, but we've had no confirmed contact. For me…us…not to hear from him is…uncharacteristic, Valentine. Yesterday, French police on the Côte d'Azur called us, thinking they were contacting the National Crime Agency in response to a flag on the Interpol database. They've got our target's fingerprints at a crime scene. Unfortunately, they've also got an unidentified male corpse…"

"Nightingale, Sir?"

"That's what I want you to determine, Agent Valentine."

"If evidence suggests it's Nightingale, Sir?"

"Then continue your investigation to discover who killed him. The number one suspect must be our reluctant witness, Miss Tamise Rivers, known as 'Tammi'. The French police have a Belgian passport in the name of Guy Montparnasse. Naturally, it's a false ID. You have permission to tell them that when you get there – if they haven't found it out for themselves by then."

"You're *sending* me, Sir?"

"As I said, your particular skillset suits this little mystery very well indeed. The situation is beyond delicate, Agent Valentine. It needs careful on-the-spot handling. There's every chance that body is Nightingale. It would explain the extremely-abrupt severing of normal communications. He is missing, Agent Valentine, and I would like you to find out why."

"Yes, Sir!"

"The fingerprints, plus witness descriptions obtained by French police, place our target on the Riviera within the last few days, and available Intel suggests she's still in France. It is *imperative* she is returned covertly and securely to the UK. At large, she's a considerable security risk…and I cannot stress enough how politically sensitive it could become if the French authorities discover who she really is."

"Wouldn't it be simpler just to terminate her in France, Sir?"

"On no account, Valentine! The information she holds *cannot* die with her! She needs to be returned to the UK for full debriefing. What she knows cannot be discussed with anyone but those of the highest level security clearance. Do I make myself clear?"

"Yes, Sir. Completely clear, Sir."

"If Nightingale is no longer able to complete his mission, you are to take it over. If he's still alive, there is no requirement for you to make any contact with either of them. You will return to the UK and report upon your findings, *directly* to me. You will not discuss this assignment with anyone else, not even your Department Head. I will deal with matters here, in order to release you from your current caseload. If the body *is* Nightingale, find out how he died – because you can bet Tammi Rivers had something to do with it."

"She's capable of that, Sir?"

"She's capable of anything, Valentine. Keep that fact in mind at all times. Use that superb analytical brain of yours to stay alive."

"Yes, Sir. What about the French police investigation, Sir?"

"You will fly to Nice tonight as a Detective Sergeant working for the NCA via Interpol. The French detectives running the case will pick you up from the airport. They're meant to have organised a hotel. Jessica, my secretary, has paperwork that'll cover you. Use your codename as your surname. We have requested you have operational seniority for the duration of the enquiry. You may come up against a bit of posturing from the Frogs already running the case, but brush it aside – this is of national importance! Mention nothing of what we've discussed today. 'Cherchez la femme', Agent Valentine. And be bloody quick about it."

****

Masson picks glutinous brioche from his back teeth and shoves the case folder through the gap in the headrests. Xavier is driving, keeping diplomatically quiet while the two more-senior officers jockey for position. Masson considers this 'his' case, but the suave individual they met off the Heathrow flight last night has seemingly been sent to run it. He looks nothing like any policeman fledgling Détective Hâche has ever seen before – smartly-tailored suit, neat haircut, leather brogues polished to a military shine. Xavier's heard the Brits are terrible at languages, but this policeman speaks French just as well as they speak English. It's useful; it simplifies communication to have two possible ways of making themselves understood. He can even read most of the Pathologist's report, only asking Masson to translate the odd word. It's a surprise. Xavier finds himself having to readdress some long-held and lazy preconceptions about the English in general, and English coppers in particular. The Englishman asks probing, sensible questions in rapid-fire style – a lot like Masson himself. The answers come from the back with equal economy.

"No DNA matches to the databases?"

"None."

"Cause of death?"

"The Forensic Pathology report is in the file."

"I find the medical terms tricky in a foreign language. It'd be quicker if you gave me the lowdown."

Masson acknowledges the irritating common sense of this with a small sigh, "We did at first suspect he may have been killed elsewhere and transported to where he was found for disposal of the body, but the Pathologist's full report confirms death as being from the fire. Apart from minor cuts suggesting involvement in some sort of struggle, there were no fatal wounds, and there was soot in the respiratory tract and airways consistent with smoke inhalation. Also, colouration; the redness on the remaining skin is consistent with carbon monoxide poisoning."

"So, the fire is what killed him."

"Looks like it…but there is a question over circumstances. You see, there's an outside chance it's suicide. Barbiturates were found in the bloodstream…and unswallowed residue in the mouth."

The English cop – Valentine – twists around in his seat to gawp at Masson's lanky frame sprawled across the back seats of the cramped Citroen, "*Un*swallowed?"

"Yes," replies Masson lightly.

"Show me the place."

****

Up on the sun-bleached, wind-scoured hillside, an unseasonable mistral is blowing in, the squall whipping up tiny dust devils that swirl around their feet. Valentine blinks and squints, unaccustomed to the bright sunlight, and pushes on a pair of designer-brand sunglasses. He looks cool despite the increasing humidity of the approaching storm. Masson stands a little aloof, hands in trouser pockets, observing the incomer with intense concentration. Valentine flicks through the case folder with difficulty in the stiffening breeze, "The body was where? Here?"

Xavier looks at Masson, who hasn't moved. Embarrassed by the Inspecteur's offhand manner, he politely indicates the exact spot, "Between these boulders, sir. Head up here, feet down there."

Xavier glances nervously at Masson again, but he's turned away, trying to light a cigarette in the gusting wind.

"One thing of note, sir. We did an experiment. I tried to walk from the car – back there where we parked today – to here, in bare feet. The corpse was found barefoot. I cut my foot within about a hundred metres – and I got thorns and things stuck in them. They were scratched, and even a little bit scalded by the heat of the rock and sand. However, the corpse had no damage to his feet at all…and yet no shoes were found here, sir."

"Suggesting he was carried…? Interesting, Détective Hâche. Thank you."

"No problem, sir."

After a final cursory glance around, Valentine makes his way back up to Masson. Xavier follows. Masson raises his eyebrows enquiringly, "Seen enough?"

"To directly address the suggestion of suicide; if he was brimming with barbiturates and sitting here waiting to die, could he simply have fallen into his campfire?"

"No."

"Because…?"

Masson responds with a degree of relish, ticking off the points on his fingers, "*Because*, if you thoroughly read the file, you'll see there *was* no campfire. The body itself was on fire. Also, he was found on his back. I suspect it's rather hard to fall forward into a non-existent fire when you're chock-full of drugs, and then wriggle into a different position thereafter."

Masson gently wrests the folder from Valentine's grasp and teases out the full-frontal photograph of the blackened corpse. It flaps sharply in the wind until the Inspecteur gets a grip of both ends and holds it up in front of Valentine. The Englishman nods in slow comprehension of what Masson's implying. All three understand it's too early to draw an official conclusion. They can't yet prove what they instinctively already know; that this is murder.

Masson continues, "If you wanted to commit suicide, you'd swallow all your pills – you wouldn't leave some in your mouth."

Valentine agrees, "And why come all the way up here to take your overdose? If it's your chap from the abandoned yacht, then why not off-himself there, in comfort?"

"And the evidence of something untoward at the aforementioned otherwise-fanatically-tidy yacht? If you're willingly swallowing enough barbiturate to kill yourself…?"

"Why smash the place up?"

"Exactly! And if you've already taken pills to do the job, why set yourself alight as well? And, that's damned hard to do, right? And where's the combustible material, the accelerant, the means of ignition, his *shoes*, even!?"

"None of which were present at the scene?"

"None."

"If this corpse and your missing yacht-owner are one and the same, then…" Valentine grins charmingly, and revolves his index finger slowly to indicate all three of them, "I think within the Circle of Trust here, it's safe to assume someone pumped him full of drugs on that yacht, during which there was a struggle. Then the same someone dragged him up here, carried him to this spot to preserve his dainty little tootsies, and set fire to him so he couldn't be identified."

Masson smiles for the first time since clapping eyes on their unwelcome visitor at Nice airport the previous evening, and nods enthusiastic assent, "Bang on, I'd say…and by how quickly the NCA jumped on our 'phone call, our chief suspect is surely the fingerprint hit, yes?"

The self-assured Valentine suddenly looks uncomfortable, "I'm sorry, lads, but this is going to be a bit one-sided, because you're sharing all your evidence with me, but I can't fully reciprocate."

Masson presses on, undaunted, "Contract killing? It's certainly efficient enough to be…" He fixes his shrewd gaze on Valentine's flushed cheeks, and suggests significantly, "But much *slicker* an operation than the usual two-shot ask-no-questions-tell-no-lies approach. A great deal of effort's been taken to ensure our boy's virtually unidentifiable. That's *professionally* thorough...wouldn't you say, *Detective Sergeant* Valentine?"

It's the first time Masson has addressed the English policeman by his official title, and the emphasis is stark. Xavier doesn't understand what the Inspecteur's getting at, but it's certainly discomfiting Valentine. He takes off his tinted glasses and glares very pointedly at Masson, who cocks his head and grins insolently back. At length, Valentine shakes his head, chuckles wryly at the barefaced cheek, and tosses Masson a crumb of information to pacify him, "All right. What can I tell you? Oh yeah, you'll get diddly-squat from the Belgian police."

"Why?"

"Because Guy Montparnasse is a false ID – that much I know for sure."

Masson's lip curls, "Thanks for the tip-off. I find it really helps to speed an investigation to its conclusion if all the officers work together. You could have told us this at the airport last night."

"Sorry..."

"Who *is* he, then?"

"I don't know yet."

"But you've got an inkling, right, or London wouldn't have bothered to send you? DS Valentine, I fully understand the need for some...*discretion* in an ongoing, sensitive enquiry, but if you won't work with me to get my job done, then how can I possibly assist you in yours...and, what's more, why the fuck *should* I?"

Xavier gasps before he can help himself. Both older men turn to stare at him, and he quickly manufactures a coughing fit. Valentine absorbs Masson's perfectly-justified attack with equanimity, responding quietly, "I'm sorry I can't give you more at this stage – but the Belgian angle is definitely a dead end. I can at least assure you of that."

He smiles conspiratorially at Xavier, and admits, "That ID's as fake as my shades…"

Xavier blushes like a schoolboy. The bloke misses nothing – not even a sidelong, envious glance to admire a pair of smart sunglasses! Xavier doesn't know where to look. He finds himself turning to the Inspecteur for reassurance. There's an expression on Masson's face he can't interpret. The Inspecteur drops his spent cigarette butt, grinds it firmly into the sand with his heel, glances at his watch, and claps his hands together commandingly, "Right! That's lunch, I think! Come on, boys…storm's on its way…"

****

When Valentine excuses himself, Xavier snatches his opportunity, "Boss, what were you getting at up there? I didn't understand…"

Masson smiles folornly, checks over his shoulder towards the restaurant toilets, and mutters, "Ever done undercover work? Anti-terrorism…anything like that?"

"No…"

"I was once attached for a few months to a unit dealing with financial crime. Industrial Espionage, they call it – selling secrets on companies and stocks for big money, so investors can clean up. Inside information on when and where to buy or sell – like knowing the Lotto numbers three days before everyone else. A lot of the profits find their way into offshore funds – tax avoidance and the like…or the money props up dodgy regimes in return for business opportunities in untapped or unregulated markets…or it winds up in the coffers of terrorist organisations. The Boston Irish business community historically financing the IRA, that sort of crap. Anyway, the whole place was constantly crawling with a succession of smarmy blokes just like Detective Valentine. They all said they were insurance investigators or actuaries – "

"But they were all cops?"

"No, Xavier, they were all *spies*! If that slicker-than-snot 'Rosbif' is a cop, then I'm Johnny Hallyday!"

Xavier's eyes are round as saucers, "A *spy*!"

"Yep. I'd stake my badge on it. And he's looking for another spy."

"How can you be so sure?"

"Because of a million things! The missing labels in the clothes, for example. I didn't say at the time because I had no evidence – I still don't – but it's fairly common for 'professional' spies to cut the labels out of their clothing, to carry toiletries in plain bottles, to transact entirely in cash, to have ridiculous fucking names…Valentine, for example."

"He *is* English…" justifies Xavier, trying to be fair to the newcomer.

"And he's *not* NCA. He's British Secret Service, I'm convinced of it! He's either here to discover who killed his colleague and why, or he's come to make sure the job's been efficiently done and the true identity of our mysterious Monsieur Montparnasse is never revealed.

You know the two nearest cameras we saw from the deck of the yacht weren't working?"

"Yeah...?"

"Well, Forensics got back to me. With him turning up and all the fart-arsing about, I didn't have a chance to tell you about it...and then I pretty promptly decided I didn't want to discuss it in front of him. Both had been disabled."

"Oh...?"

"No messing. Someone planned that in advance, prepared for it, and got it done without anyone noticing. You know as well as I do, your average burglar just isn't that bright. We are dealing with a *hit* here! A chosen target. Whoever our dead bloke is, he's mixed up in something big – and our English visitor knows that, you can guarantee it."

"What about the woman – the fingerprints on the yacht?"

"A double-agent? Another colleague whose prints were meant to be discovered? Perhaps they were left precisely to trigger the Interpol database flag; who knows? We need to keep a close eye on 'Detective Sergeant Valentine'. If my instincts are correct, he's not here to assist our investigation, Xavier; he's here to hamper it."

SIX

"Sir, they've finally turned up something on the Harbour CCTV – rear gate. The footage is a bit grainy, but it's a woman and man in a little Citroen, plates so smeared with dust and grime you can't read them at all – "

"How convenient. When; the day of the fire?"

"Early hours of the morning before the body was discovered, according to the time stamp on the CCTV. Still dark, but there is a streetlight mounted at the gate that's apparently kept on all night. It's the tradesman's entrance, basically – deliveries, refuse collection, staff parking – all the shit they don't want their fancy-pants guests to see. There seems to be a fair bit of traffic in and out…that's why it took them a while to realise what they were looking at…"

"And what were they looking at?"

"As I said, a man and woman in a little Citroen. Both match the descriptions given by our witnesses for Montparnasse and his bit-on-the-side. He's driving, and she's holding what appears to be a gun against the side of his head."

"Good Lord! You're sure?"

"No, sir, I haven't seen it, but the officer checking the footage sounded pretty certain."

"Well I never! This is like Hansel & Gretel…the trail of breadcrumbs towards the most obvious and easy-to-solve murder I've ever worked on! Doesn't it feel like that to you, Xavier, as if we're being led by the nose to the conclusion someone wants us to reach?"

"Can't stuff sometimes just be how it seems, sir?"

Masson smiles bleakly. It makes Xavier feel about ten years' old; back in the kitchen asking his mother why his father always has to work so late when everyone else's Dad comes home for dinner, and Maman smiling at him with desolate, patronising pity, and sipping her Martini in prim silence.

Masson's terse response is, "Go and find 'Monsieur M I 6'. He'll want to see this for himself, and I'd like to concentrate on his face while he watches it."

****

"So? Is it your suspect?"

Valentine squints at the screen, "I'm not sure…"

"Oh, give me some bloody credit! You're supposed to be a career copper same as I am! What does your *instinct* tell you, Detective Sergeant?"

Masson exhales in exasperation, pushes moodily against the desk to thrust himself upright, stalks to the window, and gazes out at the glittering water. Valentine's blue eyes follow him broodingly. Pursing his lips, he withdraws two identically-sized photographs from his inside jacket pocket, sliding them across the desk towards Masson, who condescends to leave the window and pick them up, returning to study them closely in the slatted shafts of sunlight streaming through the tilted blinds of the Harbourmaster's office.

Valentine wheels backwards in his chair to permit Masson unobstructed access to the computer, "You're a braver man than I if you can make a positive ID based on footage of that appalling quality, and two thirty-year-old mug shots."

Masson leans forward, holds the two pictures up to the screen, and looks back and forth, back and forth, back and forth…finally expelling a frustrated expletive under his breath, and passing the photographs on to Xavier.

The young woman in the picture is averagely pretty; a round face, a dusting of freckles, soft colour to plump apple cheeks, a mass of unruly ringlets framing her face. To Xavier, she seems a very ordinary girl, not notable either for striking beauty or jarring unattractiveness. He would find her easy to dismiss but for her eyes… Dark chasms into which you could tumble and never escape. Unnerved, Xavier shuffles the photograph beneath that of the man, and feels better immediately. The man's picture has the opposite effect. Regular-featured – not particularly handsome, no distinguishing marks – nothing of his appearance remains in Xavier's mind once he stops studying the image. It strikes Xavier he's a blank canvas upon which any picture might be painted. With a flash of inspiration, he slides the scan of the Montparnasse passport from the back of his notebook, placing it on the desk between Masson and Valentine, "It's not the same man."

Valentine taps the passport airily, "But we know for a fact this is fake…the photograph used could well be fake too. Or, it's not beyond the bounds of possibility that this guy had some surgery during the intervening decades and ended up looking rather different. Nose job, cheek sculpting, fillers in the lips… It's extreme, but it does happen, Détective Hâche."

Xavier, initially proud of his quick-thinking, is straight back to feeling inadequate again. He can't shake the peevish conviction he'd be getting on better as a Détective without this self-assured 'Rosbif' around. His despondency must show, as Masson claps him encouragingly on the shoulder as he strides past to the office door, sticks his head out, and summons the Harbourmaster. Masson doesn't dare ask Valentine to surrender the only chair – although Xavier is sure he wants to – but instead wheels one in from the outer office, places it in front of the computer, and invites the Harbourmaster to sit. Still wary of the Inspecteur, he obeys instantly. Masson points to the screen, "That gentleman on there, is he your Monsieur Montparnasse?"

The Harbourmaster cranes forward, staring intently as the security camera footage spools to the relevant point – the small car passing under the light that briefly illuminates the faces of its occupants. The Harbourmaster shrugs, "It looks like him."

Masson persists. He needs a positive ID or this case stutters to a standstill again, "I'm pushing you here, because you're the only one of us who's actually met him…so, I would like to know whether your Monsieur Montparnasse looks like *this*," here, Masson places the rather dog-eared passport scan in front of the Harbourmaster. As the man opens his mouth to give the predictably-affirmative answer,

Masson slides the picture of Valentine's mystery man beside it, "Or, a middle-aged version of *this*."

The Harbourmaster hesitates just long enough to bother Masson, "Monsieur, I need to hear your opinion, please. Take your time, to be absolutely sure."

The Harbourmaster's head ticks left, right, left, right, as he looks from one picture to the other, and back at the paused image on the screen again, "I…um…I…I only met him face to face on the date he arrived…and…I must say I looked more at the passport, really. I was more concerned with getting him moored up correctly…and I seem to remember he was wearing a hat. It was a very hot day…as far as I can recall, his face was mostly in shadow…"

"To be clear, are you saying you can't make a positive ID of Monsieur Montparnasse? You're saying he could actually be either man…and you can't be sure which of them appears on this CCTV footage?"

The Harbourmaster chews at his lip, and eventually admits, "I'm sorry…I can't do that, no…"

The Inspecteur fights to suppress his exasperation. The Harbourmaster blusters defensively, "We are an incredibly busy Marina! I personally supervise the arrival of all vessels over a certain size. Navigation into this port is complicated in a large yacht! Do you know how many boats are zipping in and out during July and August? The idea I commit to memory the features of every fifty-something man who moors here, just in case the police come calling…!"

Masson smirks despite his mounting irritation, and relents. After all, the guy's got a point.

"You're quite right, Monsieur. They all have a ridiculous tan, grey hair, and those stupid, baggy shorts, eh?"

Amazed to find the inscrutable Masson his sudden ally, the Harbourmaster relaxes enough to snigger unguardedly.

Masson tries another tack, "Did you notice *her*? Was she any better to look at?"

The Harbourmaster levels with him, "Inspecteur, if they don't have a wife, they *all* have a steady stream of women who are reasonable to look at. They're virtually interchangeable; you know how it is."

Masson sighs, "Regrettably, I'm not rich enough to know how it is. We won't take up any more of your time." He gathers up the photographs and deliberately hands them to Xavier, but they're intercepted by a grinning Valentine, who relieves the younger man of all but the increasingly-battered passport scan he evidently has no interest in. Masson scowls at an opportunity wasted, and turns back to the Harbourmaster, "Has an officer taken a copy of this CCTV disk?"

"Yes, I believe so."

"As this contains footage relevant to our enquiry, please hold onto it for the time being – don't overwrite or destroy it."

"Right."

"Thank you for your time."

"Um, Inspecteur…we're not in any trouble? About the passport? Only none of us realised it was fake…"

Masson looks pointedly at Valentine, before muttering drily, "Not to worry, Monsieur, nor did we until this morning."

****

In the back of the parked car, Masson swears loudly and thumps the driver's headrest, making Xavier jerk forward in his seat, "Tell me, Valentine, did you introduce those photographs at that precise moment just to muddy the waters, or what?!"

Valentine smiles in his serene way, and quietly counters, "You need to stop being quite so fiery and Mediterranean about this, mate."

This sends the already-apoplectic Masson over the edge, "I'm not your fucking mate! It's a good job you're in the front! 'Entente cordiale' or not, I'd smash your face in!"

Before either of them realise what's happening, the Englishman swings round in his seat, thrusts a powerful arm through the gap in the headrests, and grasps a fistful of Masson's unironed shirt, roaring, "Right! I've had about as much of this as I'm going to tolerate! I am here to do a job, ok? I know you can't stand me hijacking what you think is 'your' case, but constant needling away at me is not going to get this done! Do you understand? You either wind your neck in and treat me with the professionalism I'm *trying* to extend to you, or we drive this heap of French shit somewhere quiet and settle our cultural differences the old-fashioned way, eh? And, before you decide, consider that I went to an English Public School from the age of eight. I'm bastard good at fighting; I spent my whole childhood doing it. And I've spent my whole adulthood in the gym…not smoking endless *Gauloises* in restaurants on long liquid lunches; get it? Put this bullshit aside for a minute, and *think* about what just happened in there – because it strikes me you're a bloody good copper when you're not too busy pouting about something. Am I right?"

Masson pushes Valentine's loosening hand away disdainfully, but doesn't retaliate. He simply smooths the front of his crumpled shirt, as if the Englishman alone is responsible for its creases, and readjusts his tie.

Xavier can hear nothing but the loud rushing of his own quickening blood in his burning ears. At length, Masson asks loftily, "What are you driving at?"

"That clueless prick in there would've given you a positive ID on that passport, and you know it. It might as well have a picture of Homer Simpson on it for all the difference it makes. It's *fake*!"

"So you keep saying. You've shown us no proof."

"I can't show you proof. I don't have it. It's classified information."

Masson rolls his eyes, "Everything that might further *my* investigation is 'classified'! Can you see why that's annoying…and why I'm finding it harder and harder to assist you effectively, when all you do is put up obstacles at every turn?"

The two men glare venomously at each other in the cramped car, and Xavier holds his breath. Eventually, Valentine seems to come to a decision, reaching into his jacket pocket and producing the two photographs again, "Ok, listen to me, both of you…and listen good, because I'm disobeying a direct order with what I'm about to tell you. You *do not* repeat any of this and," here, he looks pointedly at Xavier, "you *especially* don't write any of it down. Got it?"

"Yes, sir."

"And you?"

"I've 'got it', don't you worry."

Valentine smirks sardonically, and holds up the picture of the woman.

"Tammi Rivers. Her presence is required in the UK, but she's…unwilling to return there."

He holds the other photograph up next to it, "It's this man's job to track her down and bring her back."

"Organised crime? A home-grown terrorist cell?"

"I can't tell you that. It's – "

"Let me guess – classified?"

"Do you want this fucking Intel or not?"

"By all means. Please, continue."

"You're too kind. I'm here to find this man. He's recently gone missing. If I track him down then, chances are, I'll also discover the woman too. The only recent trace of either of them was the last known location of the man in Monaco, and the fingerprint hit for the woman on your crime scene yacht."

"If your missing man is our corpse on the hill, is the woman your prime suspect?"

"Yes."

"So, the CCTV showing her holding him at gunpoint fits very neatly with the murder you suspect has taken place?"

"Yes."

"See, sir? I told you! Sometimes stuff *is* just how it appears."

"All right, Xavier! No one likes a know-it-all!"

"What's this?" Valentine is looking from one to the other suspiciously.

Masson shakes his head dismissively, "Nothing. I was just convinced we were being led by the nose, that's all. It seemed too neat – too easy. Too obvious, you know? If we track her down, what then? To Xavier and I, she's most likely a murderer against whom we're building a prosecution case. What is she to you?"

"A considerable security risk. I have orders to transport her back to London for full debriefing."

"Is that what they call it in Britain? I think the CIA use the term 'extraordinary rendition'…?"

"I'm not taking her back to the UK to be tortured, you lunatic, but she possesses sensitive information that only those with the very highest-level security clearance are allowed to access!"

"Hey, she's not running around the Riviera in a suicide-vest, is she? We at least have a right to know that. If French lives are being put at risk and the British Government is trying to cover up its bungling – "

"It's classified, Inspecteur!"

"You *do* surprise me. Will you answer me one question?"

"Only one?"

"Well, only one for the moment. Are you M I 6?"

"I'm an employee of the British state…just as you are an employee of the French state."

"Thanks for nothing. Is that all I'm getting?"

"Believe me, it's more than I'm allowed. I could lose my fucking job for what I've just told you."

"What's his name, the guy in the picture?"

"Nightingale."

Masson chortles, "They sing a beautiful song, but they're legendary elusive…isn't that right?"

Valentine runs the tip of his tongue across his top lip to disguise a sudden involuntary smile.

Masson perseveres, "Who's the geezer in the fake passport? Another 'employee of the British state'?"

"I've no idea who he is. He could be a stock library picture off Google for all the relevance he has to this investigation."

"We're no fucking further, are we?"

"I wouldn't say that, Inspecteur. I think we've come on in leaps and bounds this afternoon."

"Really? No positive ID from the one bloke who'd actually met and had a conversation with the missing yacht-owner…no proof the bloke we're searching for is the corpse on the hill, or if our John Doe is also yours. And not a sniff of our suspect woman either!"

"In terms of a police investigation, Inspecteur, we can definitely place Tammi Rivers at this location incredibly recently indeed – "

"She could be anywhere by now!"

Valentine shakes his head firmly, "She's still in France."

"You're very sure…but I suppose that 'Intel' is classified too?"

Valentine delivers an exaggerated wink, and slides both photographs into his jacket again.

Masson slumps dejectedly in his seat and gazes out of the window, deep in thought, finally suggesting, "Ok, our next step is to put out a photo-fit of the woman, and an appeal for information on her whereabouts. Emotive language, I think. 'Wanted in connection with a possible murder; potential last witness to see male victim alive' – that sort of thing. Get it on the local and regional news, Xavier. Put out the CCTV footage of him, her…but get the boffins to blur the gun out. Someone might recognise the car. Someone will remember seeing her."

Xavier thinks about those intense, penetrating eyes…and decides the Inspecteur is probably right.

"What we need to do is panic her into breaking cover. If she thinks we're already onto her, she might do something reckless that'll attract attention. Like the Harbourmaster and Montparnasse, all it takes is one member of the public…one 'phone call…"

"What else can we do in the meantime, sir?"

Masson inclines his head towards Valentine, "We can get on with finding out whether his Nightingale's still singing."

SEVEN

Tammi dresses carefully for her evening rendezvous with Guy.
She can't explain why; she just has a feeling tonight will be
significant, irreversibly altering the balance of their budding
relationship. Up until now, he's been the perfect gentleman –
charismatic, respectful; delightfully flirtatious without overstepping
the tacit boundary neither discuss but both acknowledge. To be
treated like a princess on Guy's luxury yacht has been a fairytale the
like of which she hasn't experienced since those first heady days
with the eligible Marc Pickford, way back before all men displayed
their truly vile colours – but even the disenchanted, cynical Tammi is
getting impatient waiting for gallant Guy to finally make his move.
The last couple of days they've spent together, he has been a little
more forward in his language, and has seemed to deliberately
engineer closer physical proximity. It can't be her imagination that
his every look and gesture is communicating increasing urgency, as
if something is quickening within him! Tammi cannot help but hope
it's desire for her.

She chooses expensive satin underwear – not too lacy, to prevent it
appearing lumpy beneath a simple silk shift intended to flatter her
curves. She takes time first straightening the unruly, frizzy fuzz of
her maddening hair, before restyling it into looser ringlets that
tumble and bounce around her shoulders. Dabs of perfume on

wrists, throat, and the backs of her knees create a softly-fragrant aura as she moves. Understated jewellery twinkles brightly against a golden tan acquired from many years' enforced wandering; the Caribbean to South America; the Azores to the Mediterranean – a sunkissed glow effective in disguising the inexorable march of time. She must settle soon, or the looks she trades upon will no longer attract the lifestyle she's become accustomed to. Wealthy sophisticate Guy Montparnasse might just have arrived at the perfect time for the ducking, diving, twisting, writhing Tammi Rivers.

It's therefore discomfiting to sit all dolled-up in a local restaurant as the minute hand revolves slowly around the clock face, the waiters bring her complimentary refills and exchange knowing glances, and Guy doesn't come...

Tammi waits for an hour and a half, then skulks red-faced into the sticky night, stomach swollen with cheap house wine and balsamic-dipped baguette. She's naturally incensed, but an undercurrent of concern bubbles upward like a simmering saucepan. This isn't Guy's style. He prides himself on exquisite manners and irreproachable behaviour. The likes of Marc Pickford would get drunk and forget a date. Guy wouldn't do anything as boorish...so, where *is* he? Never wanting to appear the clingy type, Tammi hasn't yet tried calling Guy, despite distractedly checking her 'phone every five minutes for the last hour. She calls him now. The 'phone rings out and clicks over to message, Guy's voice purring a mailbox ident before the beep. Uncharacteristically panicked, Tammi cuts the call, heart thudding. No matter. He'll see her number, ring her straight back, and explain himself. She tries to stroll with jaunty unconcern, killing time until her 'phone rings, but her limbs feel rigid. She only manages to strut another three ornamental palm trees down the seafront, swags of coloured lights hung between them like a Caribbean Christmas. No call. She weakens, and tries again. This time, it doesn't even ring. The call goes straight to answerphone, as if the handset has been switched off in the intervening few moments. This pricks Tammi's suspicion. After *everything* – the determined pursuit of her, the impeccably beguiling-yet-determined seduction – is she now being *dumped*? Tammi feels first bereft at the abrupt termination of this pleasant interlude; then nauseous – is this the beginning of the end, the start of being passed over for younger women by eminently-suitable men; then enraged at her own pathetic reaction, and Guy's temerity. If he thinks he's getting away with this simply by avoiding her telephone calls…!

It's a long way along the man-made promenade from the small town's seafront bars to the furthest point of the headland – the exclusive resort of Point Miroir – but Tammi has indignation driving her on, so the walk takes less than an hour. Some women might be intimidated by the deepening darkness; the deserted, winding path edged with rocky pine forest to one side and gently lapping Mediterranean to the other, but Tammi Rivers has been utterly alone in many worse places than this. She marches on quite unafraid, rehearsing the encounter she'll have with Guy at her destination, electing whether to treat him with delicacy or derision as she takes him to task.

At Point Miroir, she types in the security code only available to guests, and slips through the automatic gate as soon as it creaks apart. A couple of the late-opening bars spill swirling light, animated conversation, and pumping bass onto the promenade. Tammi scuttles past in the shadows, unobserved by the revellers. Further on, apart from a few lanterns swinging from booms, the sleeping marina is in darkness. Only the creak of mast, slap of wave, and ping of taught rope pierce the tranquillity. At Guy's yacht, a dim light in the main cabin shows as a rectangle of muted blue-grey against inky night. He's there. How *dare* he be there when he should be with her! He'd better have a damned good explanation…

Tammi feels for the chain across the end of the pontoon, unclipping and dropping it to the ground with a dull clink. She strides forward confidently in the gloom, and climbs gingerly onto the deck of the yacht, not wanting to catch and snag her expensive dress. The cabin door is slightly ajar, probably to admit what little breeze there is on this humid night. Faint silver shines around its edge, as if Guy's sitting there in the dark with only the tv on. She expects to hear his rich, deep voice; perhaps the giggle of her ingenue replacement…but no sound comes from within. If he's got a girl down there, they're being unnaturally quiet, whatever they're up to. She pushes the door, swinging it wide open, "Guy, are you there? I waited nearly two hours for you at the *Marco*!"

Indignation resurfacing at the remembered humiliation, Tammi clips down the steep stairs in her sandals, almost hoping to catch him at it and have her stomach-churning suspicions confirmed, snapping, "You could at least have had the decency to call…"

Confusion silences her. She's not greeted by the sight she expected. The tv isn't on. The cabin's in darkness but for the light shining from the open door of the slim wine fridge. It's usually amply-stocked, yet now the shelves bear noticeable gaps…and why is the door open? Is Guy on some expensive-plonk-fuelled bender, drinking half his stock since yesterday afternoon? In the inadequate, eerie, artificial glow, she can see irregular, dark shapes silhouetted against the floor, but can't make sense of what they are. She slides a hand around the curve of cabin wall, feeling for the nearest switch, flicking it on, gasping at the scene revealed.

The shapes are the carcasses of smashed wine bottles, scattered across the galley linoleum like uncovered shipwrecks at low tide. Further large shards stand proud of the thick pile of the lounge's white carpet like icebergs trapped in frozen ocean. There's spilt wine everywhere. It stains the upholstery, and shocks with its brightness against the cream sheepskin rugs. Drying runnels of claret course down the opposite bulkhead. The image that rushes into her mind is of flowing blood at a pagan sacrifice. Something hard and heavy has impacted the tv on the far wall. A spider's web of cracks spreads outward from a dark crater in the centre of its screen. It might have been the crystal ashtray now lying some feet away, the arc of spent butts describing its rolling passage across the floor. The GPS screen's survived, but the radio's been yanked from the set, leaving only two severed protruding wires.

In the midst of this madness is Guy. The curling radio cable's been used to bind his wrists together. He's slumped on the sofa, head lolled forward, mouth hanging slackly open. He's still alive. Tammi can see the rhythmic rise and fall of his chest as he breathes. He's sustained a serious beating. His face is heavily cut, bruised;

already swelling alarmingly. His forearms are criss-crossed with a tracery of coagulating blood. He's obviously attempted to fend off blows, perhaps from one of the wine bottles?

She rushes forward, dancing between the pieces of protruding glass, plonking inelegantly onto the sofa beside Guy and cupping his injured face in her hands, his blood squishing and smearing over her skin as she tries to lift his heavy head, "Guy!"

If this is a burglary, it's a botched one. They've left behind his mobile 'phone – on the sofa beside him – and he's still wearing his watch, a valuable make worth many thousands of pounds. Tammi, well-versed in this sort of thing, knows they're the very first items she'd take, because they can be turned most-rapidly from traceable booty into anonymous cash. Clumsily cradling Guy's head, desperately trying to hold it upright and clear the clotting blood from his blocking nostrils, she glances frantically around, seeking an explanation for what's happened here. Her mind is completely blank, paralysed by panic. She's clearly got to do something; she just can't decide what. Even faced with a crisis of such proportions, calling the police is never Tammi's go-to option.

A movement behind them, down the dark corridor to the bedrooms, catches her attention and makes her start. Someone's there! She leaps up and whirls around to face the threat, dropping Guy's head. His chin thuds hard onto his chest again, but not even this violent motion rouses him.

A man steps from the shadow, using one of Guy's thick cotton towels to wipe dark blood from the latex gloves he's wearing. Tammi gulps and gurgles, as if the intruder's hands are already around her throat. It's *Guy*! The same upswept silver hair. The identically-deep walnut tan. But how can that *be*?

A vivid picture flashes before her eyes. A nondescript, unremarkable Englishman-abroad, far too engrossed in his week-old newspaper... She'd been so bamboozled by her first encounter with Guy, she hadn't given the incongruous image the consideration it evidently deserved.

The man smiles distantly, as if he's being introduced to her at a cocktail party, and explains, "I'm sorry 'Guy' couldn't make it for dinner, Tammi. As you can see, he's...*indisposed*..."

EIGHT

Instinctively backing away as the man advances, Tammi yelps and hops as a shard of glass nicks the end of an unprotected toe. She stops, winces, glances down at the oozing blood forming a round, red berry beside her pink-painted nail, and croaks, "What have you done to Guy?"

The man smirks, tossing aside the bloodstained towel, "I just gave him something to help him relax. I think you'll agree it's done the trick! Sleeping like a baby…"

Tammi is convinced she's about to vomit. She retches, bringing a shuddering hand up to cover her mouth, before realising it's coated in Guy's blood, and letting it drop again. She swallows, gulps; whispers, "Will he ever wake up?"

The man frowns darkly, "Not if I have my way."

Tammi can feel a scream building inside her, and isn't sure she's either able or willing to stop it. The *first time* a man has treated her with respect! The *first time* she hasn't been controlled or coerced, bullied or beaten! The *first time* she's wanted to give herself to any man for a reason other than self-preservation, since Marc Pickford broke her heart half a lifetime ago! She tries to roar, but there's no power inside her. The intended bellow comes out as a strangled squawk, but she charges forward nevertheless, arms raised to beat the intruder about the head, to expend her fury and grief at this latest in a long and wearisome line of injustices perpetrated against her. Her spirited assault takes him by surprise. Initially, he cowers and defends himself. This lasts but a second before he takes hold of both her wrists in an iron grip, and swings her bodily. The corner of the wall rams into her ribcage, winding her severely and making her fall to her knees, helpless in his merciless grasp. The beginnings of a sob build behind her nose and in her throat. It's fortunate there's no breath left in her lungs to force out the tell-tale sound. It's a bad idea to cry in front of this man. He drives a knee into her breastbone, pushing her roughly back against the wall, legs concertinaed painfully beneath her.

Quietly, he remonstrates, "You need to calm down. I've done you a favour. You think you know what's going on here, but you really bloody don't."

Tammi fights to breathe, panting desperately, "Nightingale, Guy's not a part of this! You need to get him some medical help! What have you given him? He needs his stomach pumped or something! If you're here for me, fine – let's duke it out between us – but Guy's *innocent*, Nightingale! He's just in the wrong place at the wrong time! He knows nothing about me, you, The Cabal, anything! He's not involved…you need to *help* him!"

He chuckles softly, "You have got it bad, haven't you? I don't remember you going this gooey over a bloke since you got your knickers in a twist about Pickford all those years ago. Soon grew out of that, didn't you? I think you're going soft in your old age. Were you starting to think he might be 'The One'? Wouldn't have looked twice at him if he hadn't had a yacht and a Gold Card, would you?

Don't try to pretend you give a shit about his welfare now. You're just pissed off the fairytale's over."

This time, Tammi can't stop the keening that swells like a geyser in her head and erupts as a loud wail of anguish in the silent cabin. The man moves fast, squatting before her so quickly she jerks backward in surprise and bangs her head on the wall. He slaps a sticky, gloved palm across her mouth, hissing, "Let's keep the volume down, shall we? Wouldn't want to wake the neighbours…not when you're the one with blood on your hands, eh?"

He hauls her shuddering body upright, and supports her with an arm tight about her waist, "Can we have a civil discussion, please?"

"Or what?"

He points at Guy, "Or that. Yes?"

"Let go of me!"

He sniggers, and manhandles her ineffectually-struggling body down onto the sofa opposite Guy, "Seriously, Tammi, *enough* of this! If you want to know what's going on, you need to stop acting hysterically and start listening."

"We can't just sit here and have a bleedin' *chat*! You need to *help* him!"

"I don't need to do anything of the sort."

Nightingale rights the upturned coffee table and perches on its polished top, elbows resting on his knees, relaxed hands dangling inches from Tammi's tight-clenched thighs. He stretches to his left, fingers feeling for, hooking, and tugging a black holdall she hasn't previously noticed. Pulling it around between his feet, he unzips the top and withdraws a slim, manila folder. He jerks a thumb over his shoulder towards the comatose Guy, "Who do you think he is?"

Tammi closes her eyes, again weathering the sharp internal stab of suffering, "I don't even know who *I* am any more, let alone anyone else! I can't remember the person I used to be before you got your claws into me."

He raises his eyebrows, smiles, and jokingly admonishes, "Now, now, Tammi, I refuse to take any more than my fair share of the blame for the car crash your life has become. You didn't behave yourself. You allowed hobnobbing with the Stocker-Pickfords to go to your head. You forgot why you were there. That's your fault; no one else's. You forgot which side you were supposed to be on."

"Which 'side' would that be, Nightingale? The 'side' of truth and justice? I'm a little hazy on which one that actually *is*…aren't you? Send a thief to catch a thief, right? When judges, peers, captains of industry – key figures at the heart of the British Establishment – are the biggest crooks you've ever encountered…? The more I discovered, the quicker I realised policing my own conduct was the only sensible way forward. You know as well as I do there are no good guys in this mess."

Again, Nightingale gestures towards Guy, "There's another scoundrel to add to your clearly-comprehensive list."

"*What*?"

"I've already asked you who you think he is."

"Why do we have to go through this rigmarole when obviously you're dying to tell me; when evidently the answer's in that folder?"

He grins, and pushes teasingly at her arm, making her flinch involuntarily, "Come on, Tammi, play along! It's the most delightful fun!"

Tammi rolls her eyes, and mutters darkly, "I think he's a Belgian businessman called Guy Montparnasse. A rich fella with a penchant for the good life."

"You are quite correct about the last bit. The beginning, less so."

Tammi sighs heavily, and grunts, "Get on with it then. Swing your wrecking ball through more of my life."

"Chin up, Old Girl! You look quite defeated."

"Only 'quite'?" rejoins Tammi sarcastically, "I'm starting to believe I just don't care one way or another any more."

"This'll gee you up a bit, I promise."

Nightingale takes a photograph from the folder and places it in her lap. An old picture. A school hockey team. By the haircuts and style of the strip, she makes an educated guess it's the 1980s. Nightingale points to a teenager standing in the back row, stick aloft.

Tammi breathes in amazement, "Guy…"

"It is, as you say, the man you know as 'Guy'. And who's his chum, there, two to the left?"

"No way!" It's Geoffrey. Sir Blair Stocker-Pickford's eldest son. The heir to the peerage. The pride of the clan. The man who might have been her brother-in-law had things turned out the way she'd intended. She points unsteadily at Guy's youthful image, ashamed of how much her hand shakes, "Is he a stooge of Blair's? A 'honeytrap' designed to sucker me in? And I fell for it!"

"Not exactly, no. He's no stooge of Blair's, but he knows the family all right. It's nothing to do with The Cabal. It's just a happy coincidence. Well, happy for me, anyway. I simply wanted to illustrate how closely-interwoven this really is; how you'd better stick to me like glue if you want to make it out of here alive. That picture's interesting, in a nostalgic kind of way, but this is the one that'll knock your socks off. This is the one that'll make you realise how lucky you are I arrived when I did."

A second photograph slides into her lap. By the registrations of the cars and the style of clothing, this is later – the nineties? It's a shot that's been taken from inside a vehicle, perhaps as part of a surveillance operation. It's a meeting in a London backstreet. Such a recognisable snapshot of an England she knows so well brings on a sudden and surprising pang of homesickness, to churn amongst all the other surging emotions. The attitude of the two subjects suggests their encounter is clandestine. They face one another, but each stares over the other's shoulder and up the road – literally watching the other's back.

She knows both men.

The older, taller of the two is Guy Montparnasse. His skin looks shockingly pale without the rich walnut tan she's grown accustomed to. His hair is long, lank; so dark it's almost black. He's skeletally thin. A leather trenchcoat hangs from angular shoulders like a highwayman's cloak. The other figure, barely out of teenage, is Ricky. There's no point asking Nightingale where he got this photograph; he won't tell her.

He points unnecessarily, "Richard McAllister; your erstwhile partner-in-crime. Recall him? You killed him, didn't you Tammi."

It's a statement, not a question, so Tammi doesn't feel the need to respond. Nightingale's gloved finger slides across to the other figure, "And this man?"

She thinks, 'Guy...', but says nothing aloud. It's impossible to suppress the longing to rewind to yesterday, when the improbable fantasy was still very much alive.

"No? Nothing? I'll help you out, shall I? This gentleman's name is James Chadwick...and you're just about to kill him too."

NINE

Handcuffed in the hot, locked car, Tammi has no choice but to sit and wait. She can't call out and draw attention to herself; she's covered in Guy's blood; her fingerprints are all over the yacht! That she's being framed for his murder is incontrovertible. The question is *why*?

Nightingale must be here to transport her back to England…so why not pick her up from her hotel room? Why bother with Guy at all? What can he possibly mean by 'a happy coincidence'?

She can't explain the lookalike appearance; the obvious assuming of another identity for the purposes of…*what*, exactly? Has Nightingale precisely selected Guy for an as-yet-indeterminate reason…or does he just need a body – *any* body – plausibly similar to his own? Tammi understands the process; she's done the same thing herself, becoming her own sister to escape probable arrest, conviction, incarceration. Risks of that kind surely can't apply to Nightingale? He's on to a cushy number; a foot in either camp, able to turn towards law and duty or do The Cabal's grubby bidding, depending upon which instruction most-comfortably feathers his nest. He'd need a very good reason to leave all that behind. What could it be? She also can't make head or tail of the Jimmy Chadwick thing. She would have dismissed it entirely – but for the photograph of Guy and Ricky. It had looked genuine, stuffed with so many little details it would have been difficult to fake. Does that mean Guy's duped her with a proficiency of which she herself would have been proud? The notion causes indignation, embarrassment, confusion…and wretchedness. Why is nothing good ever *real*?

The sudden opening of the boot makes her start. The little car sinks noticeably on its suspension as Nightingale unceremoniously dumps Guy inside and slams the lid. Tammi immediately tries to open her door, but it won't budge, the locks activated. Nightingale slides into the driver's seat, puffing, "He's fucking heavy!" He smirks nastily, "Still here? You must have missed me more than you're admitting if you want to spend so much extra time with me."

He tugs at the strap of the holdall slung across his body, lifting it over his head and pushing the bag into the passenger footwell, roughly shoving her legs aside, "Move!"

"Owww!"

"Stop whining."

There are two pistols in his trouser waistband. Two. Why does he need two? She mustn't get bogged down in pointless cogitation. Regardless of the whys and wherefores, if Nightingale's got two weapons, she must get hold of at least one of them. She glances behind her, into the back seat. It's dark, but the faint dashboard lights illuminate what looks like a child's booster cushion.

"This car better be nicked."

"Why?"

"'Cos there's a kid's seat in the back!"

Nightingale chuckles, "Have I not told you my little secret?"

"Don't even joke about it. The very idea of you procreating…"
Tammi mimes vomiting, and her spiteful shot satisfyingly hits home.
Nightingale crunches the little car aggressively into gear, hissing,
"Shut up. Enough talking now."

To Tammi's surprise, they turn in the opposite direction to the
main gate, and drive all the way down the large guest car park to a
clipped perimeter hedge, passing through a gap she's previously-
presumed is a footpath up to the cliffs. Instead, she discovers it's a
narrow vehicle-access track, which doubles back on itself and curls
behind the seaview apartments. As they drive down the hill towards
the main coast road, the narrow track opens onto a stony area ringed
with high chainlink fencing. A line of commercial rubbish bins are
pushed tight against the sandy overhang on one side. To the other is
a rusting shipping container with two plastic chairs placed where the
daytime shade would be. Cigarette butts litter the yellowing grass
around the legs of the chairs like confetti, gleaming bright white as
the headlights pass across them. A few battered cars as cheap and
dusty as their current vehicle are parked haphazardly to either side of
the track. Tammi's got her bearings. They're now almost behind
the main drag of cafés, shops, and bars. Judging by the signage all
over the gate they're approaching, this is the staff entrance, and
destination for all collections and deliveries. It's the grubby reality
behind the gleaming façade. A harsh yellow light on the rear wall of
the Harbourmaster's Offices brightly illuminates the adjacent area.

Nightingale stops the car fifty yards before the gate, engine
chugging in the humid darkness. He turns to her, smiles pleasantly,
and explains, "We're about to have our picture taken. There's a

camera on that gate. I'd like to strike a lovely pose – one for the album, y'know?"

He pulls one of the guns from his waistband, and casually passes it to her. Tammi gapes, grasps it frantically, fumbles – hampered by her handcuffs – to point it straight at his smirking face, and pulls the trigger.

Click.

Empty.

Smack!

The blow comes out of nowhere. Tammi's head flies back and cracks sharply against the car window, the side of her face burning. Flashes of red and white burst before her vision. She rights herself with difficulty, gasping.

Smack!

The second blow is more shocking than the first, this time connecting with her nose and sending a dagger of agony straight up into her brain. She squeals, lolling across the seat, whacking her right temple on the dashboard. A strong fist grips the front of her once-beautiful dress, hauling her upright.

"Listening? Pull yourself together. *Now.*"

Tammi pants, sniffs…a hot, metallic glob of phlegm and blood clogs the back of her throat and makes her cough thickly as she tries to take a deep breath. She wipes her nose with her wrist, leaving a trail of blood and mucus up her arm.

"Listening now?"

She nods feebly. He cups a hand around his ear, "Sorry, Tammi, I didn't get that?"

"Yes. Yes. I'm listening."

"Good. Like I'd give you a gun with bullets in it! Honestly – use that supposedly-massive brain of yours, will you? I *know* you've killed at least one man…I *suspect* you've killed another, but I've no proof of that. I'm not daft enough to deliver you your hattrick on a plate, am I? This one, however, is very much loaded."

Nightingale produces the other pistol, and rams it so hard against her pelvis that she cries out in pain and tries to wriggle away.

"Sit. Still."

His other hand catches at the bar of her handcuffs, tugging firmly forward and bending her uncomfortably over the barrel of the gun.

"Sit up straight."

"You're hurting me!"

"Do as you're told, Tammi, or one shot cripples you for life. Sit up."

Tammi complies, wincing in pain at the pressure of metal against a pelvic bone unprotected by much covering of flesh.

"When we drive up to the gate, lean forward into the light and hold your gun up to my head. Nice and obvious. Understand?"

"Understand? *Really*? I don't understand *any* of this! Why – "

"Because, if you don't, I swear to God you'll never walk again. One shot, Tammi. You haven't enough time or room to escape the inevitable if I decide to pull the trigger. Sufficient incentive to do as you're fucking told?"

"Yes."

"Sit forward. Now. Gun up. Now. That's it. Keep it there. Face forward. Smile for the camera….perfect."

Before she can think of a way to avoid it, they're into and out of the pool of light, and he's snatching the gun back off her, dropping it into his lap, keeping his pistol rammed into her lower stomach as they drive away.

"That really hurts. There's no need – "

"If you don't shut up and sit still, it'll hurt a fuck sight more, believe me."

"Where are we going, Nightingale?"

"To a barbecue."

****

She can't passively sit here, possibly-broken nose dripping blood steadily into her lap, and let Nightingale have this all his own way. She needs to confound his plans, whatever they might be, and that means getting out of this car. How – with a loaded gun thrust against her already-bruising stomach, hands pinioned a fixed-four-inches apart, and the car moving along dark, mountainous roads with often-precipitous drops on the seaward side? She tries to forage in Nightingale's head. What's he thinking about right now? He's got to watch the dark road, steer the winding lanes with only one hand on the wheel, maintain steady enough revs to minimise the need for many wrong-handed gear changes, keep the gun pushing sufficiently firmly against her pelvis to hold her in check, and plan the final moments of the hapless Guy, doubtless already close to death from slow suffocation in the Citroen's miniscule boot...and then there's the still-unclear motive for all this, chewing away at his subconscious. Even a man like Nightingale must be feeling some pressure. Sufficient distraction for her to attempt an escape?

Suddenly, she's aware of a change in engine note. The winding road becomes narrower and steeper, the sheer rock wall looming darkly on the driver's side. To keep the gun pressed against her with his right hand, Nightingale must steer with his knees, take his left hand off the wheel, and reach awkwardly across his own body to change down a gear, rescuing the labouring little engine from stalling. The car judders violently as it loses momentum. He's got to do it now or they'll simply stop. As he pushes his knees up to steady the wheel momentarily, twisting in the dark to grope for the gear stick, Tammi seizes her moment and brings the thick metal bar of the handcuffs crunching down with all her might on the elbow of his rigid, gun-toting right arm. Mentally distracted, he's not prepared for it. Naturally the arm bends upwards under the pressure, pointing the gun towards the car roof. Released from the immediate risk of being shot, Tammi throws her body towards Nightingale, using her right shoulder to trap the arm against the dashboard so he drops the gun, simultaneously shoving frantically with her pinioned hands, forcing the steering wheel sharp left, towards the sheer rock face on the car's off-side. Left hand across his body and clumsily grasping the gear stick, right hand trapped under Tammi's full grunting, forcing weight, Nightingale is tied in a helpless knot. He struggles his hand back onto the wheel, but Tammi continues to shove it left as fast as he corrects it right. He tries to brake, but his body's still twisted. He mistakenly depresses the clutch pedal. The car bucks sharply. Tammi ducks, taking a risk with releasing his arm, and instead headbutting him hard in the stomach, doubling him over the wheel. Nightingale's foot slips off the clutch, and the car lurches again, smashing hard into the rock face, and grinding along it for several feet with a torturous screech of ripping metal and crumpling bodywork. Neither are wearing seatbelts. The impact hurls them both forward. Nightingale yowls in terror, the scream cut abruptly short by the sharp connection of the bridge of his nose with the steering wheel. His rigid form slumps, both arms limp, body collapsing down onto itself like deflating bellows. Pushing against his right thigh for leverage, Tammi wriggles backwards from the protective cocoon his body has provided, and snaps on the interior light. His forehead rests against the steering wheel, a deep cut traversing the bridge of his nose and slicing up through one eyebrow. He's alive. His breath blows bubbles in the blood streaming from his nose. Already, he's coming round, struggling to sit up, squinting in the unexpected light. Tammi wastes no time, but jabs her reaching arms past his face to thump the button on the driver's door, releasing all the locks. She whirls frantically in her seat, diving out of the passenger side before Nightingale fully collects himself. She doesn't get far. Grunting with the effort, he flings himself full-length across the front seats, grabbing at her dress, ripping the silk and getting purchase on her hips, tugging her powerfully backwards. Unbalanced, hands locked together and unable to grasp for a lever to pull against him, Tammi falls awkwardly across the door sill, body in the passenger footwell, legs flailing uselessly outside the car. She's dropped onto the holdall, and her elbow connects with something firm and cold. Of course, one of the guns! But which? Tammi squirms as Nightingale's rough fingers grip and pinch at her skin. He keeps trying to hold her in place in the footwell with only one hand. She can't work out what he's doing with the other – is he reaching for the second pistol? She tries to roll onto her stomach, cricking her neck to see what he's up to. Then she understands. The collision with the rock wall has crumpled the front of the old, cheaply-constructed vehicle sufficiently to bow the dashboard down a few inches, dropping the steering column and trapping Nightingale's legs. He's not injured, but needs both hands to pull his caught limbs free, and can't hold her still at the same time. Tammi scrabbles for the gun beneath her, jerking to her knees in the footwell, levelling it at Nightingale's shocked face, and pulling the trigger.

Click.

For Christ's bloody sake – the wrong gun, *again*!

Already he's grabbing for her wrists once more, trying to get control of her. Tammi instinctively jerks away. She doesn't have time to think about the most-practical course of action, which is probably to find the loaded gun. Instead, she wields the weapon she already holds like a baseball bat, cracking Nightingale as hard as she can across the face with the long metal barrel. His cheek splits like a ripe plum, spraying fresh blood in a fine arc across both their faces. He makes a surprisingly-contented sighing noise, as if he's had enough of fighting and has decided to nap instead, subsiding heavily onto the stained seat with eyes half-closed and mouth wide open. The blood in his clogging airways makes his deep breaths click in his throat and snort in his nose. Again, he's only out for seconds before he once more starts to splutter and regain consciousness, leaving Tammi no time to search the footwells for the useful gun.

She scuttles backwards, grabbing the handle of the holdall and yanking it after her. Glancing back, she sees to her horror that the rapidly-recovering Nightingale already has the other gun in his fist, and is flat on his back across the seats, holding it over his head and aiming out through the open door! She dashes the few feet to the rock wall, and scrambles up the crumbling edifice, scattering a tiny avalanche of pebbles across the tarmac as she struggles for purchase in near-total darkness. Six feet above is what looks like a flatter area, with the black shapes of large trees on it. She gropes upwards, tearing fingernails and skinning toe-tips and kneecaps. None of it matters. She just needs to be a moving target the trapped Nightingale can't aim at with ease. His first shot is only wide by about two feet. The bullet strikes, and the exploding rock spatters her uncovered skin painfully. She's aware she's whimpering, knows this is a foolish disclosure of her exact position, but is unable to stop. Despite her cuffed wrists, she's swift in her climb with the fear of death behind her, pulling herself up onto the plateau with an exclamation of triumph. She plunges unhesitatingly into the dark forest, swinging holdall whacking the backs of her knees, and Nightingale's bullets whining through the sticky night, and thudding into the stoic trunks of the silent pines surrounding her.

TEN

Marc Pickford stirs, starts, and his eyes snap open. He's not dreaming! There *is* the sound of a key in the lock, the jiggle and squeak of rusty bolts sliding back, and rarely-used hinges grinding into life! The sudden sunlight is blinding. He squints, blinks, and tries to focus on the silhouette in the doorway. As his eyes accustom to the brightness, he sees it's a middle-aged woman, dowdy floral housecoat over slacks and a t-shirt. She doesn't look like a fearsome kidnapper; she looks like a char-lady. She gapes at Marc in even greater consternation than he stares at her. He only manages to croak, "Help. Please. Help me…" before she starts to scream.

****

Masson snatches irritably at the ringing 'phone, "Mas-son! Yes. Really? Where? You're sure? No, no, we'll come to you. Half an hour? Yes. Ok, see you shortly."

Dumbfounded, Masson replaces the receiver and turns to Xavier, "That was Marcel. He says a cleaner's found a bloke handcuffed in a garage."

"Where?"

"Further round the coast towards Antibes."

"Dead?"

"No, alive."

"Why ring us, then? If he's alive, surely it's Marcel's problem?"

"Everyone and their Mum knows we're babysitting a 'Rosbif' don't they!"

"What's that got to do with it, sir?"

"The bloke they've found seems to be English, and none of Marcel's crew have enough to properly interview him."

"So they want to borrow Valentine?"

"They do…but they're not going to get him – not yet anyway. They're getting me first."

"Why, sir?"

Masson simply waggles his eyebrows by way of answer.

Xavier's agog, "He's *never* our missing man! The one from Valentine's photo?"

"I don't know, do I? I haven't seen him yet."

"Are we going up there now, sir?" Xavier's excitement is palpable.

Masson feels guilty as he replies, "I am. You're not."

Visibly crestfallen, Xavier asks, "How come, Boss?"

"Look, Xavier, something fucked-up is going on here, isn't it? Valentine's fed us a load of flannel. I'd be amazed if a syllable of it is true. I need someone here to keep an eye on him. I don't trust anyone else to do it but you. If we both go, he'll twig something's up…plus, my English is better than yours."

"He's only gone next door to make some calls! What shall I say when he comes back and sees you're out?"

"Tell the truth."

"What? You just said – "

"Tell him I got a call to assist a junior colleague and I had to go. That's not a lie, is it?"

"S'pose not, sir."

"Just keep him here. I need to get a step ahead of the slippery sod before he has time to throw us off the scent again. This is too coincidental not to be linked! I'll be as quick as I can. Oh, give me that passport scan of Montparnasse, will you?"

As Xavier slouches despondently in his chair and frets over how on earth he'll conceal this latest development from the eerily-perceptive Valentine, Masson's already pelting down the stairs in a whirl of gangly limbs and flapping jacket.

****

"He's in the last interview room down there. We've cleaned him up a bit and put him in a tracksuit we had going spare. All his clothes have been bagged up. The doc checked him over, swabbed him, scraped his fingernails and stuff. He didn't know how long he'd been in there. There was bowl of water with him so he'd been drinking, but he clearly hadn't eaten for a while. In the last two hours, he's had three sandwiches, and two helpings of apple tart!"

"When did anyone last go in this garage, then?"

"It's a holiday home – swanky place. The owners are coming for August…but they were last there over Easter!"

"He *can't* have been in there since Easter with no food!"

"No, he's been days, apparently…he just lost track of how many."

"Right. Why was the cleaner in the garage?"

"Said she needed a stepladder to reach the light fittings. She'd gone there to air the house and get it ready for the owners' arrival."

"And the owners don't know an Englishman?"

"Bemused as hell when I rang them! They live in Paris. They said they don't know *anyone* English. They seem legit, sir. None of them have as much as an unpaid parking ticket."

"The cleaner?"

"No previous. She's either in the running for an Oscar, or she's telling the truth. By how genuinely shaken-up she seemed, my money's on the second. She's given a statement. I let her go home for the time being."

"Any CCTV up at this 'swanky house'?"

"Nothing…doubtless why it was chosen. Frequently empty, not monitored…if you needed a place to stash someone for a few days, it's the perfect spot."

"Neighbours see anything?"

"Course not! It's really private; the drive must be two-hundred yards long! Big trees all around. You wouldn't notice a thing, especially if it was a professional job and they took him in at night."

"So, what's he told you?"

"Not too much, really. That's why I rang you. He keeps gabbling all this nonsense about being busted out of prison."

"Prison where? Done background checks?"

"I'm waiting for an email from the UK. No one's got good enough English to understand what he's getting at. He's got no criminal record here, if the name he's given us is the correct one."

"And he has no French?"

"If he does, he's keeping quiet about it. I was going to request an interpreter, and then I remembered you've got that English DS over with you. I thought you were bringing him...?"

Masson lies fluently, "He and Xavier are tied up on something to do with our burnt corpse case – they're flat out. He couldn't be spared right when you rang. Rather than delay, I came over in case I could be of use in the meantime. My English is reasonable, you know."

"Weeelll…perhaps we should wait? He's talking all sorts of crazy stuff. If he's a loony, won't it be easier for a native-speaker to figure that out?"

"Why not let me talk to him now I'm here? It'll speed things significantly for you. It might mean the difference between a satisfying collar and another one-that-got-away…?"

"You can talk to him if you want, sir. I certainly have no objection. It can't do any harm. Do you need me to sit in, only…?" Marcel glances at his watch, shifting uncertainly from foot to foot, and Masson comprehends the true reason behind his desire to delay. It's lunchtime.

He grins, "He might be nuts, but is he violent?"

"Doesn't seem to be. Just relieved to be rescued."

"Bugger off and have your lunch then. I'll be fine on my own. Just stick someone from Uniform by the door in case I need them."

"Pasquier's already in there, sir."

"Good stuff. You get off then. I can handle it."

"Thanks, sir; it's been a long morning. Shall I bring you anything back?"

Masson shakes his head, already strolling down the corridor as if the encounter is just another routine interview. Inside, anticipation churns so violently he knows he couldn't eat a bite, "No thanks. See you later."

He lets himself into the room with quiet confidence, nods and formally shows his badge to the mean mountain of Gendarme seated just inside, and turns to assess the man he's firmly convinced is yet another British spy.

****

Tammi's thirsty, but has no water. She's hungry, but there's no food either. Her bruised and battered body throbs. When she presses tentative fingertips to her swollen face, needles of pain stab so sharply they take her breath away. Half her fingernails are ripped and torn; the exposed, virgin flesh underneath stings, as do her skinned toes, grazed kneecaps, and ribboned shins. There's a deep, black bruise across her right hamstring, where it connected with the door sill as Nightingale tugged her backwards into the car. Similarly, her right elbow is inflamed and puffy where she tumbled onto the gun. She's hiding beneath a rocky overhang screened by bushes. It's a shelter out of the climbing, strengthening sun – and out of sight. She's exhausted from blood loss, constant pain, and panicky hours – she's lost track of how many – spent breathlessly zig-zagging and retracing her steps, laying false trails and eradicating true ones…just in case Nightingale returns. Although finding her is doubtless less of a pressing priority than escape from the wrecked, undriveable car, and swift disposal of Guy's body before summer dawn arrives with inconvenient promptness; he'll be back. He's nothing if not tenacious, and he doesn't leave loose ends if he can help it. Tammi Rivers has been a maddening stain on his otherwise-exemplary service record for way too long. This oasis of calm is temporary respite.

Unable to eat or drink, and disorientated by frequent loss of consciousness; she must conserve what little energy she's got left. She needs to sleep, but can't lie flat. It makes her head thump excruciatingly. Propped half-upright in this sandy hollow is not a pose conducive to slumber, but she takes heart from the fact she's resting in the shade, safely concealed from view. The problem with sitting motionless is the gradual intensifying of each individual ache and pain into a single pulse of unbearable agony. To distract herself, she thoroughly reviews the contents of the holdall. Previously, she's only searched it for food, drink, and weapons – too petrified and confused to pause for long. Now, she empties it methodically onto the dusty ground beside her. A squashed cardboard box of latex gloves. An envelope of used Euros. Nightingale's comprehensive pouch of lock-picking paraphernalia. All useful items in their own right – but no clothing to replace her ruined shift; no food to settle her rolling stomach; no drink to ease her raging thirst.

Two folders. One, the thin manila sleeve containing the illuminating pictures of Guy (if she should still be calling him that) and Ricky.

The other? Tammi picks it up, wincing as a dangling corner of ripped fingernail catches on the cardboard cover. The folder's tied with dirty red ribbon, like a Barrister's bundle of courtroom papers. Something about it feels familiar, but she's too strung-out to think straight. It hurts to unpick the tightly-tied twine, and her bloodied and sore fingers fumble ineffectually. Frustrated, she glances around, snatches up a small stone with a sharper edge, and uses this rudimentary tool to saw agonisingly slowly through the ribbon, fraying until it's weak enough to stretch and snap.

Her glazing eyes swim over the print, but even a cursory shuffle through the dossier is sufficient to reacquaint her with its recognisable contents. It's Ricky's folder, augmented by later annotations in the hands of its various owners. It's the reason she's here, now. It's what started all this. Four people have already died because of what's written here. She's determined not to be the fifth. The last time she'd seen this folder – and the first chance she'd had to thoroughly read its alarmingly-detailed contents – had been in Antigua. How had Nightingale come by it? Cold dread washes over her as she finally realises what's causing his uncharacteristically erratic behaviour.

He *knows*!

ELEVEN

Elbows on the desk, wide palms splayed flat across its pitted surface, the man's bowed head jerks up as Masson enters the room.

He's big. Not overweight; just huge. Hands like shovels, broad shoulders, thick neck, greying hair. He's bulging out of the t-shirt Marcel's crew have squeezed him into. Masson can see his long legs under the table, and the tracksuit trousers stop a good four inches above his ankles. His enormous feet are bare and dirty; doubtless Marcel couldn't find any shoes to fit him either.

Masson smiles, nods politely, and says, "Good afternoon," in his best English accent.

The man blinks, taken aback, then returns the smile readily, and replies, "Good afternoon. Your suit's pricier than the earlier chap. Am I getting shunted up the chain of command?"

Masson chuckles, "It is one of my better ones, actually. My wife bought it for me. I'm not supposed to wear it to work."

The man grins, somewhat bleakly, "I used to wear sharp suits all the time. Every day, in fact…the uniform of my lifestyle. Sometimes, I find myself wondering if I'll ever wear one again. Nowadays, it's all this crap," he picks dismissively at the jersey material, "or those jumpsuit-things where you have to get half-undressed just to have a slash."

Masson smirks, and seats himself casually opposite the massive stranger, "Ah, yes, my colleague thought you had mentioned prison somewhere...?"

The statement hangs long enough to become a question, and the atmosphere in the room cools perceptibly. The man leans back in the plastic seat. It creaks in mild protest under his weight. He narrows his eyes, and asks, "Aren't you supposed to tell me who you are before you ask me any questions?"

"Of course. My apologies."

Masson produces his identification, sliding it across the table, "Inspecteur François Masson. I usually head up investigations into unexplained or violent deaths."

"Aren't I a little hale and hearty to be on your radar then, Inspector?"

"Normally, yes, but today I am only here for my English language, not because your life is in imminent danger. Unless you know otherwise, of course, in which case I suggest you tell me before our paths cross in a 'professional' capacity."

"Honestly, if I knew...! I mean, I have literally no idea if I'm for-it or not!"

"For-it? I'm sorry...I don't know that phrase."

"Whether I'm in trouble! You see, I didn't bust myself out! This guy – he came and got me out. It all seemed legit. He said I was going back to England...and the rest is hazy, truth be told. What I'm worried about is that they'll think I was in on it – a prison break, you know? Then I'm in real trouble! I have zero proof it was nothing to do with me. It could cost me four years of good time!"

Masson takes his notebook from his pocket, flicks on his biro, and poises pen over paper, "If I could ask you to rewind a little… What is your name, please?"

"Marcus Stocker-Pickford."

"And where were you in prison?"

"I told the first chap all this!"

"He is not very confident with his English. I would like to double-check your statement. The sooner you can provide us with the relevant information, the quicker we will stop questioning you."

"Yes, I suppose that's fair enough… Ok, I was in prison in Antigua…in the Caribbean."

"You are a British Citizen?"

"Yes, I am."

"Why were you in prison in the Caribbean?"

The man takes a breath, purses his lips, exhales powerfully through flaring nostrils, and mumbles somewhat sheepishly, "Fraud. Some…um…slightly *misguided* business dealings whilst living there."

"I see. And how long were you in prison?"

"Just under four years."

"How long did you have left to serve?"

"Another year and a half, roughly."

"But someone arrived at your prison and said you were returning to England?"

"Yes – this guy! Another sharp suit…"

"Did you know him?"

"No, of course not! Just some Foreign Office Johnny, come with the right paperwork to get me home – or so I thought."

"The Antiguan prison authorities clearly believed his mission legitimate, or they would not have let you go."

"Don't you believe it! Done any time in the Caribbean, Inspector? I doubt it somehow. Money talks in a place like that. Grease the right palm sufficiently, you'll be amazed what's allowed!"

"Supposing it to be a legal extradition, were you expecting to go free in England?"

"No. I thought I was going back to complete my sentence there. I assumed my family had pulled some strings. Nice, cushy Open Prison in the countryside. No more sweating my arse off day in day out. No more cockroaches, or mosquito bites."

"If instead of a legal process, it was someone's plan to get hold of you...*why*, Monsieur Pickford? Forgive the impudence of my question, but what is so very special about you?"

The man grins wryly, and explains, "I can only think it's a ransom-job. I'm the son of an ex-Cabinet Minister; a British Lord. My elder brother was an MP until a little while ago. If someone kidnapped me, I'd *hope* my family would pay a pretty penny to get me back!"

His intended flippancy falls flat when his voice catches tellingly on the last word. Perhaps the rigours of the last few days are beginning to tell...or perhaps it's well-rehearsed bullshit delivered by an expert?

"Do you have any acquaintances in France?"

"None."

"Do you know what part of France you are in?"

"No idea! It's warm, so I'd imagine relatively far south…?"

"You are on the Mediterranean coast – the Côte d'Azur. Have you visited before?"

"Yeah, but yonks ago! Monte Carlo and Nice as a kid, with my parents and my brother. Family hols – you know the drill. Not since, though. How did I *get* here? Do you know?"

"You don't?"

"As I told your colleague earlier, I can't remember a thing between getting in that chap's car outside the prison gates in Antigua, and coming-to and throwing up in that shed where the char-lady found me. You'd think I'd recall getting on a plane or something!"

"Not if you were unconscious. Do you have any signs of needle marks on your body? Something you might have thought was just another insect bite, for example?"

"Oh. I really don't know. I'm permanently covered in bloody mossie-bites! One of your docs examined me earlier…?"

"Yes. I will be speaking to him. Do we have any contact information for your family in England?"

"I gave my parents' address and number to the other chap…"

"I just want to find out if they've been contacted regarding any sort of ransom payment?"

"Well, I wouldn't know, would I? I haven't exactly been at liberty to make chatty 'phone calls home, Inspector."

"And you have no association with France, or the Côte d'Azur specifically?"

"None. None I can think of, anyway."

"I am struggling to understand why your alleged kidnappers brought you *here*."

Masson takes his *Gauloises* from his jacket pocket, and proffers the pack, "Cigarette?"

"I don't smoke, thanks."

"Mind if I do?"

"It's your turf, Inspector, not mine."

Masson smiles, "In that case, I give myself permission."

He drags deeply, exhales slowly, "Monsieur Pickford, if I wanted to kidnap you from your prison cell, and take you somewhere the Antiguan and British authorities couldn't easily snatch you back – until I was sure I'd been paid my ransom – why would I go to the immense expense and inconvenience of bringing you to France? A short boat trip, a helicopter ride, a light plane flight, and I am on St Kitts, Nevis, or Montserrat. From there, I can island-hop my way right up to Florida, or down to Brazil... Do you see why it's odd? I simply would not bother transporting you all the way across the Atlantic without a very good reason. What is *here* that makes your presence so necessary? I can get my ransom just as easily in Nevis as I can in Nice, huh?"

"I get what you're saying...and I honestly have no idea."

"No, nor do I...not yet. But I will, you can be sure of that."

"What happens to me now, Inspector?"

"I expect you will have to go back to Antigua to complete your sentence there...but not until I have been able to investigate why and how you were brought to this country, and for what purpose. You need to resign yourself to a few days in a cell here. We will provide you with necessary washing items and some clothing to fit you better."

"But I'm to remain in custody."

"Yes. You are, by your own admission, a convicted criminal with a continuing sentence to serve…but you are possibly also the victim of a currently-unexplained abduction – "

"*Possibly?!* I was handcuffed to a bloody pipe!"

"I did not get to be an Inspecteur of Police by believing every tall tale told to me in an interview room. I will fairly and thoroughly investigate all that you have said, and I will draw conclusions based on evidence. I will not discount anything…neither will I blindly swallow it. Would you like me to contact anyone for you? Your wife, for example?"

The giant gapes, "My *wife?*"

"You wear a wedding ring."

Stocker-Pickford fingers the ring absently, as if he'd forgotten it was there.

"My wife…" He barks one harsh, mirthless laugh, "Wouldn't know where to find her, Old Chap!"

Masson shrugs, and replies mildly, "Ok…up to you… You'll have to be patient for a couple of days while we speak to the UK and Antiguan authorities about you."

"Righto… Don't suppose there's anything English to read, is there?"

Masson chuckles, "I am sure we can find you a poolside paperback to pass the time."

"Much obliged. Don't care what. I'll go mad with boredom otherwise."

On instinct, Masson chances his arm, "One final question, Monsieur Pickford. Do you know a Guy Montparnasse?"

"Golly, that's a mouthful, isn't it? Sounds like a made-up name to me!"

"You think it sounds like a made-up name?"

"Like something out of *Poirot*, eh?"

Masson produces the creased passport scan, folds it so only the photograph is visible, and places it on the table before the Englishman, who looks, starts, and tries to yank the paper closer. Masson places one finger on it and holds it still, watching every facial tick like a poker player detecting a tell.

"Good Lord! For a moment..." Pickford hunches over, peering intently, before looking up at Masson, "What name did you just say, Mont-Saint-Michel or something?"

Quietly, Masson murmurs, "Who do *you* think it is?"

"Well...it's been a few years – more than a few, really – but, if I had to say..."

"Yes?"

"It looks staggeringly like a mate of my brother's from school and University. Jim...*James*...Chadwick. They were friends for years. I assume they still are..."

Masson taps his index finger on the picture, "He's English?"

"Yes; as English as I am!"

"Any Belgian relatives?"

"No idea. Doubt it."

"Does he speak French?"

"I expect so! I daresay he speaks bloody Japanese, knowing Jim!"

"He's an accomplished man?"

"He was always one of those sickening buggers who could do everything without seeming to try. Very bloody clever. Very bloody charming. You wanted to hate his guts, but he was such a solid bloke you never could."

"Does he sail?"

"Oh yes. Cowes Week, Salcombe in the summer, all that jazz. I've stayed on a boat of his, actually, before I was married. Great fun, I must say! My brother, his tiresome wife, a bunch of simply *smashing* birds…and lucky old me! Terrific week, that was. The party did seem to follow Jim a bit. He was perennially ahead of the crowd, you know?"

"Sounds an interesting character. Is he married…or in any sort of long-term relationship?"

"Not to my knowledge. Think he's one of these types who prefer to play the field. He always seemed rather a lone wolf to me."

"Did he and your brother work together?"

"No. Geoffrey – my brother – followed my father into politics."

"And James Chadwick?"

"This and that. Investments, gambles…had his fingers in a lot of pies."

"Any criminal pies?"

"Gosh…um…I don't know…"

"Ok." Masson shoves the battered passport scan back into his pocket, feigning unconcern.

"*Is* it Jim? I haven't seen him in years. Is he in some kind of trouble here?"

"Obviously, I cannot answer those questions."

"Oh. Right. Um…"

"Your wife…you are not in touch?"

"No, no, we're definitely not in touch!"

"A result of your conviction?"

Pickford gazes distantly over Masson's left shoulder, and replies regretfully, "Not really…no… More a result of my general idiocy, Inspector."

"Your wife's name?"

"Annelisse."

"And her maiden name, please…for standard background checks."

"Her maiden name was Rivers."

****

Tammi carefully repacks all the items into the holdall, save two. Hampered by the handcuffs, she clumsily unwraps Nightingale's bundle of tools and extracts the cigarette lighter. To spare her sore fingers, she instead grips the sharp stone between her palms, stabbing at the sandy soil until it's sufficiently loose for her to scoop out a shallow pit. She places the folder in it, and touches the lighter to each corner, watching all the carefully-compiled evidence of her criminality blacken and burn. The folder is thick. It takes a while. She closely attends the fire, prodding any larger pieces of levitating ash back onto the embers, ensuring total obliteration of every illuminating syllable. When confident it's no more than anonymous ash, she pushes the lip of piled sand back over the fire, cutting off its oxygen and concealing its whereabouts, patting down the dust with the heels of her hands. She uses the hem of her ruined dress to wipe the lighter clean of all identifying prints, sliding it carefully back into the tool-wrap, tying it tight, and returning it to the holdall, her decision made.

Wincing, she rocks onto one hip, rolls to hands and knees, and gingerly edges upright. Taking a moment to weather the disorientating light-headedness, she determines the position of the sun, the angle and length of the shadows it casts upon the dusty ground, notes the distant sparkle of Mediterranean Sea visible through the trees, and limps stiffly off in the direction most likely to deliver her swiftly back to civilisation.

The last thing anyone expects is for Tammi Rivers to bowl into the local Gendarmerie and report a murder for which she is by now undoubtedly the prime suspect – so that is exactly what she must do.

TWELVE

"So, Pickford's statement is corroborated?"

"Yes, Boss. According to the prison authorities, an English representative arrived with all the correct identifications and paperwork to transport Marcus Pickford to a UK facility. They had no reason to question it. They've even sent their CCTV logs. This is the front gate feed. Look, there's the guy going in…check out the timeline…leaving about two hours later clearly handcuffed to Pickford."

Masson leans over Xavier's shoulder and clicks the mouse to pause the footage, "And who does that look like to you?"

"Well, it's not great quality, Boss…you might be able to get Technical to enhance the image a bit…but it bears a passing resemblance to the passport scan of Guy Montparnasse…or, rather, James Chadwick."

"Yes, it does…and yet according to Pickford he hasn't seen him in years. He claims he's primarily a friend of his older brother."

"So, Belgian Guy Montparnasse is actually English James Chadwick, who is also known as Nightingale…who appears to be dead?"

"It's looking increasingly like that, Xavier…and as if the gun-toting woman on the harbour CCTV is the one who did it – Valentine's 'Tammi Rivers'."

"Why, do you think?"

"Who knows? Pickford is seemingly related to her by marriage! It can't be a coincidence both have turned up unexpectedly in a foreign country within ten kilometres of one another! Oh God, Xavier, this is making my brain hurt! It's all linked, undoubtedly! But *how*?"

Xavier shrugs sheepishly, "I have absolutely no idea, Boss."

"No, nor have I. Something involving the British Government that's significant enough to have spies swarming over it…but no tangible evidence to get your teeth into! The only thing we know *for sure* is that a man got barbecued halfway up a mountain in highly-suspicious circumstances…but, despite having all this so-called 'insider info', we're no closer to discovering who he is or why it happened!"

"Valentine says – "

"That's another thing, Xavier; we can't trust a damn word Valentine says. He's not working on our murder investigation. He's purely here to keep something under wraps for the Brits, I'm convinced of it. He'll spin us any story to keep us looking the wrong way and avoid some sort of diplomatic incident."

"What do we do, Boss?"

"We keep Marcus Pickford a secret. We don't tell Valentine we've got him. Not yet, anyway. Not until we've thoroughly investigated the facts of his statement. Do all the standard checks you'd do for anyone else. Look into his family, this James Chadwick guy, Pickford's wife…and the Rivers-woman we suspect must be a relative of hers."

"What about Valentine?"

"Keep him ticking over. We're still looking for his two targets. Regardless of what we might uncover secretly through questioning Pickford, they are still at large. We need to at least *pretend* we're on the same side for the time being, until we find out what that snidey Rosbif's really up to."

A soft, polite cough behind them makes both whirl around guiltily. Thankfully, it's not Valentine, but one of the officers from the Front Desk. She frowns suspiciously at their shifty demeanours, before flashing Xavier the kind of long-lashed, dark-eyed, heart-stopping smile that, to Masson's considerable amusement, has the young Détective blushing redder than the sunburnt Germans on the beach across the road. She formally addresses the Inspecteur, "I'm sorry to interrupt, sir, but I thought you'd want to know. A woman's just staggered up to the desk in a terrible state – filthy, covered in blood and bruises, near collapse! She's wearing handcuffs, speaking English, and claiming to be a witness to the abduction of Guy Montparnasse!"

****

"How long's she been here?"

"Just over two hours."

"Two *hours*! Why did no one – ?"

"You were out, and as you never bother telling us where you're going – "

"That's rich coming from you; King of the Lunch Break!"

"Are you *nervous*, Detective Sergeant?"

"Why would you possibly think that?"

"No reason…you just seem a little on-edge. Keyed-up, you know?"

"I'm simply concerned so much time's been wasted – "

"Not wasted, Valentine. I don't know how you do things in England, but here we like to ensure our suspects aren't severely dehydrated or bleeding heavily prior to interview. It's so much more paperwork if they keel over in custody. Whilst not life-threatening, her injuries were apparently bad enough to warrant assessment by the doctor."

"Like what?"

"I don't know, Valentine, I haven't seen her either."

"Is it Rivers?"

"She has not yet provided a name. You can see for yourself," Masson stops before an anonymous entrance halfway down the grey-painted corridor, "It's this one here."

He reaches for the knob, but Valentine stops him with a hand on his forearm, "Hold on, Inspecteur. Look…I need to take the lead in this, all right? I need to be able to do this my way. The…um…British way…"

"The British *Government* way?" Masson baits.

Valentine scowls and rolls his eyes, as he does each one of the fifty times a day the Inspecteur alludes to him being a spy.

"Thinking about it, it's probably better if I do this alone."

Masson instantly steps in front of the door, barring Valentine's entry, "Oh no. No, no. You aren't getting away with that. Already you are withholding information – "

"*Classified* information!"

"And now you think you're interviewing potential suspects alone? Sorry, Valentine, but Xavier and I will be sitting in, whether we utter a word or not."

The two posture aggressively, squaring up to one another until Valentine yields, shrugging as if it makes no difference him, "Have it your way." He's more occupied with taking deep breaths, hopping on the spot, and rotating neck and shoulders like a boxer about to enter the ring, "Right, are we all ready then?"

Masson gives him a withering glance, "Of course we're 'ready'. We interview suspects all the time. We don't really feel the need to psyche ourselves up for it."

Valentine glares at Masson as if the Inspecteur is something unpleasant he's just scraped off his shoe, and haughtily enters the room without another word. Masson winks at Xavier, who smirks conspiratorially, and follows his senior officer inside.

The woman seated at the table *is* the one from Valentine's photograph! Many years older; bruised, battered, and bloodied – but the soulless eyes are unmistakeable. Despite being small and slight, her presence is undeniably intimidating. Xavier, daily accustomed to apprehending violent miscreants and questioning obstructive suspects without a flicker of disquiet, finds himself instinctively dropping behind the two older men, that they might shield him from her.

Valentine stops before the table, back ramrod straight, heels clicking together. Masson is convinced he's about to salute. He brandishes his identification like a crucifix at an exorcism, and barks in clipped English, "Detective Sergeant Valentine; Interpol! These are my colleagues, Inspector Masson and Detective Hâche of the local CID."

An even, calm stare greets this bombastic declaration; an unreadable face but for eyebrows raised in…what; amusement?

"Whoa there, Sergeant Vaseline, or whatever your name is! I'd like a *proper* look at all those IDs please."

Having never had a suspect ask to re-examine his identification in thirty years of policing, Masson is immediately intrigued. Matching and maintaining her steady eye-contact, he reopens his badge and slides it across the desk. Taking his cue from the Inspecteur, Xavier does the same. Valentine has to follow suit; it would look odd not to. She pulls down the sleeve of the tracksuit they've put her in, so she doesn't transfer prints onto the IDs as she picks up and peruses them.

"Hmmm…these two are pretty worn, aren't they? They obviously go in and out of your pockets a thousand times a day. This one, though…this one's pristine! Detective Sergeant *Valentine*, does that say? I bet you got the mickey taken out of you at school for that, eh?"

She waggles the shiny leather wallet in her still dirty and bloodstained fingers, striped with the white of so many dressings she probably couldn't leave a fingerprint if she wanted to.

"This one hasn't seen *real* action, has it? You obviously don't have much cause to whip it out, Detective Sergeant…"

Xavier glances nervously around, unsure he fully understands what's going on. Comfortingly, the Inspecteur seems to be finding the whole thing hilarious. He's grinning fit to crack his face in half, and the more puce with mortification Valentine becomes, the wider Masson beams.

After subjecting Valentine to another prolonged and discomfitingly-direct stare, the woman places the IDs back on the table and pushes them individually towards their owners, smiling genially, as if they've all popped in for tea, "Well, sit down gentlemen. I'm not the Queen."

All three retrieve their IDs and sit, with much muttering of polite apologies and interlocking of chair legs as they attempt to fit in a line opposite her; broad, masculine shoulders nearly touching in the tiny room. Bothered by the table leg, Masson eases his chair backwards. After all, he's here merely to observe 'the British way'; Xavier is making notes. Valentine takes the young photograph of the woman from his pocket and places it on the table in front of her. She looks down at it, and back up at him, "Perving over my school photos, you dirty old git?"

Masson observes her considerable effect on the seriously-rattled Valentine. He's suddenly conscious she already knows what he's only just beginning to realise – that 'Detective Sergeant Valentine' has clearly never conducted a police interview in his life! So much nervous energy is fizzing from the Englishman's erect figure, he could double as a firework on Bastille Day. His trump card played far too early, unnerved that she seems neither surprised nor intimidated by the sight of the photograph, the flustered Valentine squirms in his chair and blinks rapidly, clenching jaw working visibly. Eventually, he recovers sufficient presence of mind to growl, "It's hardly that. How old are you in that picture; you must be at least twenty! How old are you now?"

She feigns offence, "Detective *Sergeant*! You know you should *never* ask a lady her age…"

Masson openly snorts, and only makes a half-hearted attempt to cover it with a cough when Valentine glares at him. Xavier glances anxiously from the smirking Inspecteur to the simmering Valentine, worried they're making their blatant dislike of one another too obvious to their unconventional interviewee.

"May I?" she points at the photograph.

Valentine's got himself back under control, "Be my guest."

Again, the sharp tug of the sleeve over her hand so she can pick up the picture but not leave a mark. This woman knows the score.

She nods thoughtfully, and places the picture back on the table top. Valentine smiles, somewhat smugly, "You are aware I *have* your fingerprints…?"

The condescending reply deflates Valentine's pomposity like a pierced balloon, "No, you have *some* fingerprints. You *don't know* whether they're mine, as I've not been obliged to provide you with any yet."

Unable to disguise his irritation, Valentine snarls, "You could save a lot of time by just telling us what you're doing here!"

She prods gingerly at a mottled bruise on her right temple, winces, and murmurs, "You could do the same, *Agent* Valentine…but you won't, will you?"

Valentine opens his mouth to retort, before thinking better of it.

She sits back, folds her arms, again smiles in her amiably-disarming way, and says, "Stalemate, I think? I could do with a wee, if the WPC could take me, please?"

Valentine waves his hand dismissively, female plumbing definitely not within his remit. Masson cranes to mutter instructions to the attending officer, who stands and escorts the limping woman from the room.

Masson slouches in his chair, cups the back of his head in his clasped palms, stretches out his long legs, and comments lightly, "That went well."

Valentine rounds upon him defensively, "You were no help! You just sat there!"

"You told me you wanted to handle it. I left you to do it your way. You claim you're here to find a missing man, yet you asked her no questions about our unidentified corpse *at all*!" At this, Valentine looks crushed, and Masson finds himself unexpectedly sorry for the frustrating Englishman. Patiently, endeavouring not to patronise, he explains gently, "An interview is like a rally in tennis. You bat the questions back and forth. You let them reveal all the subtleties of their game as they try to get a shot past you. When the time is right, when they've used up everything they've got, you bring out your overhead smash and pummel them into the court! It's a tactical game of mental endurance. Never show your case has weaknesses or holes. Always get the ball back over the net, no matter what."

Valentine sighs heavily, "I don't usually have to deal with people."

Masson rolls his eyes at Xavier behind Valentine's back, "We'd never have guessed...what do you deal with?"

"Information. Evidence. Data."

"How do you obtain evidence without dealing with people?"

"Normally others obtain it for me."

"Men such as Nightingale?"

Valentine purses his lips, and doesn't answer.

Masson speculates, "And, because he's gone walkabout, they've taken you away from your computer screen and plonked you here – a true fish-out-of-water, huh?"

Valentine swallows his seriously-injured pride, and asks in a small voice, "What now?"

"Leave her stewing in a cell overnight, wondering what we really know about her. Before we speak to her again, and what you should have done today prior to interview – but you were too impatient to listen to common sense – is run proper background checks on her. Forget what we think we know. Concentrate on what we can actually discover and prove. We need to get a set of prints off her if at all possible. We have to *confirm* they're the same as the ones lifted from the yacht, instead of just *assuming* they are. We can only hold her for a certain amount of time without charging her with something, whether her face matches an old photograph or not."

"She was bloody careful about handling stuff."

"She knows our game...but she'll slip up eventually – they always do. Patience is the key."

Masson clasps Valentine's shoulder in one firm, friendly palm, "Listen, I do this crap every day. I can be of considerable use to you...*if* you tell me what's really going on here; who she really is. Come to that, who *you* really are! It strikes me you're all theory and no practical. Xavier and I, we're one hundred percent hands-on. We can turn the tide of your case like *that*!" Masson clicks his fingers with a flourish right under Valentine's nose, making him recoil in surprise, "*If* you trust us as colleagues…"

Valentine rubs his tired eyes, and mutters, "I'm sorry Inspecteur, I have my orders."

Hand of friendship spurned, Masson smiles sorrowfully, claps the Englishman forcefully on the back, and drawls, "Best of luck with your bull-in-a-china-shop interview technique, then! I'm going for a smoke."

****

"Where's Valentine, Boss?"

"I don't know…sobbing in the Bogs, probably. Quick, while he's not around – what else did you find out about Pickford earlier; anything good?"

Xavier beams expansively, "Oh, yes, sir!"

From the lockable drawer in the bottom of his filing cabinet, Xavier extracts a thick wadge of paper.

"Crikey, what's that lot?"

"Marcus Stocker-Pickford, sir! Articles about his fall from grace. Dodgy deals in the Caribbean, allegations of historic insider trading – apparently the reason they had to leave the UK in a hurry – "

"They?"

"Marcus Pickford and his *wife*, Annelisse!" Xavier is clearly delighted with what he's discovered. He lays the internet printouts in a row across Masson's desk. All pictures of the same woman.

The woman from downstairs. The woman Valentine had told them was Tammi Rivers.

Masson gapes, "Xavier, are you *sure*?"

"Yes, sir."

"Just like that?"

"Yes, sir!"

"Because?"

"Because...long-dead women don't leave fingerprints on expensive yachts, or arrive beaten up and handcuffed at police stations."

"*What?!*"

"Admittedly, I can't find a photograph of her, but internet searches for Tamise or Tammi Rivers all return the same result. She's *dead*!"

Masson shakes his head, "Another Tammi Rivers, surely?"

"No, sir, it has to be our girl – the one Valentine says he's looking for!"

"Why, Xavier?"

"Because, several years ago, Tammi Rivers fell to her death from an airport multi-storey car park. Sixty feet! Pavement pizza; no getting up and walking away from that! At the time she fell, she was involved in a police chase, because – coincidentally – she was holding yet another prisoner at gunpoint...her *own sister*, Mrs Annelisse Pickford! There might be another Tamise Rivers...but I'd say it's pretty unlikely there's another Tamise Rivers with a sister called Annelisse Pickford – and there's Madame Pickford's photo again, sir; it's the *same woman*."

"Shit...what's the hell is going on, Xavier!"

"I've got a theory, sir."

"Come on, let's hear it. It can't be any more insane than all the notions that are whirling around my head right now."

"Valentine's been sent here to find James Chadwick/Guy Montparnasse/Nightingale – whatever you want to call him, as seemingly they're all the same man – because he's helping the Pickford family do something illegal that's of interest to, or a source of embarrassment for, the British Government. Pickford's 'kidnapping' from prison was arranged, the house he was found in was a scoped-out hiding place, and he was always going to meet his wife here…because here is where the boat is! What if it had been agreed that old-friend-of-the-family and apparently-expert-sailor James Chadwick brought it in…and the Pickfords were due to sail it out again? It was all going great until the cleaner showed unexpectedly at the location where Marcus was hiding out, and cocked up the plan!"

"But Chadwick and Marcus Pickford look nothing like each other! How was Pickford going to pass himself off as 'Guy Montparnasse' in order to escape on his yacht with a readily-supplied false passport?"

Xavier sighs, and acknowledges the Inspecteur's intelligent observation, "I hadn't thought of that. I don't know, sir."

The Inspecteur's on a roll, "Also, how do you explain the handcuffs Pickford was discovered in?"

"That's easier – they're cover, sir! He could have put them on himself when he heard the cleaner opening the garage door! He's a criminal! He's got links to the British Government. His Dad was a UK Cabinet Minister, and is now in the House of Lords. His brother was an MP. It's all in here!" Xavier waves his reams of research under Masson's nose, blurting breathlessly, "His elder brother – the MP – lost his seat in the UK Parliament because it came out in the press that he'd been heavily-invested in his little brother's illegal schemes…and couldn't explain where the money had come from."

"Misappropriated public funds?"

"Could be. The one theme throughout all these articles is the allegation that the Stocker-Pickford's myriad investment funds launder ill-gotten gains. The number one investor, if the British press is to be believed? 'Businessman' James Chadwick! Rumoured to be a player in South London's criminal underworld. There's healthy speculation about the Dad too; suggestions that he abused his influential position, past and present, to appoint Government contracts. He places publicly-financed initiatives with the companies who'll give him the greatest preferential kick-back. Regardless of whether the bridge, railway, motorway, or hospital actually gets built, Sir Blair Stocker-Pickford and his cronies clean up! Allegedly, anyway… He's the original Teflon-man – nothing seems to stick to him…unlike his sons, who've respectively lost career and liberty within the last four years because of the media storm. British newspapers were alive with it for weeks! Where did James Chadwick go? He disappeared when all these allegations first surfaced, and no one's seem him since. Similarly, as soon as the Antiguan police knocked on their front door, Annelisse Pickford also completely vanished. Reading this lot is a conspiracy-theorist's wet dream!"

"Anything pointing to James Chadwick being a British spook, rather than a crook?"

"Nothing so far. I haven't got to him properly yet, I'm still digging on the Pickfords. There's a tonne of dirt! Do you think my theory holds up, sir?"

"It's certainly got merit, Xavier," Masson skim-reads the uppermost article, "I mean, why would Valentine be sent to find a woman who's been *dead* for nearly seven years! The one conclusion I simply can't dismiss no matter how charitable I try to be towards the abrasive bastard, is that our 'friend' Valentine has even less idea what he's doing here than we do! He's obviously spent his career churning through data in a basement somewhere, leaving the dirty work to the more competent operatives. Your assertion that Valentine's been sent to recover money the Stocker-Pickfords have pinched from the British Government is certainly plausible...but how do we prove any of it?"

As the Inspecteur frowns and massages at the headache forming behind his eyes, another grizzled old Detective, with salt and pepper beard and weekend sailor's tan, glances up from his computer screen, catches sight of a junior colleague entering the room, and bellows, "Hey, Bourdey – nice romantic lunch? Grope the right sister today?"

The entire investigative unit erupts into guffaws as Bourdey blushes beetroot and throws the department comedian an ill-tempered V-sign. Noticing Xavier chuckling along with the rest, Masson asks, "What's this now?"

"Twins, sir. One's been here ages, and her sister's just started working downstairs as well. Bourdey asked the new one out. It was going great, by all accounts – and then he got a hefty slap yesterday for feeling the other one's arse outside the girl's locker room."

Masson, still distracted by his whirling thoughts, squints in incomprehension until Xavier spells it out, "Twins, sir! Identical! He couldn't tell 'em apart! He felt-up the wrong sister and didn't even realise! He had to have it pointed out to him! Imagine not being able to recognise your own girlfriend; embarrassing, eh?"

Xavier's already chortling again, but Masson doesn't join in. Instead, he abruptly snatches up one of the recently-taken colour pictures of husband and wife from a Caribbean lifestyle magazine soirée, and compares it to a black and white shot from an English society periodical with a date way back in the early noughties. He peers intently at them for some seconds under the brightness of his desk lamp, before shooting to his feet, sending his wheelie chair scudding across the office, and making Xavier jump.

"Boss, you all right?"

"I've just thought of something!"

"Where are you going?"

"To test a hunch, Xavier! I'll be back in a minute."

****

Masson takes the stairs to the basement an eight-step flight at a time, splaying his palms against each wall and swinging himself from landing to landing with great flat-footed leaps that echo back up the winding staircase like slaps on bare skin. Bounding through the door with his customary energy, he greets the Custody Sergeant with the breezy, "How's our tourist in Number Four?"

"Snores like a locomotive. Everyone's been complaining."

Masson chortles, "The English! So great at making friends wherever they go!"

The Custody Sergeant snorts disparagingly, and finishes his coffee in one swig.

"I need a word with him. Can you unlock please?"

"Yes, sir."

Pickford is wedged on the concrete shelf topped with an inadequately-thin plastic-coated mattress, that serves as a bed within the narrow cell. To straighten his long legs fully, he has to rest them at an angle several feet up the wall. He's reading the book they've found for him. Clearly a man accustomed to incarceration, he merely glances as the inspection panel opens, the door is unlocked, and Masson steps inside.

"Am I off then, Inspector? Does my Caribbean private jet await?"

"Alas, not yet, Monsieur Pickford. How is your book?"

"Absolutely awful."

"You did say you didn't mind what it was…"

"And I'm regretting that."

"Apparently, it was the only one they could find. You don't have to read it."

"What's the alternative, go bonkers with boredom? My French isn't even good enough to read the graffiti in here!"

Masson chuckles, "A question for you – related to background checks. By any chance, was your wife a twin?"

"Oh. Um. Yes…?s"

Masson thinks the reply is delivered cautiously, as if Pickford's concerned what the next question might be.

"Identical?"

"Er, yes…scarily so, actually."

"Your wife's name was Annelisse, yes?"

"Yes."

"Maiden name Rivers?"

"Yes, as I already said."

"What is her twin's name, please?"

"Tamise…"

"Otherwise known as 'Tammi'?"

"Yes…"

There's a note of resignation in Pickford's voice, as if he's been expecting this all along.

"Thank you, Monsieur Pickford."

Masson turns to go.

Pickford asks, "That's it?"

Without looking back, Masson answers, "That's it."

The clang of the closing cell door is loud in his ears as he walks away.

THIRTEEN

From the upstairs office window, Masson watches the little car containing Xavier and Valentine turn out of the staff car park and up the main road towards Valentine's hotel, before striding purposefully to the evidence store to check out a recent item.

Time being of the essence, he's seated at the desk in the interview room well before the female officer arrives with the summoned Englishwoman. He doesn't bother to stand, but indicates the chair opposite, "Good evening. Please sit down."

"I didn't think the French did overtime. I'd better not miss my dinner, Inspector. You lot cock up a lot of stuff, but you never ruin a meal...I'd imagine not even in prison."

"You are not in prison, Mademoiselle."

"I'm not free to go, am I?"

"Be a little more forthcoming with your information, and I'm sure you will be back to your French Riviera holiday in no time at all...if, indeed, recreation is your reason for being here."

"And, in the meantime, I go hungry..."

Masson rolls his eyes in exasperation, and intones, "I will ensure you are adequately fed when we are finished here."

"Too kind."

"De rien."

"Just us two? Got shot of the Apprentice and the Posh Fop?"

"Détective Hâche is an experienced and capable officer with a bright future…and I have a feeling you know more about my new friend Valentine than I do."

She smiles, shrugging non-commitally.

Masson ventures, "M I 6?"

She shakes her head, "Doubtful."

"M I 5, then?"

"Possible."

"What's he doing in France?"

"Hasn't he told you?"

"Oh yes, he's told me."

"A pack of lies, right?"

It's Masson's turn to be coy, simply responding, "Do you know him?"

"No…but I've encountered his kind before. I don't wish to be coarse, Inspector, but I came here hours ago to report witnessing a crime, and no one seems to give two shits! In fact, I'm the one being treated like a criminal! Are so many people assaulted and abducted on the Riviera these days that no one bothers to investigate any more? You're not remotely interested that I witnessed a serious life-threatening attack!"

"On the contrary," Masson swings Nightingale's dusty holdall up onto the table, "I am very interested."

He slides the manila folder from the bag, opens it, and takes out both photographs, placing them on the table before her. He points to the 1990s London street. He taps his finger on Guy…Jimmy. Whoever he is…*was*…it doesn't matter now.

"This man. Identify him please."

"His name is James Chadwick."

"Does he have any aliases?"

"I know he has a good line in fake tan and French accents."

Masson withdraws the tired passport scan, presses it as flat as he's able, and shows it to her. She nods, willingly enough, "Yep."

"So, to be clear, James Chadwick is also known as Guy Montparnasse?"

"To my limited knowledge."

"Thank you. This picture now. This young man…James Chadwick again, yes?"

"Looks like him. School photo?"

"And this boy here?"

Masson's finger slips efficiently down the line to stop at the only other familiar face, "Marcus Stocker-Pickford?"

Tammi lurches in her chair. She tries to disguise the involuntary reaction by pretending to fidget in bruised discomfort, but when she glances up, the shrewd eyes are fixed intently upon her. She clears her closing throat, and croaks, "No, that's his brother. Geoffrey Stocker-Pickford. The elder son."

"The MP?"

"I don't believe he holds office any more…some sort of scandal…?"

"Involving Marcus?"

"You're very fixated on Marcus, if you don't mind me saying."

"He's the brother with the criminal record."

"I see."

"*Do* you?"

"I'm still not clear what this has to do with the crime I've been trying to report but no one wants to know about. I'll try again now, if you don't mind, as I seem to have your undivided attention. I'm witness to an abduction, Inspector! As you can see from my injuries, I only just made it out alive myself...and yet you're showing me forty year old Hockey Team photographs and questioning me about them! Don't you *want* to find Guy Montparnasse?"

Masson lifts his ongoing-case folder from the seat beside him, produces the full-frontal photograph of the blackened corpse, and whispers, "I think I already have."

There's nothing to prove this picture is of Guy, but Tammi knows it anyway. It shouldn't come as a surprise – Nightingale was always going to kill him – but seeing it still has the power to shock and sadden. She shouldn't care; Jimmy Chadwick lied to her...but it hurts nevertheless. What she mourns is the shattering of yet another dream.

Masson watches the fleeting shadow of regret pass across the thin, drawn face, and presses home his slight advantage. Wafting the passport scan back and forth in her peripheral vision, he murmurs gently, "What alerted us is that there is no such person in Belgium with this name, of this age, of this appearance...and at this fictional Bruges address. The road name is genuine, but the building number is not. It is a completely false ID. However, there *is* a British Citizen called James Chadwick. He has multiple addresses and business interests. He has a passport, but he never seems to use it. He's apparently been missing four years, yet – within the last six hours – I've received *two* apparently-independent corroborations of his identity...and even charming school photographs! He *exists*. What he's doing in France under this false passport, I am hoping you will tell me."

"I can't. I don't *know* James Chadwick! Well, I know him by report and reputation. I didn't think I was intimately acquainted with him! I thought I was making friends with a Belgian called Guy."

"How did you discover they were one and the same?"

"It was...brought to my attention."

"By?"

"A little birdie told me."

Masson's eyes twinkle mischievously, "A Nightingale?"

The woman gasps, as Masson hoped she would, and spontaneously laughs aloud, "I've come here to tell you something it seems you already know, Inspector!"

"Far from it, Mademoiselle. I have been travelling swiftly down the wrong road, I think. I've been firmly convinced James Chadwick is also the British Agent Valentine calls 'Nightingale'."

"Chadwick? No, Inspector, he's not Nightingale. Reportedly, he's a gangster, a murderer, a dealer, a trafficker, a moneylender...a thug. Jimmy Chadwick has a reputation as a nasty piece of work, back where I come from."

"A 'nasty piece of work' with no criminal record."

Flirtatiously, she teases, "Plenty of criminals have no criminal record, Inspector."

"Does that include you? You see, neither Tammi Rivers – nor her identical twin Annelisse Pickford – have any sort of convictions we can uncover…although, as you so astutely point out, it doesn't mean they aren't criminals."

"My, my, Detective Hâche *has* been busy, hasn't he?

"I told you, a bright future."

"Well, Inspector, despite his brilliance, I'm not telling. Your protégé needs to work it out."

"And he will. Everyone has their theories. We've just got to test them against available evidence. Valentine maintains you are Tammi Rivers, the woman he's been sent here to find.

Xavier is sure you are Annelisse Pickford, because the evidence he's uncovered supports that assertion."

"And you, Inspector?"

"I believe I have a foolproof way of determining the answer. Come with me, please."

The Inspecteur stands, mutters a brief instruction to the attending officer, takes Tammi insistently by the elbow, and guides her from the room, leaving the WPC behind.

As they reach the door at the head of the stairs, Masson suddenly trips, his greater weight toppling the unprepared Tammi forwards. She instinctively puts up her hands to shield her already-injured face, and both bodies bounce lightly off the toughened glass.

Masson is all concern, "Oh, I am so sorry! So clumsy of me! You are all right?"

Tammi can feel the pads of her three unbandaged fingers pressing firmly against the clear pane. The crafty bastard! Those prints would be enough to match whatever they already had off Guy's yacht, and the ancient records Sir Julian Franklin had no doubt sent to France along with the wet-behind-the-ears Agent Valentine.

Tammi sighs wearily, acknowledging she's been outclassed, and endeavours to smear the prints as she eases her fingers off the glass.

Having attained his objective with comparative ease, the Inspecteur is all affability, jauntily bashing in the security code and politely opening the door for her to precede him down the stairs. Rather than being returned to her cell for more hours of worry and wondering, the Inspecteur instead propels her firmly along the opposite corridor, stopping before the door to Number Four.

"This afternoon, one of the things Détective Hâche discovered is that only one twin is still alive. Initially, this caused us confusion, so I decided to speak to an individual intimately acquainted with both sisters. That person did something very notable. They know which twin still lives…and they revealed that truth to me without even being aware they'd done so. Quite unconsciously, they referred to Annelisse Pickford in the *past* tense, and Tammi Rivers in the *present*."

The woman's intelligent eyes roll and dart, as if the agile brain is somersaulting like a gymnast behind them.

Masson reaches forward and opens the inspection panel in the cell door, peering through, then stepping aside and inviting the woman to take his place.

Tentatively, still with suspicious eyes fixed upon him, she edges closer, finally condescending to peek inside. If she's at all surprised by the sight that greets her, she betrays no outward evidence of it. Masson is impressed by her admirable self-command.

Positioned behind the woman so he can see over her shoulder and into the cell, Masson watches Pickford glance towards the opening panel with his customary insouciance. The Inspecteur is well-placed to observe the big man's amazement and consternation at the sight of all-too-familiar features staring in at him, and is consequently fully prepared for what happens next. Pickford leaps from the bunk as if it's been electrified. It takes but one enormous stride for him to cover the few feet to the door – but Masson's faster. Yanking the startled woman aside, he slams the panel shut on the advancing figure with a clang. He's already hauled her struggling body halfway back up the corridor before the giant begins to hammer furiously on the impenetrable barrier, yelling, "Hey! Open this door! Hey! Masson! Inspector Masson! Hey! Heeeeeyyyyy!!!"

Despite her attempted resistance, Masson maintains his vice-like grip on her upper arm. Their progress is relentless; along the corridor, out through the security entrance, and back onto the cavernous stairwell, where they pause momentarily, Masson listening intently for tell-tale footfalls above, before spinning her body violently around and thudding her face-first against the cold plaster, pulling her arms up her back so viciously that pain knifes across her swollen elbow joint. The accompanying jolt through her battered head as it thumps the wall makes her whimper in agony. The Inspecteur's body is thrust tight against her back, his feet splayed for stability. It crosses her mind to hook up a heel and drive it as hard as she can into his unprotected groin…but even if that gets her free of him, what then? She's in the bowels of a police station! Every section door she's seen so far has a coded keypad, into which a number must be typed to release the lock. Doubtless every door has the same code, but that's immaterial if she doesn't know it. Realistically, how far might she get? The top of this staircase? The far end of the next corridor? If she wants this hell to be over, what's the point of continuing to run? Yes, Masson holds power here; admittedly, Valentine poses a problem that must be dealt with – but the man who presents *actual* danger is the only one who knows the full truth: Agent Nightingale. Everyone else who's ever discovered it is dead! There must be a way to leverage her current predicament. There's *always* a way if you think hard enough…

It means she doesn't surrender to her first temptation to fight, and run. Instead, she waits for Masson to make his play.

His breath is hot against the side of her face as he growls, "The sight of you is the first thing to get that big bastard off his bunk in nearly a week! I want to know who you are, what you represent, and why you're causing such a stir on my stretch of coastline. Either you tell me, *tonight*, or I wash my hands of it. I turn you over completely to Valentine, he takes you back to England as soon as he can, and the very best of luck to you!"

"I can't go back to England, Inspector. I'm dead if I go back."

"So, level with me, Mademoiselle Tammi Rivers… Perhaps I could help you?"

It goes against everything she's ever believed, "I'm no grass, Inspector. What exactly are you asking me for?"

"*Exactly?* I don't want British Secret Service, posing as Interpol officers, sniffing around my unsolved cases and deliberately interfering for unexplained reasons. I want Valentine gone! I have a murder and a kidnapping frustratingly unresolved; both investigations going nowhere because of his meddling. All I uncover are more questions and no answers! I think you can give me answers."

"I can do better than that! I can give you the bloke who perpetrated both acts…but what can you give me in return, Inspector, except a sentence and a cell?"

The pressure at her back lessens perceptibly. Her arms are allowed to drop an inch or two lower, mercifully easing the burning pain in her straining shoulders and throbbing elbow, "What do you want?"

"I want a legal British passport in my own name. I lost mine, you see…a long time ago. It hasn't mattered for a few years, but I need it again now."

"Which would beg the question, 'whose passport have you been using', but I think I already know the answer to that. I think you've been using the identity of your identical twin – Marcus Pickford's wife – am I right?"

"I'm not saying anything without some assurances."

"I can soon check whether you entered France on your dead sister's passport."

"Do what you feel you must, Inspector. You should be aware that the more you dig, the more I clam up."

"Don't threaten me, Mademoiselle."

Tammi scoffs, "*I* threaten *you*? I'm not the one abusing my position to illegally physically restrain a cooperating witness, am I?"

The Inspecteur stiffens behind her, before she detects a low chuckle rippling through his body, "You've got some balls, I'll give you that."

Blessed release follows swiftly. She totters sideways, exhaling with relief, circling her shoulders and reaching to rub her sore elbow. He waits just long enough for her guard to drop, before gripping her upper arms roughly. She cries out in alarm as he shoves her aggressively back against the wall, holding her in place with a firm hand against her sternum, demanding, "Is that *all* you want; a passport?"

Tammi toughs it out, smiling sweetly up at him despite the gnawing pain and mounting terror, "And a sporting head start…but I doubt you'll give me one of those, will you?"

"I do not have the power to obtain you a new British passport."

"I understand that…but I reckon Valentine does."

"What are you suggesting?"

"I'll give you what you need to solve your cases, if you let me handle Valentine as I see fit."

"I cannot sit back and allow you to break the law – "

"I'm not asking you to, Inspector! Please. This is bigger than you, than me, than Valentine! All I'm asking is you allow me to fight my corner, without interference. You want Valentine gone and your life back to normal? Trust me, this'll be the quickest way to get us all out of your hair."

Masson takes his time considering the carrot she's dangled.

"Valentine wants to reinterview you tomorrow. I will take a disinterested back seat in his incompetent process – much in the way

I did today – only if you've already given me something tangible to progress my own investigations."

"Agreed."

"One thing you should know." Here, the Inspecteur smiles quite unexpectedly. It's charming; white-toothed and wide, it lights up his brooding features, "Valentine has no idea I have Marcus Pickford. I would like to keep it that way. If he chooses to withhold information from me, then I will withhold information from him. It's childish, but satisfying all the same. You like pizza?"

Taken aback by yet another abrupt shift in the rhythm of the encounter, Tammi replies hesitantly, "I suppose…just not the one with pineapple on."

"I promised you something to eat…and it might be a long evening."

Tammi beams enchantingly, as if Masson has asked her on a date, rather than subjecting her to ongoing interrogation, "I currently have nothing better to do, Inspector. Without my passport and your cooperation, I'm not going anywhere."

Masson steps away from her, indicating she should precede him back up the echoing staircase, "In that case, Mademoiselle Rivers, let us trade…"

FOURTEEN

Nightingale watches the lukewarm water in the stained basin turn increasingly pink as he dabs gingerly around the cuts on his face with a bunched wad of wet paper towel, trying not to disturb the congealing blood that's already forming protective scabs over the deep wounds. In the speckled service-station mirror, red-rimmed eyes stare blankly back from his damaged face. The cut across the bridge of his nose definitely needs stitching. The one along his cheekbone probably does too, but he's got nothing to do it with. His backup operational equipment – including his medical kit – is safely hidden, but he can't go and recover it because the key to the hiding place is in the lining of his holdall, and fucking Rivers has that! Fortunately, there's nothing else in the bag that can be linked back to him. Even if she were to discover the key, there's no explanation where it's from. He'd be reasonably relaxed about losing it but for the fact it's now in Tammi's possession. If he's learnt anything about that bloody woman over the years, it's *never* to underestimate her.

****

Masson wipes his mouth with the paper napkin, bunches it in his long fingers, and tosses it into the empty pizza box. He takes a swig from the can of soft drink, leans back in his chair, lights a cigarette, and balances a notepad on his knee, "When you're ready, Mademoiselle Rivers."

"I'm not dictating my memoirs, Inspector. If you want information, you need to question me."

"And you need to answer me truthfully."

"To the best of my ability."

"How very cryptic. Ok. Question one. What are you doing in France?"

"I'm on holiday, Inspector."

"On a false passport?"

"If I *had* a passport in my name, I'd be *using* it."

"*Would* you? Are you M I 5, Mademoiselle Rivers?"

"Me? Of course I'm not!"

"You expect me to believe – with the way you behave – that you are a civilian?"

"Yes, Inspector!"

"Then explain to me why Valentine knows your name, has been sent here specifically to find you (despite records stating you died seven years ago), has an old photograph of you that looks as if it was once intended for an official identification of some kind…oh, and how he has your fingerprints when you have no criminal record?"

Tammi absorbs the sarcasm equably, relishing the opportunity to lock horns with a worthy adversary for once, and explains, "I was approached to join the Service from University. I don't know how they do it in France, but in England they aptitude test and recruit a lot of people that way. I considered it, but I…um…decided against it in the end."

"And Marcus Pickford – is he M I 5?"

"Marc? He can barely tie his own shoelaces – they'd never have him! He's rich and privileged, Inspector. In England, you don't need anything else. That carries you comfortably through life without a skill to your name."

"He's two-thirds of the way through a Caribbean prison sentence. That doesn't seem too comfortable to me."

Tammi scowls, and snaps irritably, "Well, he's out of danger! That's the important bit. Or, at least, he *was*, until Nightingale picked him up."

"Ah, and so we come to Nightingale. Valentine is very interested in him too. How do you know it was Nightingale who took Pickford from prison?"

"Because, if you think about it, it's the only thing that makes any sense! Marc Pickford and I are witness to things some powerful people in Britain would rather keep hidden – six feet under, if that's what it takes. Nightingale's in their employ. I mean, Her Majesty's Government pays his wages, but someone else pulls his strings. That's why the British authorities are so keen on having Marc and I back – to give evidence that unmasks Nightingale and his puppeteers…and also why we're not over-anxious to go, if I'm honest. Fall foul of the people who control Nightingale, and we're as good as dead whatever side we're on."

"Where does James Chadwick fit in?"

"Take you, Inspector. If you've had enough of nobly fighting crime and decide to retire to Provence to grow lavender or something, you just hand in your notice and leave, right? However, if you're Nightingale, you've taken on a job you can never leave. You know too much. What you've heard and seen across thirty years compromises both sides. There's only one way to give up his chosen career, and that's to die. He's been after us for years, Inspector. He wants to take us home. We don't want to go. I had to make it tricky for him; put some obstacles in his path to hold him up. Who do you think was ultimately responsible for Marc's Antiguan arrest?"

Masson gapes, "You?"

"Yes, Inspector. It was all getting a little too close for comfort. I needed the freedom to move at a moment's notice! I'm assuming you don't know too much about Marc…but, believe me, he's an encumbrance when he wants to be! I needed to put him somewhere safe for a while – until the heat was off – and come back for him at my leisure. I thought I had five years' grace, to shake off my pursuers, and get back to the Caribbean in time to fetch Marc on his release…but – "

"But, despite your best efforts, Nightingale got there first."

"He follows me all the time. That's his job. Sometimes I know he's there, but invariably I don't. Nightingale is superb at blending in to the background. He's been biding his time, waiting for just the right moment. The world's known where Marc Pickford's been for the last four years. There was a load of scandal in the British press about it. It's not a secret he's serving a sentence for fraud in Antigua. I wondered why Nightingale had waited so long to nab him…and then it hit me! When I started getting friendly with Guy Montparnasse, Nightingale would have checked out who he was, discovered what I didn't know – that his identity was false – and decided now was the perfect time to retire. My new boyfriend wasn't who he purported to be. He was, in fact, a notorious villain in a foreign country under a false passport; who would miss him? Nightingale needs a body roughly similar in height and build to his own? Bingo! A white male of similar chronological age? *Double* Bingo! Someone no one is looking for because actually he doesn't exist? Jack-bloody-*Pot!* Worth waiting for, I'd say."

"Have you considered perhaps Nightingale and Chadwick were working together to entrap you?"

"Not for a moment, Inspector. Agent Nightingale works alone. Always has; always will. He doesn't make friends."

"For security?"

"No, because he's a complete arsehole."

Masson sniggers, scribbles a couple of notes on his pad, lights another cigarette from the stub of the first, and grunts, "Describe to me the events of the night you claim James Chadwick was both abducted and murdered – and not by you."

Tammi sighs, rubs her forehead with one bandaged hand, and begins, "I was supposed to be meeting the man I knew as Guy at a seafront restaurant called the *Marco Polo*. He made the booking, and told me when to meet him. It wasn't the first time we'd eaten there together."

"What were you wearing?"

"The clothes I had on when I arrived at this police station."

"Did you have a handbag?"

"Yes, I did."

"Where is it?"

"Nightingale took it off me at Guy's yacht."

"The yacht has been thoroughly searched. No handbag was discovered."

"I can't help that. The yacht is the last place I saw it."

"What was in it?"

"About €100 in cash, a small makeup purse, a 'phone…"

"What did the bag look like?"

"A rectangular cream clutch with a thin silver chain strap."

"Thank you. Carry on."

"He didn't show up. That wasn't like Guy. In the couple of weeks I'd known him, he'd been the perfect gentleman. We'd never even kissed! Well…on the cheek…or he used to kiss my hand. Old-fashioned, you know?"

"You had not slept with him?" Masson recalls the report on the crime scene. Only one set of fingerprints found in the yacht's main bedroom…and they didn't belong to Rivers.

"No."

"What did you think about that?"

"Nothing! I just thought he had good manners! I thought I was being *romanced*. Is there anything wrong with that? It makes a flippin' change, I can tell you. Usually you lot get in a girl's knickers first, and ask her name afterwards…if you bother at all…"

"What do you think now you know his true identity?"

"There's a chance he was looking for revenge. I was the one who threw the scent off me and onto the Pickford boys. I tipped off a journalist. I was responsible for people starting to probe where they'd never bothered to look before."

"You suppose he was gaining your trust in order to exact later retribution for throwing unwelcome light on his previously-secret criminal dealings?"

"I think there's a good chance, yes."

"So, you go for a romantic dinner. Your date does not arrive. What then?"

"I left the restaurant. I stood outside on the seafront, and tried to ring him. No answer. I was…concerned. I had nothing better to do with my ruined evening, so I thought I'd walk down to Mirror Point and check he was ok. He could have been taken ill, or had an accident. He could have stood me up – in which case he was going to get a piece of my mind."

"I can imagine," comments Masson drily, "But, when you arrived at the marina?"

"I went in through the access gate from the promenade. I walked along by the shops – some of the bars were still open, but I didn't speak to anyone. Right down the bottom of the marina, it was all dark. It was a cloudy, muggy night. People were below already – there was nothing to sit on deck for. The cabin door was open. There was this weird, artificial light around it, like the tv was on. I called to Guy, but there was no answer. I went into the boat. The wine-fridge door was open. That's where the freaky light was coming from. I put on the main overhead light, and the room was a mess – broken bottles everywhere, spilt wine all over the cabin, place totally trashed. Guy was in the middle of it all, on the sofa;

breathing, but unconscious. He'd been beaten up pretty badly in the course of whatever had happened. At first I thought it was a burglary or something…but he was still wearing his watch – and it was an expensive make, one worth nicking. Also, his 'phone was beside him on the sofa. A thief would have taken that too. You know better than I do how quickly you can turn a stolen 'phone into cash. I tried to revive Guy, but he wasn't waking up. When I opened his eyelids, his pupils were pinpricks. I assumed he'd been drugged. It was only then I realised Nightingale was there – "

"Yet, only two sets of prints were recovered from the yacht. Yours, and the set we assume belong to James Chadwick."

"Nightingale is a *professional*, Inspector! He always wears gloves for everything. What did you find in that bag I nicked off him? A massive box of latex gloves, that's what! He probably wears them to wank, knowing him! I tried to get him to help Guy, but he wouldn't. Instead, he roughed me up a bit to ensure I behaved myself, took the same pictures from his bag as you showed me earlier, and told me the unconscious man I'd been dating was the notorious Jimmy Chadwick! He said it was a 'happy coincidence'. At first, I didn't understand what he meant by that. He handcuffed me and locked me in a car. Then, I presume, he cleaned up the crime scene, including doing away with my handbag and any evidence of his presence. He was in the yacht a while. Eventually, he lugged Chadwick out, put him in the boot, and told me I was going to kill him…so, I guess at that point he was still alive…? Nightingale drove us out of the marina. I assume the car was stolen, because it had a kid's seat in the back."

"Which direction did you take?"

"Don't you have all this on CCTV?"

"Which direction, Mademoiselle Rivers?"

"Up a track behind the main car park, and down to the Service Gate that comes out on the coast road."

"You made no effort to call for help, or try to get out of the car while Nightingale was still inside the yacht?"

"At the time, my head was spinning! I couldn't make sense of the Jimmy Chadwick thing, or work out why Nightingale was there! I only figured it out later. I just knew I was covered in Guy's blood, my fingerprints were all over that yacht, and I was being framed for his murder. I knew I had to get away so Nightingale wasn't in control any more. We fought in the car. I made him crash, out where the coast road turns inland and starts to climb into the hills. I grabbed his holdall because I thought there'd be an explanation in it. There wasn't. There was just some of his operational gear – the folder, some cash, more gloves, his lock-picking kit. He had a gun! He tried to shoot me! I legged it. I was terrified. I was losing a lot of blood. At the time, I thought he'd broken my nose. I kept staggering on until I couldn't walk any more. I remember I just flopped down for a while in the dust and thought to myself, 'I'll rest here for a minute and then keep going', but I must've passed out. When I came to again, it was light. That scared me, because I didn't think I was far enough away from the road. I managed to get back up and keep going, but it wasn't easy. I was dehydrated; disorientated. I was convinced as soon as Nightingale could dump Guy's body somewhere, he'd be back for me. I tried to lay false trails. I just ended up stumbling around in the heat, falling over, blacking out. I don't know how long I spent doing that. I was so out of it, and so confused about the time. In the end, I decided the safest place to be wasn't stumbling around in the woods, but somewhere he'd never dare come and get me – so I managed to get my bearings, find the town, and hand myself in. If he was going to try and frame me for Guy's murder, I wanted to give a statement to refute any evidence he might have planted at the scene. I only worked out his motivation later! Guy's body needs to be identified as Nightingale by someone sent specifically from London for that exact purpose – so everyone who *matters* thinks Nightingale's dead. He probably hasn't contacted his handler in a few weeks – intentionally – setting up his plan. I expect he's submitted plenty of reports about how he was closing in on me. His file's probably already been stamped M.I.A. What he'd intended was to do the job, pick up Marc from wherever he was hidden, get back to the marina, and get the three of us away on Guy's yacht, sailing merrily off into the rising sun before you'd even finished picking bits of cornflake off your tie."

"I understand your assertion that Nightingale needs a plausible corpse to allow him to disappear without any consequences…but I'm unclear why it is necessary for him to take both you and Pickford with him?"

"That's the bit I can't tell you, Inspector…the bit the spooks'd call 'classified'."

"Oh, 'classified'. Valentine's favourite word."

"Although, in his case, I expect he's using it because he has no idea what's actually going on. He's been briefed sufficiently to get a very specific job done – find Nightingale, dead or alive. He has no idea why."

"Yes, he increasingly gives me that impression the longer he remains here."

"So, Inspector, have I given you enough to be going on with?"

"Why do you conclude Nightingale put Marc somewhere safe and elected to go back for him later?"

"It's neater, isn't it? It's what I'd do in that situation. Break Marc out of jail first (because it's the longest and riskiest part of the whole operation), bring him to France because Nightingale knows I'm already here, cosying up to the man he's chosen as his stand-in corpse. Secure Marc somewhere temporarily, frame me for murder to ensure my onward cooperation, sufficiently disfigure the chosen body to prevent clear identification, return to pick up Marc, disguise yourself as the chap you've just barbecued so no one questions you sailing his yacht out of a busy marina just as it's getting light…? Not a bad plan, really…but for the fact I wouldn't play ball, and Pickford's already back in the slammer. I'm sure Nightingale didn't bank on breaking Marc illegally out of one cell only to see him end up in another within a matter of days!"

"No, he wasn't supposed to be in my cells at all. He was discovered secured in a remote location."

Rivers' body-language is gleeful. She clasps her hands together in delight, and bubbles, "That's it, then! The jigsaw fits. Except, he's cocked it up, hasn't he? I'm here making friends with you, Marc's reading Jilly Cooper in your holding cells, and no one (except perhaps naïve Valentine) believes that burnt body is Nightingale! He's buggered this up good and proper!"

Masson regards her thoughtfully. He's starting to comprehend how best to deal with her. Just when she's feeling most comfortable is the time to change the rhythm. He *wants* to continue talking to her. He *needs* more information. He has so many more questions to ask…but she's gaining confidence, getting into her stride. He cannot allow her to take control of their encounters. He therefore suppresses his constant, ravening desire to *know*, smiles his charming smile, stubs out his cigarette, and beckons the attending officer forward with a flick of his finger, "Unfortunately for you, Mademoiselle Rivers, because we cannot currently prove the identity of that corpse, we also cannot prove you did not murder him – or, indeed, that James Chadwick and Nightingale are two different individuals, as you claim. You remain a prime suspect until I am satisfied otherwise – and time is ticking for you. Valentine is *very* keen to take you home. To add weight to your statement, I must find this 'Nightingale' still alive…and be sure I have the right man when I do."

Frantically, she holds up a palm to stay the advance of the Gendarme, and blurts, "I hit him – twice! Well, once…but he also headbutted the steering wheel when the car crashed. He's got a massive cut across the bridge of his nose. Then I hit him with a gun."

Masson raises a sardonic eyebrow, and asks provokingly, "Wouldn't it have been simpler to shoot him with it?"

"It wasn't loaded! The *loaded* gun was jammed against my pelvis. I had to do as he said! He could've shattered my spine if he'd chosen to fire. I couldn't take the risk, not then. I had to wait until he was distracted by driving the darker, windier roads. Later, when we fought – when I made him crash the car – I hit him across the cheek with the gun. It split the skin. It'd be a bad cut, even a few days later. That'll be the way to know you've got the right bloke."

"Again, unfortunately for you, I have absolutely no reports of crashed cars on the coast or mountain roads…only a severely burnt male corpse and your glib story." He turns from her to give a brief instruction to the Gendarme.

There's a note of desperation in the voice that cries, "I'm telling you what happened, Inspector!"

Easing slowly to his feet, tucking his paperwork under one arm, gathering up the detritus of pizza boxes and drinks cans, and standing aside as the officer takes Tammi by the elbow, compels her to stand, and propels her firmly towards the door, Masson drawls, "And I am correspondingly grateful for your cooperation, Mademoiselle Rivers. By the time Valentine interviews you in his own inimitably-hopeless style tomorrow, Détective Hâche and I will have investigated everything you have told us so far."

The Inspecteur waits until she's halfway down the corridor, before calling, "You can play games with Valentine all you like, but do the same to me, and our deal is very definitely off! Enjoy your evening, Mademoiselle."

FIFTEEN

"And here we are again."

"Lovely day for it, Agent Valentine."

"I'm a Detective Sergeant."

"And I'm the Queen of Sheba."

Valentine smirks stiffly, and loftily replies, "Inspector Masson's team have efficiently obtained and processed your fingerprints, Miss Rivers, proving your identity beyond doubt. What's more, the matching of those prints places you on the yacht of a missing man; a location being treated as a crime scene."

Tammi ignores Valentine, and instead fixes Masson with her steady stare, murmuring, "That *was* efficient of Inspector Masson, wasn't it?"

Surprised, both Valentine and Xavier turn to look at Masson, whose face remains impassive but for the slight raising of one eyebrow.

Tammi smiles to herself, and the extreme weight of her gaze thankfully slides off Masson and back onto Valentine, whom the Inspecteur notes wisely avoids direct eye contact, instead staring fixedly at a point just over her left shoulder, and stating imperiously, "I have informed the authorities at home of your positive identification, and they are issuing the documentation to permit your return to the UK for questioning there."

Xavier thinks he detects the flicker of the woman's eyes towards Masson again. It's so fast, he's left wondering whether he really saw it at all.

"You don't hang about, do you Valentine?"

"Detective Sergeant Valentine."

"Whatever you say. Don't you have to take Nightingale back with you too?"

"As you well know, Nightingale is in the mortuary."

"No, Detective Sergeant, Agent Nightingale is still alive."

Valentine purrs indulgently, "Miss Rivers, we have CCTV footage of you holding Nightingale at gunpoint – "

"Show me."

"I beg your pardon?"

"Show me the footage. Please."

Before Valentine's even turned to Masson to ask, "Can that be arranged?" the Inspecteur's waving Xavier out of the room to action the woman's request.

Valentine turns back to her, "In the meantime – "

"No. If it's all the same to you, Detective Sergeant, we'll wait for Bright Future to come back with his *Etch-A-Sketch*."

While Valentine blinks in confusion, Masson finds himself fighting the very unprofessional urge to giggle. He turns his face away and wipes his mouth with his handkerchief, as if that will erase the grin that tugs at the corners.

Naturally, Xavier isn't gone long. He returns with four mugs of coffee on a tray, and a laptop computer under his arm. He dishes out the coffees, places the laptop in front of Tammi, clicks to the correct file, and plays the relevant section of the recording. She watches it in silence, "Ok, can you run it back, please?"

Xavier returns the footage to its previous starting point.

"Can you play it any slower?"

"Yes…half-speed."

"Ok, and can you run it back a bit further, to before the vehicle approaches the light?"

Xavier rewinds more.

"There! See?" Tammi turns the computer one hundred and eighty degrees, so Masson and Valentine can view the screen, "See that there?" She stabs at the image with a bandaged finger, "See the two shafts of light there? Watch the timeclock. Those are the headlights of the car we're in. Note how long we sit there before going through the camera. Nightingale's driving. The yacht-owner Guy Montparnasse is unconscious in the boot. Nightingale stops the car a hundred yards or so from the gate in order to beat me up, threaten me with a loaded gun, and coerce me into holding an empty gun to his head for the purposes of the security camera footage. He's scoped the place out. He knows the location of the cameras."

Masson scribbles a note on his pad. Someone took out the cameras nearest Chadwick's yacht; someone who knew they were there. Nightingale?

"Nightingale is setting me up precisely to create the illusion you're falling for now! Look at the state of me, Valentine. Do you think, if I'd been the one in control of the situation, I'd have ended up looking like the loser in a boxing match?"

"If you expect me to swallow this bunch of – "

"I don't expect you to 'swallow' anything! I'm asking you to *look*, Valentine, that's all! Spool it forward?"

Xavier complies. She's jabbing passionately at the screen again, "Look! Look at the attitude of his body. It's unnatural, yeah?"

"He's being held at gunpoint…"

"*Look*, Valentine! One hand on the wheel. Surely, if I wanted to control him, I'd have *both* his hands where I could see them? Look at the angle of his upper body. It's twisted towards me. Pause it there, please. See his right shoulder? It's rolling out, yes? See his upper arm? It's turned back, towards me. That's because, below the dashboard, out of sight, he's got a loaded gun rammed into my stomach. He said he'd shoot me if I didn't comply. Run it on again? *Look*! Watch as we go into the light. See, a jab of his right arm towards me, and it makes me lift the gun up…he's *ordering* me to do that! Pause it again, please. See that silver there, around my wrist? That's not a lovely bangle, it's the handcuffs he put me in; the ones I turned up here still wearing? Look there…see that dark patch round my mouth? That's blood running out of my nose like a tap, because of where he hit me. How can you not see that all this is bullshit fabrication by a professional!"

"Explain to me how, if you're being held at gunpoint in a moving car, you manage to escape…?"

"*Think* about it, Valentine! If you're using your right hand to shove a loaded gun into someone's guts, how do you change gear in a left-hand drive, manual car? He had to keep using the wrong hand, literally reaching across his body, contorting himself to get his left hand on the gear stick. I seized my chance. We fought in the car, and I managed to trap his hand so he dropped the gun. I pushed the steering wheel. The car impacted the rock wall. It caved the whole front of it in. I had to fight him to get out of the car. That's how I bashed my leg and my elbow. He got his hands on the loaded gun again, and he was shooting at me as I ran away. I had to scramble up a bank with handcuffs on – that's how I lost half my fingernails, and shredded my arms and legs. I was trying to get off the road and into the cover of some woods – "

"Where's the car?"

"What?"

"The car. Where did this happen?"

"I don't know exactly. It was dark. The situation was rather stressful; I wasn't exactly checking out the scenery! I know we were going away from the coast on a narrow road winding up into the hills. I remember there was a drop on one side and a rock face on the other. I steered us into the rock face to stop the car so I had half a chance of getting out."

Valentine turns to Masson, "Any likely damaged cars reported?"

Masson shakes his head, "Xavier's been trying to trace the car since we first got the CCTV footage. No luck so far."

Valentine turns back to Tammi, shaking his head in mock regret, "Oh dear, Miss Rivers. Perhaps it was *Chitty-Chitty-Bang-Bang*, and it just flew away?"

"I'm telling you, when I got out, Nightingale was still alive, Montparnasse was in the boot, and that car was undriveable!"

"Yet, we have no evidence of the car; still less of Guy Montparnasse. Inspector Masson's team have confirmed that identity as false, by the way…and no sign of Nightingale apart from CCTV footage of you with a pistol to his head…followed by the discovery of a burning corpse within less than five miles of the marina."

"What about this, huh? This? These?" Tammi points at her bruises, and holds up her bandaged fingers.

"Oh, I don't deny you fought one another. I don't dispute that dark patch showing on the footage is probably blood from your injured nose. I just don't think any of it happened in the car as you claim. I think it all took place on that yacht, where you sought to subdue him. Perhaps more occurred on the hillside where you forced enough barbiturate down his neck to floor a herd of elephants, then burned the poor bastard alive!"

Tammi groans in frustration, "Valentine, you're being used! They haven't told you anything, have they? Nightingale wants out! He needs you to believe that body is his so everyone stops looking for him. He picked up the first poor bugger he found who bore a passing resemblance…a chap who just happened to have a false passport, a nice yacht, and doubtless his own reasons for not wanting to be discovered. Nightingale is *still alive*! Tell London that. Tell them he can go anywhere with what he knows – same as I can, in fact!"

"*You're* not going anywhere."

"Maybe not right now…but Nightingale is, I can assure you of that. *Tell them.* It'll sharpen their thinking."

"Tell them yourself…when we get home."

Tammi throws up her arms in exasperation, and turns to Masson, a desperate, silent plea in her expressive eyes.

In English, so she can understand, Masson calmly enquires of Valentine, "How many days for the passport and the transfer paperwork?"

Valentine doesn't notice. His reflex response is also in his mother tongue, "End of the week."

Masson turns back to Tammi, holding her gaze for a beat longer than necessary, "Mademoiselle Rivers, we will review your assertions regarding the CCTV footage. We will attempt to get our Technical team to enhance the definition. We will also continue to make enquiries concerning the car."

"He couldn't have driven it away, Inspector! The front was all smashed in!"

"We will check it."

Frustrated at his stonewalling, Tammi snaps, "How long are you going to keep holding me here? Surely we're over the limit by now? If you have nothing to charge me with, you have to let me go."

"Push me, Mademoiselle Rivers, and I *will* arrest you on suspicion of murder. Would you like me to do that?"

"Of course not."

"Then permit me to do the job which may exonerate you."

"For how much longer?"

"For as long as it takes. If you are innocent, you have nothing to fear. You will just have to wait."

When the door closes behind Tammi and the attending WPC, Masson tugs the laptop round so it faces the three of them. He rewinds the recording and plays it again, "There's foundation in what she says, Valentine. Look at the position of his right arm and his shoulder. It *is* open towards her...and the blood all over her face? Xavier, we need to get this quality enhanced."

"I'll talk to I T, Boss."

Valentine fidgets and frowns, searching for reasons to contradict Masson.

"Come on, Valentine, you can't deny she's been comprehensively battered by someone!"

"But in self-defence as she claims...or in the course of force-feeding him the drugs your pathologist found in his mouth and bloodstream?"

"Disregard what you've been *ordered* to believe, and just address the *facts*! She's a tiny woman; five feet tall? I don't care how fit and strong she might be – not withstanding the physically limiting effects of her own considerable injuries, five feet nothing of slightly-built woman against six feet two of well-built, reasonably muscular man? Who would the sensible money be on?"

The image of Tammi thrust helplessly into the wall by the weight of his own body flashes into Masson's mind, "Any one of us could physically overpower her if required...and yet you continue to insist she got the better of this man sufficiently to force him to ingest drugs?"

"At gunpoint she could have done."

"Maybe – but how did she get him all the way up to the location of the fire? No evidence of dragging through the dust. We've already determined he didn't walk, and he wasn't driven right up there. Are you saying *she* carried him? Does it truly seem possible?"

"Where's your proof she didn't, Inspecteur?"

"Where's your proof she did?"

"I don't need any. My job is to track the whereabouts of my missing colleague, recover this woman alive – both of which I've already done – and escort her back to London for debriefing."

"And what if your colleague is *not* the roast in our freezer? What if he *is* still at large, brimming with British secrets he's just desperate to sell to the highest bidder? If she's right and you're wrong, Valentine, are you *sure* you'll have a job to go back to?"

****

Outside the interview room, Masson lets Valentine stomp moodily off down the corridor, grabbing Xavier's arm to hold him back.

"Xavier, I want you to check the town CCTV for the night before the body was found."

"Boss?"

"Any cameras that pick up the *Marco Polo*, the seafront, and the promenade out past the beaches to Point Miroir."

"What am I looking for?"

"Rivers. In that cream dress, carrying a handbag, coming out of the *Marco*, making a telephone call, walking to Point Miroir. Ok?"

"Sir, how do you – ?"

Masson's already striding up the corridor after Valentine. With uncharacteristic irritation, he barks over his shoulder, "Just get it done, Xavier…and find that damn car! No more excuses. It didn't just bloody *vanish*!"

****

"We've got the car, sir. Found a couple of days ago, crashed and abandoned on the coast road going up to the mountains."

"*Days* ago? Why was this not brought to my attention sooner?"

"I think it's been on someone's To-Do List, Boss."

"Despite the fact we've been actively seeking the self-same vehicle? Do you know, Xavier, I think the next job on *my* To-Do List might be ripping him a new arsehole! Who was it?"

"Not quite sure, sir."

"Very diplomatic, Xavier. I'll be finding out later...so you'd better warn whoever-you-don't-know-it-is, all right?"

Xavier looks at the shiny toes of his brogues, and mutters, "Yes, sir."

"In the meantime, let's avoid further delay – what have you got?"

Back on safer ground, Xavier flicks open his notebook and rattles through the information, "Reported stolen in Marseille about three weeks ago. Plates match – "

"Was there a kid's seat in the back of it?"

Xavier checks the notes. There's amazement in his voice as he replies, "Yes, sir. How did you – ?"

Briskly, Masson responds, "Basically, it's the car from the CCTV?"

"Yes, sir."

"Everything corroborates her story! Did you check the town cameras like I asked?"

Back to the notebook, "Comes out of the *Marco* just before ten pm. Walks up and down the seafront on her 'phone, puts it in her bag, and marches off down the promenade, just like you said. Spotted passing the camera on the Lifeguard Station about ten-forty pm. Arrival just after eleven on the Guest Access Gate camera at Point Miroir. Tracked across the main square about eleven-fifteen...and off towards the private moorings...but then we lose her, of course, because the cameras down there were tampered with, and it was too dark for others further away to pick her up. Next sighting on CCTV is just after midnight – the clip we've already seen, in the car with her possible gunpoint captive, leaving the marina via the Service Gate."

"It all fits. I think she's telling the truth, Xavier!"

"Valentine doesn't believe her."

"Yes, granted, but I maintain he's been ordered not to, regardless of what the evidence shows. In his defence, he doesn't know about half of this, but he's come here with his mind made up...and I think he's mistaken! The more we investigate, the more evidence we uncover that backs up her version of events."

Xavier can't refute the Inspecteur's words, but he'll never trust the woman with the pitiless eyes, corroborated evidence or not.

"Any clues in the car? Was it like she said – caved in at the front; undriveable?"

"Yes, sir. It's early days for the forensic investigation, but there's a lot of blood in the front, and some evidence of blood in the boot, too."

"Right, Xavier, I'm going to make a prediction here! The blood in the boot will match our burnt corpse. The blood in the passenger seat of the car will belong to Rivers. Any other blood...for her story to stand up, it has to be Nightingale's. If we're being thorough, we really should compare the blood in the car to Pickford as well, even though he has no injuries – just to rule him out."

"Yes, sir."

"The longer this goes on, Xavier; the deeper we dig, the more I trust her."

SIXTEEN

"Boss, Pickford's asking for a telephone call."

"Has he had one before now?"

"No."

"I rattled him yesterday, Xavier."

"Why, sir?"

"I showed him we had Rivers. Just through the panel in the cell door, but he went mental! Apparently, he yelled and thumped the door for half the evening."

"Well, the Custody Sergeant says he's demanding a 'phone call now."

"We can't deny him one, in case he does want to ring his lawyer."

"Do you really think that's who he wants, sir?"

"Not for a moment – but rules are rules. See if you can listen in. I want to know who he calls."

****

"Dad."

Silence on the other end of the line, then the cautious, "Marc?"

Pickford doesn't respond immediately. He wants to see what else his father might say. He hasn't spoken to him in nearly ten years. He knows his father will never forgive him for dumping Tammi and marrying Annelisse. No one would listen to him when he tried to explain. They'd all been so obsessed over the damn money; about keeping the secrets – Tammi included. Dad's little puppet. Annelisse had been different to all of them. Clueless about the money, blissfully ignorant of the undercurrents swirling around her, she'd just been *fun*…and pressured, struggling, undervalued Marc Pickford had needed that. Geoffrey had always been the favourite son. Marc had one use – possession of the correct name, the right genes, the required ingrained loyalties – to be the attention-monopolising figurehead, while Tammi Rivers covertly ran the whole corrupt show for his overbearing father. Marc understood he wasn't up to it. He'd never denied being a bit of a dope. What hurt was that no one bothered to make a secret of their contempt for his lack of ability – not even his mother! It was true that his elopement and whirlwind wedding to Annelisse Rivers had derailed everything a bit. Arguably, however, if his father had trusted him a little more, and not placed everything under Tammi's exclusive control…? Sir Blair blamed Marc for not securing her via the age-old avenue of marriage. At the time, Marc had tried to point out how ridiculous this was but, as usual, no one had been listening. *Tammi* controlled Tammi. Marrying her wouldn't have made a damn bit of difference to that. In fact, it would have rendered them all even more vulnerable to her than they currently were! In his father's eyes, everything that had happened since, including his brother's very public fall from grace and his own arrest, directly stemmed from useless bloody Marcus plumping for the wrong twin nearly thirty years ago. Guilt surfaces briefly. Poor Annie. He feels regret whenever he thinks of her…but also relief. His marriage *hadn't* been happy. She *had* been the wrong twin. He should have married

Tammi, regardless of whether he'd have been able to control her – and certainly not simply to please Sir Blair. Tammi had cared for him much more than the avaricious Annelisse ever had. Annelisse had enjoyed the money and prestige. Tammi had certainly used his familial influence to advance her own career, but for both their benefits – and she'd seemed to actually like *him*, instead of only what he represented. She'd taken a great many risks on his behalf, and invested considerable personal effort in his advancement and prosperity. She'd tried to build the two of them a future, the only way she knew how. He'd thrown her efforts back in her face. Small wonder their subsequent encounters were tinged with awkwardness, and the recollected pain of past injustices inflicted and suffered on both sides.

He idly wondered whether he'd garner any thanks or respect for calling his father now, or quite why the selfish old goat deserved the warning he was about to gift him. The reason was the same as always: Marc was a Stocker-Pickford. Family and reputation mattered infinitely more than any personal regard. It was his *duty* to do this.

"Are you all right, Marc?"

"Yes, Dad."

"Where are you?"

"I'm in a police station on the French Riviera."

"Good God! Why?"

"Because someone took me from prison and brought me to France."

Another pregnant pause, "Yes. I did know about the removal from Antigua. We couldn't discover your whereabouts thereafter."

"Is this something to do with you, Dad?"

"Heavens, no! How can you ask me such a thing?"

"I just wondered, as you seem so well-informed."

"Marc, you are my son. Regardless of what's happened, I still have concern for your welfare."

Marc can't keep the genuine amazement from his voice, "*Do you?*"

"Of course I do! How could you think otherwise?"

Marc decides it's most prudent not to answer this question. Instead, he smiles grimly to himself, and delivers the vital intelligence that's the sole reason for this call, "Dad, I only get five minutes. I just wanted to tell you that's she's *here*."

A sharp intake of breath on the other end of the line – a considerably-greater emotional reaction than hearing the voice of his estranged son for the first time in a decade, "Under arrest?!"

"I don't know…but in this police station." Here, Marc stumbles through the French place name with such appalling pronunciation he can almost feel Sir Blair wincing down the 'phone, "I saw her yesterday. I haven't spoken to her. I have to go, Dad, my time's up. I just wanted you to be aware."

His time isn't up. When he replaces the receiver, he has another two minutes on this call…but Marc Pickford has nothing else to say to his father. He's also sure if he remains on the line, he'll cry.

****

"He called his father."

"To say what?"

"She's here."

"Really?"

"Yes, sir. Here's the transcript of the call."

"She's here... And he said that to his father, the prominent politician with the questionable past?"

"As I said, nothing proven, sir. All press speculation, but no criminal convictions. Same with the brother, Geoffrey. Allegations of this and that, but no concrete proof, and no convictions. Same with James Chadwick. A load of press chatter about his serious criminality, his past association with Geoffrey Stocker-Pickford, but not a speck of evidence. Marcus is the only one with an *actual* criminal record."

"Sounds as if he took one for the team, doesn't it, Xavier?"

"Boss?"

"Tammi Rivers told me *she* reported Marc's dodgy deals in Antigua! She deliberately ensured he'd be arrested! She said it was to keep him safe – out of Nightingale's clutches. She also tipped off the British media about both James Chadwick *and* Geoffrey Stocker-Pickford. Why do that? She implied it was to create a diversion...but a diversion from *what*?" Masson strokes several days' growth of stubbly beard ruminatively, "How's this for an idea, Xavier? Tammi Rivers *works* for Sir Blair! She's not some helpless pawn in a bigger game – she's the Pickford family *Fixer*! She's here to rescue Marcus and get rid of Nightingale once and for all! The British authorities are on the tail of the Stocker-Pickfords. They want to turn the obviously-corruptible and financially-desperate youngest son. She's in France to make sure they don't succeed!"

"It's a great theory, sir...but how do we prove any of it when all the evidence continually stacks up in Rivers' favour?"

"We've simply *got* to find this Nightingale! He's the only guy who can tell us the truth about Rivers and Marcus Pickford...and, unlike Valentine, I do believe her that he's still at large. I genuinely think he and James Chadwick aren't the same fella, and he wanted James Chadwick's corpse to pass off as his own. What I still can't fathom is *why*! If he's an Agent working for the British Government – charged with returning Marcus Pickford to the UK and capturing the elusive Rivers once and for all – what's his motivation for staging his own death and doing a disappearing act? Back to the evidence, Xavier! There's *got* to be a clue somewhere!"

SEVENTEEN

"Sir, there's something in here!"

Xavier's manipulating the holdall between deft, gloved fingers. Masson glances up from the case folder he's comprehensively re-reading for the umpteenth time, still convinced it already contains the answer to this perplexing mystery.

"Well, tip it out. I thought we'd had everything out of there already…?"

"No, sir, it's between the two layers."

"No way! How many times have we been over that?"

"A few…but we were examining the items inside it, not so much the bag itself. Can I cut it, sir?"

"Yes, yes, get it out, whatever it is!"

Xavier takes a scalpel from his desk drawer, and slices carefully through the canvas, wriggling and pushing until a small, blue object drops onto the desk. He snatches it up, "A key, Boss!", holding it out in his open palm. Masson scrabbles for gloves from his jacket pocket, taking the key by the metal end and revolving it in the sunlight, "Doesn't tell us much."

There's a number – 16 – crudely painted on one side of the chunky plastic body in what looks like *Tippex*.

"Where would you get that kind of key, Xavier?"

"It's like a locker key, sir. A gym, a station, a school, an airport…?"

"Yeah…and no name, no logo… Let's get it dusted anyway, but I bet you €20 there isn't a fingerprint on it."

"How can we find where it came from?"

"I have no idea. It could be from anywhere in the world! Why don't we try another appeal? You never know. Get on the local evening news, hold it up with the number on it, and ask if anyone owns this key or knows what it opens."

Xavier shakes his head, laughing in disbelief, "A long shot, sir!"

Masson wags an admonitory finger, only half-teasing, "Not necessarily! Everything about this case so far has been really 'local'. We've been functioning within a radius of about fifteen kilometres at most. The yacht at the marina, the location of the body, the wrecked car on the mountain road, the discovery of Pickford…so why can't this key have come from somewhere around here too? Let's face it, Xavier, even the longest shots strike something eventually."

****

"Boss, I've got to say – you're a bit of a genius!"

Masson smirks, blushes, and quips, "Only a bit? Why, what brilliant thing have I done now?"

"We've only managed to find out where the key's from!"

"No!" Masson's embarrassment's forgotten. He gapes, incredulous.

"Yes, sir. The station, sir!"

"*No!*"

"The Stationmaster rang this morning, after watching my stellar press conference performance on the regional news last night. It's his number 16 locker key. He rented it out about two weeks ago. The chap paid for a week, then didn't come back and didn't renew.

No contact number or anything. The Stationmaster was going to give him a few more days, and then open the locker with his master key."

Masson crows jubilantly, as delighted as he is amazed, "That *never* should've worked, Xavier! Not in a *million years*!"

"Well, it did, sir…and your instinct was dead right. This case *is* all going on right under our noses. We're practically tripping over crime scenes and evidence everywhere we turn!"

"Yet still scrabbling blindly for a proper explanation of why all this stuff is happening. That's what I'm finding so infuriating about it. It feels tantalisingly close, and yet still so totally out of reach!"

"I'm going up to open the locker now, sir. Do you want to come?"

In the car, rattling along the narrow road, Xavier elaborates, "There's CCTV of the day the chap organised the locker but – surprise, surprise – it's shoddy quality, he's wearing a baseball cap and, like with everything else we've seen, it may or may not be either James Chadwick or the man known as Nightingale."

"It's taken out in whose name?"

"G Montparnasse, of course! He pays cash, takes his key, and leaves. He doesn't put anything in the locker at that time, or go anywhere near it."

"But he comes back later?"

"I've got someone spooling through two weeks of footage, but the camera is fixed, and frustratingly only films the main door and the ticket booth. The lockers are round a corner, and not covered. There's another camera on the platform, but that obviously doesn't pick up the lockers either."

"Convenient. Given how aware our man seems to be of CCTV observation, it could explain why this flyblown little dump was chosen."

"Could do, sir."

"One step forward, two steps back…"

"We don't know that, sir. There might be vital information in the locker that'll blow this case wide open!"

"Or, the damn thing could be empty, because whoever is meant to be depositing something in there now can't."

"What?"

"*We've* got the key *they're* supposed to have."

"Oh…"

Xavier's shining face falls, and Masson feels guilty for quashing his youthful enthusiasm, "No, you're right, Xavier. I'm being too negative. Let's just get there and see what's what. We should also get the locker door dusted for prints, just in case any match our current cast of dodgy characters."

"I did request that, sir. Someone's going up there later, I think."

"Good. Well done. At least we're doing everything we reasonably can with the paltrey leads we're getting."

"This'll be the one, Boss. I'm sure of it. The missing piece!"

****

The Stationmaster hangs back a polite but curious distance. Xavier unlocks the dented metal door and cautiously inches it open. Inside the locker is a small, wheeled suitcase of the type executives take on short-hop business flights. Xavier hesitates. Masson nudges him with characteristic impatience, "Come on, then!"

"It…could be…a bomb, sir. Booby-trapped or something…"

Masson rolls his eyes, "Get a grip, Détective, this isn't *Die Hard*," elbowing his younger colleague out of the way and manhandling the case from the locker, as Xavier and the Stationmaster exchange alarmed glances. Plonking it on the floor, Masson squats, unzips it, and riffles through the contents. A small envelope of used Euros, several sets of underwear and socks, a few shirts, a couple of pairs of trousers, an extremely-comprehensive first-aid kit for such a small suitcase, a rolled towel, a sponge bag containing masculine items. Exploratory sniffing around the unopened caps of various muskily-scented plastic bottles suggest they're filled with shampoo or shower gel – but they're plain; no product names or identifying stickers. Masson thoroughly examines a pair of underpants and a shirt or two, "No labels. All cut off tight against the seams. Men's clothing. Male toiletries. No other clues in the first-aid kit either – all plain packaging…no labels, no language…"

"A spy's suitcase, sir?"

"I'd say so, wouldn't you, Xavier? More points in Rivers' favour! More corroborations of her assertions regarding British Government Agent Nightingale…"

As he speaks, Masson absently squishes the satisfyingly-crackly plastic-lined sponge bag in his fingers. Suddenly, he cocks his head, eyes widening. Speedily unzipping the bag again, he upends its contents into the suitcase, turning the emptied pouch over and over, palpitating it between his fingers, "He's at it again, Xavier! There's something in the lining of this too! Got a penknife?"

Xavier hands the Inspecteur the medical scissors the Boss has just tipped from the first-aid kit, watching Masson run his gaze down the edge of the zip, before using the curved ends to unpick a small area of stitching, "This has been done before – look! It's not quite as uniform as all the rest. The stitches are bigger, and more irregular. It's a neat job, but this bit's been done by hand, not by machine."

Masson pushes down inside the separated lining, "Yessss…"

He withdraws a credit-card-sized piece of plastic, and holds it up triumphantly. Xavier whips it from his fingers, "Hotel card-key! For *La Méditerranée*, right here in town!"

Masson shakes his head, chuckling, and muttering, "What are the bloody chances…?"

Xavier is exultant, "I *told* you, Boss! I *said* this would be what blows it wide open!"

Masson bounces to his feet, re-energised both by the unbelievable discovery and Xavier's unconfined delight, "Right! Get all this into the biggest evidence sack we've got, seal it up for the time being, and stick it in the car boot. We'll explain later why we've opened and fiddled with everything. Tape off this locker area until the Forensic van can get up here to dust that door…and…"

"Yes, sir?" Xavier's like a sprinter on the blocks, poised for the crack of the starter's gun.

The Inspecteur smirks indulgently, "I've been thinking of treating Madame Masson to a dirty weekend away for our anniversary…I wonder what *La Méditerranée's* like these days?"

Xavier chortles, already halfway across the tiny station concourse to the door, "I'll just get the tape, Boss!"

****

He isn't meant to be here, doing this. It's not supposed to be necessary. This is one backup he never thought he'd need. He should've known. Put Rivers in the mix, and nothing ever follows its predicted path.

He can't contact the usual channels for assistance, because he's meant to be dead – and if he starts lifting wallets and nicking cars, he'll attract the wrong kind of attention. He was never supposed to be returning to the town at all. From the yacht to the house; collect Pickford, leave Chadwick behind for the cops to wrongly identify, speed back to the yacht before sunrise with his two shell-shocked and vital captives, and set sail for the beginning of the rest of his life. He hasn't given this once-perfect plan up for lost…not yet…but the unforeseen problems mean he needs his second bag of gear from the down-at-heel station locker. Without the key, he's going to have to spin a good yarn about how he lost it, and why he's a week late settling up the rest of his rental bill. He's already spent the small float of cash he had on him the night of the burning. He stinks. He's dusty, sweaty…and his face is shocking. Perhaps he'll tell the guy he's been mugged? That'll explain the absence of a wallet. Whilst it'll be tricky convincing the Stationmaster, it's preferable to an attempted return to his swanky hotel looking as bad as he does. He pictures approaching the glamorous Receptionist, about to explain he's mislaid his room key and needs another. She'll call the Police before he's even drawn breath! Pistol-whipped, sweat-stained, blood-soaked men are doubtless not encouraged at *La Méditerranée*. It's a shame he can't go back there. There's a huge envelope of emergency cash in his hotel room safe, as well as a number of useful passports, and a bottle of dye to turn his artificially-greyed hair back to brown. No matter. The bag at the station contains a sufficient cash float for emergencies. It'll buy him a day or two more to regroup, properly tend to his cuts, and revise his onward plans. Losing Rivers remains a source of intense, humiliating frustration – how could he have been so careless? Forced to abandon the undriveable car, he'd taken his bag of fire-starting equipment from the boot, hefted the insensible body of Chadwick onto his back, and carried the man as far as he was able before sun-up. Exhausted, he'd arrived at the boulder-strewn gulley as dawn broke. There were apartment blocks directly across the valley. If he tried to walk further, he'd risk being spotted by an early-riser, out on their balcony drinking their breakfast coffee, watching the sun's first rays strike the opposite hillside. He'd dumped Chadwick between the rocks, and collapsed beside him, recovering from the arduous climb and loss of blood; waiting until mid-morning, when he suspected most people would be at work and the apartments quieter. He'd set fire to Chadwick with the items from his bag, and left as the blaze took hold, the smoke blackening and drifting higher into the clear blue sky behind him. On foot and remaining hidden, it took a considerable time to return to the place he'd left Pickford. Perturbed to find it already swarming with Gendarmes and Forensic units, their presence at least enabled him to discover which Police Station his erstwhile hostage had been taken to. He's busted the guy from one jail this month already. There's nothing to stop him removing Pickford from another, especially a backwater Gendarmerie during the height of a sultry Mediterranean summer, when no one cares about rules anything like as much as they should; particularly when confronted with a pile of temptingly-untraceable Euros it'd take a year or two to earn the honest way. This delay's also gifted the authorities ample time to discover his burnt body. London *must* have sent someone by now! He'd left an evidence trail a moron could follow: hints about Rivers; the sudden cessation of all communication as he apparently got closer to 'apprehending' her; Sir Julian Franklin would be having kittens! It's maddening to have to adapt his peachy plan, but twenty years of pursuing Rivers has accustomed him to the unexpected. He's neatly framed her for his murder – that's something she won't have seen coming – but he's still guilty of underestimating her, after all these years! He'd reckoned without her daring escape, taking his bag containing the secret dossier. Read it, and she'd comprehend his motivation for all of this. If you keep Tammi guessing, she's easier to control. Once she understands what drives you, she can get inside your head...and that's the last place he wants her. He's comforted by the knowledge she needs Marc Pickford just as much as he does. It'll keep her close by. They're all united by the same grubby secret. This isn't over.

He pelts across the dusty station car park, takes the narrow steps two at a time, and pauses to the right of the concourse entrance, out of sight of the inadequate sweep of the CCTV camera. He's distracted by a flat, slapping sound away to his left. Curious, he jogs the length of the building and peeks through the chainlink fencing onto the platform. Feet away, the Stationmaster perches on a rickety wooden chair, tilting a watering can inaccurately into a hanging basket, a large proportion of its contents missing the container entirely, and spattering the platform with the most moisture it's received in months.

He whirls around, sprints back the way he's come and, head down to confound the camera, shoots through the door and scuttles to the lockers, penknife already in his palm. With the Stationmaster thus occupied, can he force the lock and escape without needing to explain himself at all?

Dismay stops him in his tracks. Locker 16 stands wide open and clearly empty. Police tape cordones-off the entire area, flapping in the warm breeze that funnels through the propped entrance door and out onto the sun-baked platform.

He doesn't linger. By the time the Stationmaster dismounts the wobbling chair and shuffles back inside with his empty can, the concourse is deserted.

****

"And the last time the room card-key was used?"

The Receptionist traces a manicured fingernail down the screen, "Four days ago – to access the room. 16.27pm."

Masson twinkles charismatically, "I don't suppose we can have a little look at the CCTV for that floor at that particular time?"

The Receptionist's apple cheeks dimple angelically, "Yes, sir. Of course. I'll ask someone to organise it for you."

The young Front-of-House Manager is clearly desperate for every juicy detail, but knows it's unprofessional for a man in his position to gossip like a fishwife. Instead, he sits edgily before the computer at his postage-stamp of a desk, with Xavier leaning over his shoulder, and Masson circling the small room like a caged tiger.

"Sir!"

Masson's around the desk in two strides, "Ah...*there* you are..."

A tall, slim man in linen slacks and a white shirt, collar unbuttoned, sleeves rolled up to expose an expensive watch and deep tan, wears a Panama hat at exactly the right rakish angle to completely obscure his face from the security camera.

"And when do records show he left the room again?"

The Manager shakes his head, "They don't. The card-key is required to unlock the room. When the door closes, it's automatically locked unless there's a fire, or the key deactivates it again."

"So you only have a record of when he entered the room...not when he left it."

"That's correct."

"How do you know he isn't in there now?"

"Housekeeping went into the room the day before yesterday. There was no one there. They went back in again this morning...the room was as they had left it."

"The last time he went in was four days ago, and you know it's been left at least three days?"

"Yes, Inspecteur."

"My colleague and I need to see inside this room, please."

The man hesitates. Masson lofts a quizzical eyebrow, and the explanation tumbles out, "I can't authorise...I mean, I need to ask permission from...higher up... From the Manager of the *Hotel*!"

Frustrated by further delay, Masson waves an irritable hand and snaps rudely, "Chop-chop, then! Oh, and Monsieur?" The red-faced Manager turns, hand on the doorknob, "While you're there, get permission for us to open the safe as well."

****

"Sir...!" Xavier holds up two envelopes in his gloved hands.

"Is that all that's in there?"

"Yes, sir."

"Well?"

"Euros. Thousands!" Xavier thumbs the used notes in wondering envy.

"And the other?"

"Passports, sir. A stack of 'em! Some English...Irish...there's a New Zealand one here!"

"All the same name?"

Xavier shuffles a few out and checks them, "No, sir. Various different names. No duplicates."

He holds one up at random towards the Inspecteur, "Same bloke, though."

Masson unfolds the tired passport scan from his wallet and compares it to the picture, "*Not* James Chadwick..."

"No, sir. Definitely the chap from Valentine's photograph!"

"Call him."

"Sir?"

"Call Valentine. Get him over here. He needs to see for himself how much we know. It might finally persuade him to stop being so bloody obstructive..."

EIGHTEEN

Summoned, the put-out Valentine stands in the centre of the hotel suite, and takes in the haul piled on the coffee table. The wheeled suitcase in its clear evidence sack, recovered from the station locker. The envelopes of currency and false passports, found in the hotel safe. A printout of the room-access log, taken from the Reception computer. He shakes his head, and turns judgemental eyes upon Masson, "And you had the gall to whine at me about withholding information…"

Masson snaps peevishly, "You weren't *listening*, Valentine! Proof was the only way to persuade you…so I had to find some. Rivers is telling the truth; certainly about the circumstances surrounding our burnt corpse – "

"Are you sure, Inspecteur?"

Masson exhales exasperation into the air-conditioned metres between them, "*Now* what's your problem?"

"How do you know the chap on the hotel CCTV is Nightingale? You can't see his face! It could be this Chadwick-character."

The Inspecteur almost growls with frustration, "Look, Valentine! In this suitcase, here…in the closet in this very hotel room…all the clothing items have had their labels removed! On the yacht, Chadwick's clothing bristled with labels of every shape and size – "

"The corpse was dressed in *un*labelled clothing…?"

"Have you never heard of a corpse's clothing being changed to hamper identification?"

"Have *you* never heard of a crime scene being staged to befuddle the dozy Police?"

Masson turns to Xavier, "Give me that email from England, will you?"

Xavier slides a printout from the back of his notebook.

"No doubt you'll recognise this as a British passport? Take a good look at it. That is James Chadwick. That is his real passport, and we've also seen younger photographs of him that confirm his physical appearance and his identity...beyond question."

Masson extracts the now-flimsy scan from his pocket and unfolds it gingerly, holding it up next to the passport printout, "James Chadwick is Guy Montparnasse, see? And I'll bet you my life savings he's the fella in our freezer. The man *you're* looking for is the chap from your photograph, as you well-know. His real name? Pick one!" Masson snatches up the pile of passports, "Clive Lewis, Michael Lunnon, Christopher Teal, Eric Parker – " Masson discards each one as he reads it, tossing them carelessly to land on the couch between the two men, smacking flatly onto the pvc cushions and making Valentine twitch.

The Englishman recovers quickly, rolling his eyes and sighing theatrically, as if dealing with Masson is a gargantuan trial of his monumental patience, drawling sarcastically, "All right, Masson, you've made your point. However persuasive your argument, we still don't have conclusive proof of the identity of that corpse. You know I'm right! Yes, you've managed to prove the identity of your yacht owner. Yes, I accept that Nightingale has definitely used this location as a base, but – !" Valentine holds up a hand as Masson opens his mouth to argue, "He isn't here now, is he? Whatever crumbs you've been able to uncover, we're still a step behind! We're still no closer to tracking him down!"

****

The Receptionist finishes the surreptitious typing of a text message to her boyfriend. She hears the suck and sigh of the rubber seal parting, and the automatic door sliding back. She adds a couple of kisses, arranges her bored features into a welcoming smile in anticipation of lifting her head to greet the guest who's just entered the hotel foyer…but no one approaches the desk. Instead, a tall, slim man with grey hair walks straight past, suspiciously briskly, face deliberately averted. Given the events of the last hour – the arrival of the police, the rumours already circulating below-stairs of false passports, envelopes of cash, missing persons, and murder suspects – his behaviour pricks her attention. She's not supposed to leave the desk unattended, but mid-afternoon is a quiet time of day in July. Everyone's on the beach, making the most of the Mediterranean sunshine. If she can just stop him before he reaches the lift…get a look at his face…?

"Monsieur. Monsieur! Just a moment, please. Monsieur?"

He doesn't look around. That in itself is odd. Instead, he starts to trot, so she does too, high heels clopping on the terrazzo floor.

"Excuse me! Monsieur!"

He reaches the lift, and jabs frantically at the button. The light above the door illuminates. The bell pings. The door slides open.

He dives in, any pretence at subtlety abandoned, wiping his palm down the control panel, selecting almost every floor in his desperation to get the doors closed. She rushes up, "Monsieur!" reaching out to push her forearm into the diminishing gap. Her eyes meet his reflection in the lifts' mirrored interior. His face is a mess – bruised, cut, and swollen. The front of his shirt is caked in dried blood. She gasps, and involuntarily withdraws her hand.

There's a gun in the waistband of his trousers!

The lift doors *thunk* shut.

Without pausing to consider the wisdom of her decision, the Receptionist kicks off her high heels, hoiks up her pencil skirt, and charges up the adjacent stairs two at a time.

****

The lift stops at virtually every floor, there being no way to override the bank of buttons he thumped in haste. He has to suffer the agonising suspense of the lift doors opening onto an expanse of bland carpet and uniform décor, and endure the eternity they take to close again, leaving barely time for one shaky breath before the process repeats on the next floor. How the hell did the Police find the locker? Because he didn't pay for it? Thankfully, there aren't any clues in there...except the card-key in the sponge bag lining; what are the chances of some backwater bobby noticing that...? He's come straight from the station to get this done – now – before the French cops join the dots. Upon reaching the correct level, he's going to smash the nearest fire alarm, empty the safe, and make his escape in the ensuing confusion. That jobsworth Receptionist will be stopped in her officious little tracks by having to deal with a full-scale building evacuation. Not ideal, but the best he can come up with under the circumstances. He needs cash. He needs at least one passport. Fresh clothes wouldn't go amiss either.

****

Thighs burning, heart hammering, chest bursting, the Receptionist plunges through the fire door from the staircase, thundering along the carpeted corridor in her bare feet, tight skirt hampering her stride. She arrives gasping for breath, perspiration beading at her hairline. All three policemen turn to gape as she stumbles in and has to hold her panting body up with a delicate palm against the flocked wallpaper, collecting herself sufficiently for coherent communication.

The good-looking Inspecteur smiles cautiously, and queries, "Mademoiselle?" Before she can respond, the fire alarm begins to jangle deafeningly from the ceiling speaker.

Masson, noting her bare feet, assumes the lift's been disabled and she's rushed up to warn them of the fire and request their assistance. He swiftly begins to gather the evidence from the coffee table, hefting the suitcase into his arms and directing Xavier to collect up the other items. Thus distracted, he's utterly unprepared for either Valentine's shouted expletive, or the Receptionist's chilling scream.

NINETEEN

It's the weirdest three minutes of Inspecteur François Masson's life; the one event he knows he'll replay during each wakeful hour of every sleepless night from now until the day he dies – racked with guilt and mortification. Despite the piercing fire alarm, Valentine's curse and the Receptionist's squeal are loud enough to turn Xavier and Masson's heads towards the narrow hallway. A tall, slim man stands there. He has grey hair, a deep tan – and he's filthy and covered in blood. He's got the Receptionist in a headlock against his stomach, a gun rammed into the crown of her head. Bent double, his arm tight around her neck, it's impossible for the young woman to struggle and breathe at the same time, making the petrified girl an opportune hostage.

Two very obvious injuries stand out from the mess of bruising and swelling on his face. There's a deep purple cut tracking the bridge of his nose and bisecting one eyebrow. There's a second split across his cheekbone, which glistens wetly with fresh blood, as if it might need a stitch or two to heal it.

Nightingale.

It *has* to be!

While Masson simply gawks at the unexpected sight, normally-agile mind utterly blank, Xavier reacts with admirable decisiveness and speed. Diving full-length like a rugby forward going for a Try, he barrels into the unprepared intruder and tumbles him backwards. The man has to release his prisoner to regain his own balance. Xavier seizes his chance, grabs the startled Receptionist in more than one place her mother would disapprove of, and bundles her straight through the closest door, into the suite's tiny bathroom. The action rouses Masson from his horrified trance. Dumping his armfuls of plastic-wrapped evidence, he tries to dart around the obstacle of the sofa before Nightingale can recover. He isn't fast enough. The man's arm snaps up, gun aimed directly at Masson's chest. In perfect French, he states calmly, "Keep still, Monsieur. This gun is loaded. I won't miss."

From the corner of his eye, Masson notices Valentine fidgeting around in his jacket as if he's lost his wallet. In amazement, he realises the Englishman is also producing a pistol he isn't supposed to have, ineptly waving it around. Nightingale simultaneously detects the movement. Seemingly without needing to aim, he jerks the gun barrel minutely left, and drops the incompetent pen-pusher with an accurate shot to the upper thigh. Valentine flies backwards as the spray of blood, bone, flesh, and trouser fabric erupts from him like a miniature meteor-strike. His loosely-clasped gun falls from his fingers, bounces across the carpet, and slides under a chest of drawers. The blood is squirting high and pumping fast. Masson leaps sideways, gripping Valentine's ankles, ignoring the infuriating Rosbif's squeal of agony as he drags him behind the relative safety of the sofa. Swearing under his breath, Masson hunkers behind the couch, slaps both hands onto Valentine's leg, and presses down as if seeking to flatten the Englishman beneath his palms.

The gunshot immediately brings his courageous fool of a junior colleague back out of the relative safety of the bathroom. Xavier attempts to grapple with the British Agent, gripping the spy's wrists and pushing them upward with all his might. Masson, unable to leave the thrashing, groaning Valentine, can only watch in dismay as Nightingale lifts his knee and drives it into Xavier's groin. Xavier squawks in predictable pain, and his legs buckle involuntarily. As the young policeman's body curls protectively around his throbbing privates, Nightingale brings the butt of the gun cracking down upon Xavier's skull, striking him expertly just above the right ear. Xavier subsides against the man's blood-encrusted shirt with a shuddering sigh. Nightingale scoops him up with a powerful wrist under each armpit, and drags him bodily from the room – an infinitely more valuable hostage than a hotel Receptionist. Masson is powerless. If he gives chase, there's every chance Valentine will be dead in minutes. Instead, he yells, "HELP! *HELLLLPPP!*" at the top of his voice. The sobbing, shaking Receptionist appears in the bathroom doorway, a mess of disordered hair and streaked mascara. Too agitated for professional politeness, Masson screams over the deafening jangle of the fire alarm, "Don't just *stand* there, you idiot girl! Get a fucking *ambulance!*"

****

Valentine's had surgery, a transfusion, and now he lies in a hospital bed in a recovery room, with Masson squirming in the uncomfortable plastic seat beside it.

There's no trace of Xavier anywhere. Half the station's been looking for him since the alarm was raised. Masson sits with elbows on knees and head in hands. Valentine's dried blood crusts his rolled-up shirtsleeves and the legs of his trousers, where he knelt in the ever-widening pool maintaining pressure on the wound until his whole body ached, counting the wasted minutes to the ambulance's arrival. Minutes when he should have gone after Xavier. Minutes when he should have let the Englishman die. After all, what loyalty did he have to Valentine? He didn't even know who he really was! Xavier had leapt out of that bathroom to save *him*. He'd put himself in harm's way deliberately – twice within two minutes – for the sake of the hotel Receptionist *and* his undeserving senior officer, while Masson just stood in the middle of the room with his mouth open.

Hot tears rush into Masson's eyes, and he knuckles them away. To find Xavier, he needs to think straight. Emotions like guilt, embarrassment, regret...they all need to wait until the young Détective is safely back where he belongs. The Inspecteur tries to reason out what might happen next. Nightingale can't get anywhere without money or paperwork. What brought him back to the hotel at such considerable risk was the contents of that safe. Evidently, he has no compunction about inflicting serious injury to attain his objectives. He'd likely have shot Xavier at point-blank range if the lad was of no use to him. Nightingale can only have taken Xavier alive for one reason: to bargain with...and Masson has nothing. He doesn't know enough about what's really going on here to make a sufficiently-persuasive trade.

Masson stands and leans over Valentine, raking the serene face for signs of animation. When the Englishman awakes, he's going to wish he'd bled to death on that hotel carpet.

TWENTY

Valentine's too groggy to put up much of a fight. He's barely conscious before Masson's in his face, growling descriptive threats, promising comprehensive vengeance that's going to make being shot feel like a bee sting. Valentine holds up his hands in shaky surrender as the incensed Frenchman grips a fistful of hospital smock, jerking his helpless torso off the pillows like a ragdoll.

He slurs out one word, "Rivers…"

"What?"

"Rivers! She's the one London want. She's the only thing my bosses are interested in. Not Nightingale. Track her down, bring her home. That's it."

"Why? Who *is* she, Valentine?"

"I have no idea… I just know they want her more than anything else."

"What are you saying?"

"You want Xavier back, offer Rivers in exchange. She's the key…"

Masson's just about to ask how he's supposed to negotiate with a man who's disappeared off the face of the planet, when his mobile begins to ring. Masson immediately drops Valentine, in order to root frantically in his jacket. The Englishman slumps back onto the pillows with relief, head lolling, hooded eyes already closing again. Masson turns and strides to the window. The screen says, 'Xavier'.

"*Xavier!*"

At the exclamation, Valentine's eyes snap open and fix themselves unblinkingly on Masson's broad back.

A dry chuckle on the end of the line. The same clipped, textbook French as earlier this afternoon, "Regrettably not…although he did very kindly allow me to use his 'phone. Am I talking to an Inspecteur Masson?"

"You are. Am I talking to the M I 5 Agent known as Nightingale?"

The man doesn't answer that question. Instead, he drawls, "You have something I want, Inspecteur…and I have something you want."

"Is Xavier all right?"

"Well…he's alive. How long he remains so rather depends on you."

"We'll find you – "

"Will you? Will you *really*? And will you do it fast enough to save your poor little colleague, here?"

"I swear to God – "

"Whatever deity you invoke, Inspecteur, it's earthly concerns that trouble me more. You're holding a gentleman called Marcus Pickford." Masson instinctively glances behind him, but Valentine's asleep with his mouth open. Masson's thinking fast. Eyes on Valentine's immobile, ashen face, he asks, "You looked in a bad way this afternoon. Things been pretty troublesome for you since that crash on the mountain road?"

There's a fractional hesitation on the end of the line; enough to confirm a theory for the intelligent Inspecteur. Nightingale knows they have Pickford…but it's doubtful he's aware they have Rivers too. Cautious – ever-mindful of the presence of Valentine – he volunteers, "I do have what you're after, yes. I have something infinitely better though."

"Impress me."

"I've got a woman called Tammi Rivers."

Silence. Absolute, cold, crisp silence. It goes so quiet, Masson removes the handset from his ear to check the connection, "Monsieur Nightingale?"

"Prove it."

"I'm not sure I can, not over the 'phone…but give me back Xavier, and you can have her. She's a smart-talking, trouble-making pain-in-the-arse. I'll be glad to be rid of her."

The tempo of the voice quickens, "I need to see for myself, Inspecteur. I'm not accustomed to trusting the word of others."

"And I need Xavier…alive. Intact. Unharmed – "

"I wish you'd said earlier, Inspecteur. Some of that could be a problem now."

Masson feels bile rise in the back of his throat, and gurgles faintly, "Just don't hurt him any *more*, all right? Or I won't give you anything!" For some reason, the image that pops into Masson's mind is of the petite, dark-eyed Desk Officer flashing that flirtatious glance at his Détective, making Xavier blush like a schoolboy.

"You want your lad back, Masson, you're going to have to give me *both* of them – Pickford *and* his moll."

Given how intensely embroiled he is within this baffling investigation, and how ordinarily-tenacious about unearthing truth, Masson is amazed at the ease with which he makes his decision. What does it matter if he never discovers what's really going on here? What *matters* is that twenty-six-year-old Détective Xavier Hâche gets the chance to find out whether a flash of dark-eyed promise might become more? What *matters* is that Détective Xavier Hâche gets to fulfil the immense career potential he displays every day. Why should an overworked Inspecteur of Police in a rural French district care whether two British citizens commit crimes against their sovereign government; or the cold, pompous Valentine looks a fool in the eyes of his employers? He suddenly, passionately, emphatically wants every one of these duplicitous foreign bastards off his turf and back in their own country where they belong, ruining someone else's summer.

"You know what, Agent Nightingale, you've got yourself a deal. Return Xavier – harmed *no further* – and you can have your request, provided you get the hell out of my country within twelve hours."

"I'll do it faster than that, Inspecteur, I can assure you."

"When shall we exchange? Where?"

"I'll come back to you on that. Double-cross me, and he dies…immediately. You understand?"

"Yes…I understand."

"No 'phone triangulation. No call tracing – "

"I want Xavier back. Why would I do a thing to jeopardise that? The rest is your problem to solve."

"I'll be in touch, Inspecteur."

****

Valentine waits until he's sure Masson is gone; hearing the door thud shut, listening to the departing footfalls recede down the corridor, and counting to fifty before cautiously opening his eyes.

The room is empty. He'd pretended to be asleep throughout Masson's disconcerting call. Obviously, he'd only heard one side of the conversation. He might be hopeless at tackling assailants; inexperienced at verbal thrust and parry in an interview room – but Valentine's a detail-obsessive, and he can detect a man concealing his true intentions when he hears one. Masson had been holding back, delaying before responding...not because of Nightingale, but because of *him*. Wincing at the daggers of pain from his injured leg, Valentine inches up the mattress until he can reach the locker beside his French hospital bed, groping inside the cubby hole to unearth his mobile 'phone, and dialling the number he memorised in the taxi from his flat to the airport a few days ago.

It's answered immediately, "Yes?"

Valentine quells his nerves. He's got a justifiable reason for this call.

"Sir. It's me, Sir. You told me to only contact you, and only on this number."

"Correct. I also told you only to contact me in the gravest of emergencies – "

"I've been shot, Sir! I'm in hospital – "

"I'm not your Mother. What you're describing is an occupational hazard – "

"Sir, I'm not calling about being shot. It's the circumstances."

"I thought you were hours away from returning with her?"

"I was, Sir...but...Nightingale's not dead, Sir!"

"*What?*"

"He abducted and killed someone else…he staged his own death. It was neatly done; the evidence was persuasive…but…I've seen him today with my own eyes. *He* shot me, Sir! If it wasn't for the French Police Inspector here, I would have just bled out at the scene. I've had surgery, a transfusion – "

"*Operational* detail! This isn't 'what I did on my holidays'."

"It *is* operational detail, Sir! Whilst the Inspector was trying to keep me alive, his younger colleague was attempting to apprehend Nightingale singlehanded. Unsurprisingly, he failed. It's evident Nightingale has him as a hostage now. I overheard the Inspector on the 'phone… He's just agreed to swap Rivers for his colleague!"

"He…he…*can't*!"

"That's just it, Sir, he *can*! She's in his cells, she's not under arrest, her new passport and necessary paperwork arrived by courier at his police station this morning…and I'm stuck in here powerless to take any action. I'm on drips, a catheter…I can't get out of bed and stop him! All he wants is his colleague back. He doesn't care what I want… We haven't exactly hit it off, so doubtless he feels no loyalty either to me or this investigation – "

"I couldn't give a damn about the 'investigation'! I *must* have that woman! This policeman *must* be stopped! What the bloody hell is Nightingale *doing*?"

TWENTY-ONE

The hastily-convened meeting of the secret society known as The Cabal takes place in an anonymous East London function room – the kind of serviced office building where you book by the hour and take your chances on the freshness of the patisserie and the cheapness of the coffee. It doesn't do for the high-profile individuals seated around this table to be seen congregating at one another's offices. You never know who might be watching. They haven't survived this long by being careless.

Sir Blair Stocker-Pickford deliberately times his arrival for exactly two minutes before the meeting is due to begin. He likes making an entrance. He's entertained by the notion they're all beginning to glance at their watches and wonder where he is. He enjoys annoying them. They were all so quick to crowd behind Julian, to point fingers, to apportion blame...yet none would be here at all if it wasn't for him. He'd had the original idea, taken the initial risks, blazed the trail. They would do well now and again to remember quite how much they *all* owe him. Sir Julian Franklin is a prime example of a nobody lifted from obscurity to influence by membership of The Cabal. The spymaster would still be writing lemon-juice letters to his handler from a Vladivostok bedsit without it.

Sir Blair checks his watch, and enters the room with one minute forty-seven seconds to spare.

"Gentlemen."

He takes the one remaining seat around the circular table, smiling affably at the collection of flushed and troubled faces that turn his way. They don't take a room unless it has a round table, reinforcing the lie that none is master here. Officially, they're a committee who make decisions by majority vote…but, as any idiot knows, all committees need a Chairman.

Blair observes Julian looking pointedly at his watch, but he isn't late, so there's nothing the two-faced Secret Service snake can do but glower, and call the muttering assembly to order.

Today, Sir Blair feels invigorated; reborn! All he knows about this meeting is that it concerns Tammi Rivers – when do they ever discuss anything else? For the first time in four dispiriting years, Blair is supremely confident he is the only person around this table who knows precisely where Rivers is – because of his boy. Dull-witted he may be, but Marc understands his duty. The intelligence he's so lately provided is about to reinstate his ol' Dad to his rightful position. It's going to lay the ghosts that have haunted Blair since the first raft of articles appeared about Geoffrey, and he understood his heir's bid to reach Number 10 Downing Street was permanently scuppered. Julian swooped so fast to undermine Blair he's still not completely sure Geoffrey's downfall wasn't Julian's doing – despite him laying the blame very firmly at Rivers' door; a convenient scapegoat for Julian's machinations. It almost doesn't matter now. Sir Blair devised The Cabal, nurtured it, made it the powerhouse it is

– and thanks to his youngest son, he's finally about to retake control. He's going to succeed where Sir Julian Franklin has so spectacularly failed, despite all the supposed insider knowledge at his fingertips. Whatever Julian's secretly up to, it's too late for him. By the end of today's meeting, no one will ever dare to question Blair's authority again. He smirks into the sudden silence, juts his thick neck forward – bullishly intimidating – and queries witheringly, "So, Julian, what's upset your delicate digestion this time?"

****

Masson's in the cell doorway. A different Masson. No longer languid, laconic, ironic. Now, his watchful eyes roam as if anticipating trouble at any moment.

He beckons, "Up, Mademoiselle Rivers. Time to go."

She stands, but that's all, "Go where?"

"With me."

"*Where*?"

"Out of this police station. You want to do that, don't you?"

Tammi folds her arms defiantly, "Depends where I end up."

Masson tuts impatiently, gets a good grip of her elbow, and lugs her out into the corridor, where the smirking Custody Officer surveys her contemptuously, before clicking a pair of handcuffs spitefully tight around her thin wrists.

"Owww…what – ?"

She looks up and down the corridor. Her. Masson. The Custody Sergeant's already loping back to his desk, job done.

"Where's Valentine?"

"Not here."

"Where?"

"That is no concern of yours, Mademoiselle Rivers."

"It flippin' is if you're taking me to the airport to meet him, isn't it? I thought – "

"I have decided I don't care what you think."

"Am I going back to England, Inspector? The least you can do is tell me that."

"I have no idea where you are going, Mademoiselle Rivers. I only know you are leaving France…and that's what matters to me."

She tries to pull away from him, but his grip's like iron, strong fingers no doubt creating another bruise to add to her comprehensive collection, "Who's got to you, Masson? Who's paid you to pass me on?"

"*I* don't accept bribes, Mademoiselle. Unlike you English, I'm not permanently for sale…"

"So, where are we *going*?"

"For a lovely ride in the countryside."

"Are you dumping me over the border? Do you think that's going to solve your investigations?"

Massons smiles nastily, "You wish. For you, it will not be that easy. You pretend you're part of the solution, but it's becoming increasingly evident to me that you are the entire problem."

"What – ?"

"Enough. No more talking. You were just confounding me while you played for time…having a little fun with the stupid Frogs, huh?"

Indignant, Tammi snaps, "I've told you nothing but truth!"

"I cannot deny that everything you've told me is supported by evidence – "

"Well, then!"

"But that does not mean it is the truth. The 'why' is absent from all of this, Mademoiselle…and the 'why' is *all*. Tell me *why*, and I will treat you very differently."

"I'm unable to do that, Inspector."

"And so you embark upon another adventure, Mademoiselle. One over which I have no control."

They're out of the main door and into blinding sunlight. It glances off the sea across the road, flashing so brightly her eyes water after many hours in a gloomy cell. Masson's grip on her arm loosens, slides away, and a different hand grasps her instead, pulling her towards the baking bodywork of a police car. She tries to look round to see who it is, but a hot palm pushes down on the back of her head, forcing her to duck awkwardly as she struggles inside the vehicle.

The brown eyes of the driver briefly meet hers in the rear view mirror, before flicking right to observe the exchange between his colleague and the tight-voiced Masson, all conducted in low, rapid French she can't decipher.

When the other copper also gets into the car, she realises what's most troubling about them. Both wear stab-vests on their torsos, and pistols at their hips, but the guy in the passenger seat also rests a rifle across his lap. Is Masson having her taken somewhere quiet and disposed of? How's he going to cover that up, given her very public arrival at the station – distressed, bloodied, handcuffed? Plenty of people have seen her. He can't just make her disappear…can he?

TWENTY-TWO

"Off we go, Monsieur Pickford. I'll just put these on you."

Handcuffs click over Marc's thick wrists. He doesn't react with pathetic wincing and complaint like he used to. These days, he's inured to it.

"That it, then? Done with me, Inspector? Am I off back to the Tropics? No offence, but I'm not sure I'll be choosing the Riviera for my holiday next year. It's nothing like the brochures."

Masson chuckles, and asks, "I trust you received a change of clothes this morning?"

"I did, yes...in anticipation of my long and sweaty journey?"

Masson merely smiles. Wary since the shocking sight of Tammi's horrifyingly-injured face through the panel in his cell door, Marc's been waiting for something to happen. That's what Tammi does – makes things happen. He placidly allows himself to be steered from the cell, but keeps his head up and his eyes moving, seeking her at every turn.

****

Masson's had time to sleep on yesterday's rash decision. Or, rather, to toss, turn, fidget, and pace his dark house, muttering to himself until he fears he's going mad, trying to work out how to renege upon the irresponsible bargain he so impulsively made, without fatally imperilling Xavier in the process. He's *got* to let both suspicious

Brits go in order to recover his Détective, and that's not negotiable. Getting Xavier back is all that matters! Almost all, anyway… François Masson's a career detective. He believes in the law he's employed to uphold, and he detests unsolved mysteries. It's self-evidently dangerous for an apparently intelligent, highly-trained British Secret Service operative to risk arrest and exposure on foreign soil; what's so damned important about Rivers and Pickford that Nightingale will go to such lengths to obtain them? Masson *has* to know. They've spent too much time, money, and effort on this investigation to allow three highly-suspicious criminals to simply walk away without consequence or explanation. Besides which, no one messes with Masson's team and escapes unscathed. He has a responsibility to Xavier; a duty of care to the dedicated young man. He's got to see justice done. He wants to put the morally-bankrupt Nightingale in a prison cell and never let him out. He wouldn't mind doing the same to that infuriating Rivers-bitch either.

By 5am he has the answer. By 7.30, he's in the station's IT department, gabbling like a lunatic. That's why Marc's been dressed in a fresh tracksuit. There's a tiny GPS transmitter sewn into the centre back of the trouser waistband. Wherever Nightingale takes Pickford – and for whatever reason – Masson and his team will be able to follow for as long as the signal lasts…and the determined Inspecteur isn't going to let them get far. He glances in the rear view mirror of the car in which he's driving himself and Pickford to the agreed exchange location. It cheers Masson immensely to think the clueless fool has no idea he's beaming a signal from the top of his arse-crack directly to the laptop of the geek-in-chief back at the station. The Inspecteur smiles grimly. He's got unmarked cars stationed at strategic points where significant roads bisect…and a motor boat lurking at Point Miroir, just in case Nightingale is arrogant enough to revert to his original plan of sailing away. Masson *wants* Nightingale to assume he's being followed. He's banking on it adding unwanted pressure to the frantic escape; forcing the British spy into the sort of rash, panicky decisions he'd spent all of yesterday making himself.

His mobile rings. He takes a chance and answers it hands-free, praying Pickford knows as little French as he claims, "Mas-son!"

"A change of plan."

Masson curses inwardly. If he's had time to repent his haste, so has Nightingale.

"What change?"

"A new location."

"You can't move it now!"

"Why not? Because you've surrounded the original place with too many officers to shift in a hurry? I may have been temporarily wrong-footed a day or two ago, but I wasn't born yesterday, Inspecteur. Did you really expect me to stick trustingly to the plan?"

Masson swears under his breath, and growls, "Where now?"

The voice rattles off map reference coordinates.

"Hold on, I need to write it down!" Masson skids the car to a sharp halt, beaching it on the rutted verge, and sending a cloud of grass pollen puffing into the humid air around the bonnet like a bow wave before a boat. He wriggles out his notebook and pen, "Again please."

The code is repeated. The call ends abruptly.

Muttering furiously, Masson gropes under the seat for his map book, frantically flipping to the index and seeking the closest grid reference point. He dials the other car.

"All right, Inspecteur?"

"Fermier. He's changed the swap location!"

"But – the team…"

"I know! We haven't got time to move units now. *We'll* just have to do it – the three of us. Ok with that?"

"Yes, sir."

"He's given me a grid reference," Masson rattles it off, and he can hear Fermier's own map rustling and flapping as he seeks the spot, "Looks like a forest clearing up above that abandoned Chalet Park. You know, the one that burnt out in the last lot of big fires?"

A muttered exchange between the two armed officers in the other car, "Yes, sir…Martin knows the place, sir."

"Good. I'll see you there. Radio through to the others what's going on, and tell them to sit tight 'til I give the word. We don't know what direction he's coming from, so we can't have a sudden load of cars diverging on very few approach roads – he'll notice in seconds. I can't take that risk with Détective Hâche's safety."

"Understood, sir."

"Just wait for me to arrive. Whether he's there or not, don't do a thing until I show up. I'm not that far behind you."

"Ok, sir. No problem. See you there."

Masson cuts the call, and shoves the car furiously into reverse, meeting Pickford's even stare in the rear view mirror as he does so.

Poker-faced, Pickford states, "This isn't the way to the airport, Inspector."

Masson snarls in frustration and accelerates too fast, wheels spinning on the dusty surface. He's just got to get poor Xavier back in one piece. After that, the gloves are well and truly off.

TWENTY-THREE

The police car is alone in the woodland clearing. Masson's vehicle bounces in across the rutted surface and swings round swiftly, the rear wheels disturbing an arc of pink dust that hangs in the unmoving air.

Masson jerks up the handbrake, "Wait here, Monsieur Pickford." Locking the Englishman in, he jogs over to the other car. Marc peers intently out of the back window. There are three silhouettes in the other vehicle – two in the front, one in the back – but he can't decipher their features. The driver rolls down his window as the Inspecteur approaches, and Marc sees it's a uniformed policeman. He jerks his strong wrists against the handcuffs a couple of times, but naturally they won't budge. He didn't really expect them to. He's locked in, the Inspecteur has the keys; he's just got to sit, watch, and wait.

"Sir."

"Did you radio the location change?"

"Yes, sir. All units standing by."

"Yeah…twenty minutes away." Masson's rattled. He can't disguise it. Fermier and Martin exchange glances, "We can always call in the Coastguard chopper if we need it, sir."

Masson sighs wearily, suddenly craving those hours of sleep that had eluded him, "Yes, I suppose so…"

Fermier grins encouragingly, and pats the pistol in the holster on his hip, before lifting the rifle illustratively, "Don't worry, sir, we'll get Détective Hâche back. We can take this guy."

Masson glances up, over the roof of the car, "I fucking hope so, because here's our boy now by the look of it. Ok, he's armed and dangerous. Expect him to be as competently firearms-trained as either of you – and be aware he's already shot one cop this week. Let him see Rivers…in fact, make sure he does – but, if anything happens to me, don't let him anywhere near her until we have Xavier secure. Apparently, she's the one he really wants."

"Yes, sir. Understood, sir."

"Be ready, gentlemen. Eyes on Xavier at all times, yes? I want everyone out of here alive…including our suspects, in decent condition for arrest and questioning, ok? We don't shoot unless it becomes unavoidably necessary."

"Don't worry, sir, we're on it."

The car – Xavier's car – executes its own clumsy handbrake turn, and parks facing the way it came. More dust. Masson can feel its abrasiveness on his teeth. The driver's door opens. Nightingale steps out. The butt of the gun protrudes from the waistband of his trousers.

There's no sign of Xavier.

He calls across, "Inspecteur! Got what I came for?"

Keeping his hands in full view of the crack-shot, Masson points towards the police car. Clearly visible is a wriggling Tammi, held helplessly against the glass by Fermier's powerful forearm.

Nightingale nods slowly, and turns back to Masson, "And the other?"

Masson walks to his car, and helps the handcuffed Pickford out into the sunlight, holding him by the elbow. Marc doesn't know what's going on here, but he wants a look in the rear of that police car. He staggers a little on the uneven ground, his considerable mass unbalancing the Inspecteur sufficiently to move them both a few feet to the left, providing Marc an unobstructed view of the bruised and battered face held at the rear window of the adjacent vehicle. Somehow, he'd known it would be her. What did it mean?

Masson swiftly gets them back on course – upright and moving away from the cars. Marc manages another look behind him. It's the minutest of gestures, but as she's released by the big cop in the passenger seat, she points sideways, little fingers waggling, miming a running action. Is she telling him to do it now?

Unsure, Marc does nothing immediately, but instinctively hesitates nonetheless, making Masson snap, "What?"

Marc's squinting into the sun, focusing with difficulty on the individual in front of them, "Is that Jim over there?"

Masson sighs, "No, Monsieur Pickford…but he'd like you to think it is. Would it have made a difference if it was?"

"What's going on here, Inspector?"

"Stop here, please, Monsieur."

All too aware of Nightingale's faultless aim, Masson stands slightly behind Pickford, hand firmly on his shoulder, calling, "There you are, Agent Nightingale. As promised. And now for your side of our bargain?"

Nightingale opens the rear door of Xavier's car, and drags the semi-conscious, horrendously-beaten Détective from the back seat as if he's a sack of flour. Xavier's legs slide and plonk into the dust like two unbaked baguettes. Pickford feels Masson's grip on his shoulder tighten tellingly. A low sound like a moan of agony escapes from between the Inspecteur's gritted teeth. While Masson's distracted by personal anguish, Marc snatches another glance over his shoulder. Tammi is still at the rear window of the police car, eyes fixed on him.

Nightingale hefts Xavier to a standing position. Xavier's hands are roped together behind his back. His ankles are also hobbled, permitting him to shuffle, but not to run. Nightingale wraps a strong arm around Xavier's waist and propels him closer to the waiting figures as if he's a dressmaker's mannequin. Xavier's head lolls. He's red all over – skin, hair…a mess of blood. Masson's shallow breathing falters completely. For a second or two, he thinks he might suffocate with guilt and shame…and that he'd deserve it if he did – but he's here to rescue Xavier, as Xavier had saved him yesterday. He cannot fail him.

"What now, Agent Nightingale?"

"Release Pickford. Let him walk forward."

"Release Xavier too!"

"Pickford first, Inspecteur."

The British Agent takes the gun from his waistband and presses it against the side of Xavier's drooping head, "Any funny business and your boy dies where he stands."

Masson calls, "I'm letting Pickford go now!" Quietly, he growls, "Walk forward, Monsieur Pickford, straight towards them. Be aware two armed officers in the car behind you have their weapons trained on you."

"Is this legal, Inspector?"

"*Go*, Monsieur Pickford."

There's something undeniably familiar about the man a couple of hundred yards in front of him – and it isn't just the striking similarity to his brother's old friend – but Marc can't work out what's triggering the sensation of déjà-vu. Playing for time, he pretends to stumble again in the flip-flops they gave him, permitting another surreptitious glance behind. One small, decisive nod from the back of the car. Now.

Pickford takes another exaggeratedly-unsteady step, then darts surefootedly sideways and sprints like a gazelle for the closest tree-cover. All too absorbed in watching each other – Marc, as usual, an afterthought – it takes vital seconds for anyone to react. Masson only has time to scream, "*Noooo!*" – convinced Pickford's just cost Xavier his life – before all descends into horror and confusion.

Nightingale, ever the first to respond, removes the gun from Xavier's head to track Pickford's surprisingly-fleet progress. Easy as it would be, he can't shoot the troublesome tosser. He needs him alive.

Masson turns to the police car in impotent panic, but Fermier's already out and pelting after the escaping Pickford, rifle clutched tight against his body as he runs. In the car, Martin lofts his own firearm and levels it at the British spy through the open driver's window. Nightingale clocks the racing Fermier, and is just about to drop him with a shot instead, when he finds himself flying sideways, landing heavily on his hip in the dust, a bullet whining through the air above his prone form.

As soon as the pistol's pressure leaves his temple, Xavier seizes his chance, ramming his pelvis as hard as he can into Nightingale's middle, and dropping the unsuspecting spy like a stone. It means Martin's intended 'incapacitating' shot misses by several feet, but it buys Xavier temporary liberty. He can see Masson already dashing towards him, so he wobbles at the Inspecteur as fast as his bound ankles and battered body will allow. It's the best he can manage, but it's woefully inadequate. Masson can see what's going to happen. It's yesterday afternoon all over again. Despite the fact he's barely hit the dirt, Nightingale's already rolling, arm outstretched, sunlight flashing off the gun barrel. Masson roars in frustration and fear, diving forward, gripping Xavier's legs in a bid to drop him to the ground and disrupt Nightingale's unerring aim. It works, after a fashion. Given the state he's in, Xavier crumples unresistingly to the floor, Masson crawling desperately on top of him to protect the young man's body with his own, but Agent Nightingale doesn't miss. His shot is off-target thanks to Masson's ungainly tackle, but it finds its victim nonetheless. The bullet penetrates the back of Xavier's knee, and shatters it to fragments. His scream is blood-curdling. As Martin fires another shot over Nightingale's head, designed to subdue but not to injure, Masson drags Xavier around the back of the police car to relative safety. Panting in horror and fright, the Inspecteur tugs off his belt to use as a tourniquet. He can hear Martin's voice chuntering powerfully into the radio. By the sound of it, he's calling in every backup he can think of, from the Coastguard to NATO. Masson's penknife slices swiftly through Xavier's bonds, to lie him flat and elevate the damaged leg against his chest and shoulder. Tugging his belt as tight as it will go around his colleague's thigh, he grips the bruised, cut, and bloodied fist that gropes blindly for his own, "Hold on, Xavier. Help's coming. I promise. Hold on."

TWENTY-FOUR

There's no boozing in prison. There are no expensive Cuban cigars. There are no night-long games of high-stakes poker; no liquid lunches at the yacht club; no snoozing the afternoons away in your luxury pool, while someone infinitely more capable than you digs you out of the messes you've unwittingly got yourself into over the preceding twenty-four hours. There's only heat, mosquitoes, the sour smell of stale sweat and inefficient drains, and the same four walls to stare at for endless hours as the pent-up frustration bubbles and boils. Marc Pickford hadn't realised how much he drank until he'd sweated his agitated way through his first few days of incarceration. It had shocked him. When had he become so dependant on alcohol that his hands shook uncontrollably without it; that his head span, his stomach churned, and he spent nights puking into the plastic bucket that now served as his en-suite bathroom.

The ancient cot in his prison cell collapsed under his weight. The replacement bed also bowed alarmingly, until the sniggering, sneering guards braced it with an extra plank of wood or two.

He couldn't keep up at Recreation, when the rest ran on ahead and he wobbled after them at barely walking-pace, heaving like a consumptive, absorbing the abuse that pursued him inescapably. He found himself recalling University Rugby – the freedom and self-confidence that stemmed from effortless fitness and natural strength.

There were no mirrors, but there was a stainless steel door to a storage room on the way back from the showers. Walking naked in line, he didn't need to see detail. The bloated, sunburned mess that quivered past the reflective surface was humiliation enough.

Some people slept in their cells through the long, steaming days and nights. Some cried. Some shouted. Some plotted. Some read. Some simply stared at the light travelling across the ceiling, marking time. Marc Pickford got off his fat backside, and put the work in. In the miniscule space where, arms outstretched, his fingers could touch either wall, he did sit-ups, press-ups, lunges, squats, handstands, star jumps, shadow-boxing...and the weight melted away. Along with his intimidating size re-emerged the fit physique that had disappeared in his thirties as debauchery took hold, filling the chasm created by estrangement from his family, distance from his wife, and the emasculating failure of his once-illustrious career.

He didn't know what he was preparing *for*, but the compulsion not to quit was all-consuming. The balance shifted, from laughing-stock to...what? He only knew if he strolled into the prison yard and said he wanted to use the free-weights, no one argued. It was common knowledge he had money – was that what made the difference? It seemed as if no one quite knew how to take him on – so they didn't bother. He got tougher, stronger, and something hardened within his previously-boyish, vulnerable core: a resolve never to be the victim again.

Therefore, upon plunging into the woodland, Marc Pickford stops and uses his brain for the first time in years. He doesn't crash onward through the lush summer undergrowth until he tires and is recaptured. Instead, he identifies a tree with trunk and branches meeting in a low, accessible V-shape, and sprints over to it. He bounces, wobbles, and stumbles to get his balance as he places one foot in the hollow, thrusts with his newly-muscular legs, and propels himself high enough to grasp the most-substantial overhanging limb in his cuffed hands. He swings his long legs to gain momentum, curls – grateful for all those hours of agonising crunches – and hooks both his legs around the branch, rolling up and over to lie full-length, shuffling along it until he reaches the camouflage of the leafier end. It bows under his weight, but holds. He clings on with feet, knees, inner thighs, elbows, and awkwardly-contorted hands, recovering his breath and waiting for something to happen. He can hear shouting, and then gunshots in the clearing behind him, but can't turn to see what's happening. He'll fall straight out of the tree if he does.

A very short interval elapses before a figure leaps into the bushes metres from his hiding place. He tenses, holding his breath. It's one of the policemen from the car. Is that Tammi's intention; divide and conquer? The officer spends some time examining the trodden undergrowth, eventually noticing footprints in the sandy soil. He follows them as they travel towards the tree, while Marc curses his foolishness in not rubbing them out as he went. Fortunately, they turn in confused circles at the base of the trunk, and unjumbling the overlapping pattern of tracks keeps his pursuer near-stationary beneath Marc's motionless body. It's only a matter of time before the guy realises the footsteps go no further, and decides to look up… Marc can clearly see he holds a rifle in his right hand, and has a holstered pistol on his hip. His precarious position prevents an agile ambush, so Marc just has to roll.

He's toned up, but he's bulked up too – fat replaced with dense muscle. A conservative estimate of his weight is perhaps eighteen stone, maybe more. Regardless of the size of your gun and the quality of your training, eighteen stone of dead weight dropping onto your unsuspecting shoulders from ten feet up is enough to knock anyone over. The policeman grunts and flops helplessly to hands and knees, flying rifle bouncing into some nettles. Seriously winded, his hand nevertheless goes instinctively for the pistol, kneeling up; turning. With a coldness he's never possessed before, Marc lunges powerfully forward and rams the heel of his hand hard against the cop's Adam's apple, causing him to hack and heave as he fights for breath. Thankfully, it's enough. Marc springs into the nettles, grabs the rifle, and drives the stock aggressively into the bridge of the gasping policeman's nose. He subsides sideways, blood already gushing from his flaring nostrils, and lies very still, face-down in the dry leaf-litter.

Marc wastes no time, takes the pistol too, grips the rifle firmly, and swiftly retraces his steps towards the clearing.

Their fates are entwined. He can't go without her.

****

Tammi's impressed. She hasn't seen Marc move that fast in years. Evidently, prison's been good for him. He looks almost the same now as when she first met him, all those arduous years ago. There's a split second, as Marc pelts athletically for the closest undergrowth, when everyone stands gawping at one another with no idea what to do…and then all hell breaks loose. Marc's in the forest within seconds, but Nightingale's already pointed his gun, aimed, and elected not to shoot him. As for the armed coppers, the big one is out of the passenger seat and sprinting after Marc almost as soon as he starts running, but he still vanishes into the trees before the policeman's halfway across the clearing.

As soon as the shooting starts, Tammi wriggles herself into the comparative safety of the tiny footwell behind the passenger seat, ears straining for information. A hideous howl of agony echoes, but Tammi can't work out who's been hit. Her companion mutters darkly to himself as he hunkers down and levels his rifle through the open window, delivering several steady shots which seem designed to prevent Nightingale shooting back. Who might be hurt – Masson, or Bright Future, the young detective he defended with almost paternal protectiveness? The copper's barking staccato French into his radio, which crackles, hisses, and squawks with unintelligible replies. Tammi knows why Nightingale's being cautious in shooting at the police car. As with Marc, he can't take the risk of a stray bullet hitting her. Not until she's outlived her usefulness.

Another shot. The bullet zips straight through the car, missing the French cop by inches, and shattering the passenger window, showering them both in cubes of toughened glass. Tammi dives forward, hands over her face to protect it, shaking her head frantically to drop the chunks of glass from her curls. The driver slithers even further down in the seat, rifle up, blindly pumping another pointless shot out through the open window.

There's silence for a second or two. Tammi cautiously lifts her head, and realises she's nose-to-holster with the policeman's pistol.

Another shot. In through the driver's window, embedding itself in the roof lining with an audible whine and thud. The French copper's edging across the car, below dashboard level, contorting himself awkwardly over the gear stick and handbrake to get out via the passenger door. So absorbed is he in making stealthy progress, he doesn't detect the little, practised fingers reaching around the edge of the seat, hooking the weapon free as his body slides past.

TWENTY-FIVE

Tammi's brain's working overtime. By the state of him, Bright Future's in no condition to put up a fight, so if he's the one who's been shot, potentially Masson's fully-occupied with trying to keep him alive, somewhere behind the cars. If it's Masson who's been hit, neither of them now present a threat. That leaves Nightingale, and the two French cops. The one in the woods is Marc's problem for the time being. Currently, she's in a good position; armed, and valuable to Nightingale. That temporarily places two sworn enemies in uneasy alliance, leaving only the one remaining French policeman to deal with. He's inconvenient, but he's not *involved*. He's here because he's been told to be, and that's not his fault. She needs to do this with competence, but compassion.

He's out of the passenger door, pushing it gently closed behind him, edging along the bonnet at a crouch, obviously seeking to confuse Nightingale with the altered direction of his suppressing fire. Tammi takes a risk on inching upwards to peek out of the police car's rear window. She can't see Nightingale anywhere. Is he hiding the other side of the little Citroen? The policeman is squatting mid-way along the car bonnet, sliding the barrel of the rifle onto the bodywork, intent upon the vehicle across the clearing.

Does it matter to Tammi if the copper shoots Nightingale? Well, yes, it does…because armed cops are mostly trained to wound and not to kill. She doesn't want Nightingale recuperating from a minor gunshot in a French hospital, trying to assure his freedom by singing like a canary to Inspecteur Masson and whoever else might be listening…Agent Valentine, for example; faithfully reporting her precious thirty-year-old secret back to Sir Julian Franklin! No, if the French cop's going to shoot Nightingale, it needs to be right between the eyes – and the guy won't willingly do something that'll cost him his career. *She* must dispose of Nightingale, and that means getting the cop out of the way, quickly, before all the support he's requested shows up in force.

As the policeman leans forward, tenses, and focuses down the sight to take aim, Tammi mutters a silent apology to the innocent man, pokes the pistol in the gap between passenger headrest and door pillar, and shoots out through the shattered window. No *Calamity Jane*, the pistol bucks wildly in her unsteadied hand, and she rocks sideways as it discharges, thumping her head on the rear window. She's aimed for the fleshy part of his upper arm, but almost misses him completely, the bullet fortuitously skimming a crouching buttock, gouging out a big chunk of flesh, and making him yell in shock and pain. He springs forward, headbutting the car with such force his body ricochets before he can stop it, rifle rattling away, out of reach across the mud. He squeals as his burning bottom thumps the dirt, rolling instantly onto his front to ease the agony, one palm slapped protectively over the wound, the other reaching for the emergency pistol, scrabbling with frantic fingers at the holster as realisation dawns. It's *gone!*

Tammi's already trying to clamber through the centre-console gap to escape the locked rear of the police car. Hampered by the handcuffs and her efforts to avoid all the broken glass, she's making a considerable meal of it when a movement catches her eye. It's Nightingale. Flitting across the front of the police car, he kicks the rifle away too hurriedly. It skitters under the vehicle, and Nightingale swears in irritation, dropping to his knees beside the French copper, pistol to the helpless man's head. He uses the cop's own handcuffs to pinion his arms behind his back, and leaves him lying on the ground not daring to move, one side of his face thickly coated with pink dust, panting and grunting with the pain in his bottom.

Tammi calculates speedily, "Nightingale, get me out!"

He ducks inside the car, and plucks the stolen pistol from her fist, "First, I think I'll have that."

"Get me *out*!"

He laughs – like a man who thinks he's won – reaches under her arms, and hauls her like a parent pulling a toddler from a high chair, until she has enough room to put her feet down. She's barely recovered, trying to brush glass from her hair and clothes, when he has her by the throat, hissing, "Fucking Pickford! What does he think he's playing at? Where's he *gone*, Tammi?"

****

In the trees, Marc only sees that the policeman is shot, and then the blood-caked figure – who looks so uncannily like Jim Chadwick – pelts across the open ground between the two cars, and puts the Plod out of action. At first, Marc thinks he's fired a bullet into the side of his head, but then spots him being handcuffed, and observes the policeman continuing to writhe in pain, flat on his face in the mud – thankfully still alive. There's no sign of the Inspecteur, or his horrifically-assaulted colleague.

Not-Jim is already at the passenger door of the police car, leaning inside, pulling at something...

It's Tammi, of course, dragged bodily from the vehicle, also handcuffed. As Marc watches, Not-Jim grabs her around the throat and dangles as he strangles. Only her reaching tiptoes touch the ground.

Marc edges further forward. He still can't see Masson anywhere. One cop is out for the count several hundred yards behind him, but he won't remain unconscious for long. The other is handcuffed and bleeding at the kidnapper's feet. He can't hear what the guy's saying to Tammi, but it's getting heated. Her exposed toes, in their police-issue sandals, draw swirling patterns in the dust as he shakes her aggressively by the throat. He's apparently getting nowhere, because he rapidly raises the stakes, pointing the gun at the prone policeman instead, evidently making an innocent man's life the condition of Tammi's cooperation.

Marc's been many things in his time: spoilt, selfish, lazy, greedy, petulant...but he's not by nature a cruel man, and the idea of some poor fellow being caught in the crossfire simply for doing his job troubles his ingrained British sense of fair play. It jolly well isn't cricket, and Marc's not about to idly spectate upon cold-blooded slaughter, policeman or not.

Posh wally he may be, but Marc Pickford's not entirely useless, despite what everyone says. He can mingle effortlessly at parties. He can flirt with the best of 'em. He can – or could, once upon a time – score a stonking Try, and convert it with aplomb. He can bowl a mean 'googly'...and the upper-class, country-estate-dwelling, silver-spoon-supping Lord's son can't half shoot too. Grouse, pheasant, venison, rabbit...and, it turns out, suspicious, armed kidnappers with murderous intentions.

Not-Jim pulls Tammi's face close to his, bending to hold his pistol a menacing foot from the policeman's skull. It's impossible to hold the rifle properly in handcuffs, but before he has time to doubt himself, Marc hurriedly jams the barrel against the tree he's hiding behind, rams the stock tight in the hollow between collarbone and shoulder, takes aim, and fires. The bullet goes in through Not-Jim's waist, and out through his oblique muscle. Blood bursts from the back of his shirt, before spreading downward in a thick, dark line, sticking the fabric to the seat of his trousers and staining them too. He drops Tammi, who instantly dives back in through the open door of the police car, taking prudent cover. Not-Jim whirls, crazed eyes raking the woods, waving the pistol violently.

Another shot, this time penetrating the right-hand pectoral. Not-Jim stares down in utter amazement at the fresh corona of blood spreading across his already-revolting shirt, before pitching to hands and knees, convulsing and vomiting a copious quantity of blood and stomach-acid into the dust between his gripping fingers. He sags slowly onto his side, curling into a foetal position, body beginning to jerk spasmodically like a struggling fish on a hook.

Marc sprints out into the clearing. By the time he reaches the figure, it's stopped twitching. Blood trails from slack lips onto the ground beneath his cheek. Marc averts his eyes and snatches up the pistol, pushing it into his trousers. He's built quite an arsenal in the last five minutes.

Crouching in the passenger seat footwell, Tammi flinches and gasps in alarm as his enormous shadow falls across her…before realising it's him. Her body slumps in relief, "Thank fuck! I didn't know who was firing!"

He helps her out of the car, demanding, "What the bloody hell is going on?"

"Jesus, Marc, not *now*! Hear that?" She cocks her head like a little bird, pointing towards the distant sound of sirens, "Escape now, explanation later."

She tugs one of the pistols from his waistband, and darts round to the back of the police car. Marc follows curiously. There's Masson, on his knees in the dirt, Xavier's injured leg elevated against his shoulder. The Inspecteur doesn't even try to fight – just holds up his hands in exhausted surrender as Tammi levels the gun at his head, "Your handcuff keys, Inspector?"

"Right hand trouser pocket."

Marc fishes around, pulls them out, unlocks Tammi swiftly, and points the rifle clumsily at Masson while she unlocks him in return. Masson mumbles, "Fermier…Martin…?"

Tammi shrugs in incomprehension, glancing at Marc, who offers an apologetic grin and the reassurance, "Your two chaps? Both alive, Inspector. Bit worse for wear…"

Masson exhales deeply, eyes closing with what might be relief. Characteristically unsympathetic, Tammi prods him in the back with the gun, as if to rouse him, "My new passport, Inspector? I presume you have it?"

"Inside jacket pocket."

Marc removes that too. Tammi grunts, "Get his wallet as well…we could do with some cash."

Marc finds it, opens it, "70 Euros in here!"

"Take it. We'll need it."

Marc shoves the cash into his pocket, discards the wallet on the ground, and starts to jog towards the little Citroen, calling, "The keys are in this one!"

Tammi ignores him, concentrating on Masson; intelligent eyes holding his with hypnotic intensity, "I guess this *is* my sporting head start after all, eh?"

"You won't get far."

"We'll see about that. I've spent twenty years confounding everyone's expectations, Inspector; I'm not about to stop now. I hope Bright Future makes it."

She turns to Marc, who's already folding his long legs into the tiny car. The sirens are getting noticeably louder by the second. Irritated by the short-sightedness of his choice, Tammi yells, "Not that, you moron!"

Offended; defensive, Marc retorts, "Why?"

"What are you going to do, drive straight at that lot?" She points illustratively at the narrow dirt track – the only means of vehicular entry or exit to the clearing, "We're *not* taking that car!"

Peeved that despite saving her life, she's still not allowing him to make any decisions, Marc snaps, "Are you mad? How are we going to get away with no transport?"

"On foot, stupid! I bet every single vehicle route down this hill's got a copper parked at the end of it! We'll be caught in seconds!"

Tammi's already running towards the rear of the clearing, "On foot, we can go *anywhere*! We can *hide* anywhere! Come *on*!"

TWENTY-SIX

"Where did you learn to do that?"

"The Scouts."

Marc blows powerfully on the small, smoking pile of brush and kindling, sitting back on his haunches with a satisfied grin on his face as the first few flames crackle and take.

"Impressive. What else are you good at? Washing people's cars? Helping old ladies across the road?"

Annoyed, Marc retorts, "Why is it when *I* do something useful, you belittle it, but when *you* do something useful, the whole world has to notice?"

Tammi glowers, pouts, and rejoins, "All right! What's rattled your cage?"

"Why couldn't we have taken that car?"

"Are you *still* sulking about that?"

Marc tips the last few chunks of crispy chip into his big palm, tossing them into his mouth and chewing noisily. He crumples the paper container and overarm-bowls it into the small pit in which he's built their campfire, "We could've been over the border by now!"

"Because we'd definitely have got that far!" Tammi replies sarcastically, sucking her thick milkshake up through its straw.

Marc mumbles, "We might have done…"

"Marc, there was *one track* up that mountain! Were you not paying attention on the journey?"

"Well – "

"We both came from the same police station, right? Through town, up onto the mountain road…and I counted five, maybe six, turnings off it…all the way up to where we left the tarmac completely and bounced up that dirt track to the clearing. Are you telling me a bloke with the gumption of Masson wouldn't have put a Bobby in a car down every one of those little turnings, just in case? And yet you wanted to drive straight down the mountain and into his clutches?"

"I s'pose…"

"Do you? You 'suppose'. That's big of you."

"I don't know why you're acting as if all of this is my fault!"

Tammi gapes; incredulous, furiously throwing the drink cup into the fire. The dregs of liquid inside it hiss against the flames.

"You *are* having a laugh, aren't you?"

"What?"

"All this *is* your fault, you flamin' moron! It's been your fault for twenty bloody years!"

"Why?"

There's an expression on Tammi's face he's never seen before. It's unsettling – like looking into the eyes of a stranger.

"You never knew I was pregnant when you dumped me at the altar, did you?"

"*What?*" Marc lurches up from his reclined position, half-eaten *Big Mac* rolling unnoticed from his lap into the dirt.

"That's right, I *loved* you! I thought I was working towards our shared future!"

He's shamed by the contempt in her eyes, "But it seems you wanted your ego massaged, and you weren't prepared to wait for my efforts to bear fruit. You let my shallow tart of a sister turn your head…"

Acknowledging you've done wrong is hard – even when you know it's true. Marc whines, "You were always at *work*, Tammi! You cared more about Dad and the money than you *ever* did about me – "

He's immediately silenced, flabbergasted by the emotion in her voice, "Don't you *see* it was a means to an end? Your Dad, the funds, the control I had…I could never, never have done what I did for *both* of us without *total* vigilance and dedication! Can you not understand it was *necessary*? What a *life* we could have had – !"

Her voice catches. He's hot all over, face burning.

"If only you'd used your brain, been patient, let me do my job…instead of thinking solely with your cock…"

He struggles out the beginning of a sentence he has no idea how to finish, "Tammi…I…"

Her voice is quiet, but firm, "There's no justifying what you did, in my eyes…if that's what you're about to try and do."

"I – "

"You dumped me, ruined everything, broke my heart…and *that's* why all this is your fault."

Troubled; confused, he still resists, "How is *this* anything to do with what happened when we were twenty-seven years old?"

"Because I never wanted to hurt anyone as much as I wanted to destroy you and everything you supposedly stood for…so I took what I knew – which was rather a lot – and I fucked off."

Marc slumps back against the fallen tree again, "Yes…the whole reason my father's never forgiven me."

"Because if you'd kept it in your trousers for a few more months, we'd be living the life of riley now, not sitting in the French dirt with pine needles in every orifice, wondering how we're going to dig ourselves out of this latest mire! Although, let's be honest, only one of us is going to do any digging. The other's just going to sit here until the solution's spelt out to him."

"Hey!"

"Am I wrong?"

Marc snorts humourlessly, but can't look her in the eye.

Tammi sighs, and flops theatrically onto her back on the ground, staring up through the tree canopy. The pines are stark silhouettes against a muted, milky dusk.

"Just tell me, truthfully, how easy did Annelisse make your life?"

Marc smiles ruefully, absently rolling a pebble with the toe of his flip-flop, confessing, "She didn't. It got really bloody complicated straight away."

It's too dark for him to see the spiteful smile of satisfaction on her face, "Do you now concede I made things simple? Can you now admit it all *worked* with me in charge…and didn't once you'd tossed me aside?"

"Now who wants their ego massaged?"

"I just want you to admit responsibility – culpability – for once. If you hadn't treated me like crap, I wouldn't have fallen apart. I placed all my hopes in you, Marc…in *us*…and you trampled over every dream I had. Your selfish actions set in motion a chain of events that rendered me susceptible to Ricky McAllister's manipulation – and all that entailed for both of us."

Marc's expression darkens. He growls, "That little worm…"

"Oh yeah, there's no denying he was larvae…but God, he was clever! He found out about the money, Marc. Our money."

"How? Did you tell him?"

"I don't know how. Of course I didn't tell him! He never trusted anyone, so I guess he did a lot of digging on me. When you became an intended 'Mark' of his, I expect he did due diligence on you too. He'd have joined disparate dots no one else would ever have connected. That's the kind of bloke he was. Once he was on to a scent, there was no shaking him off…and Ricky could smell money like the *Bisto-kid* smells gravy. When he died…"

Here, Marc fidgets and coughs his way through the uncomfortable recollection of the Scotsman's body at the foot of his palatial staircase, neck broken, unseeing eyes staring. He tosses the dusty burger into the fire, and prods it prissily with a long stick. Disturbed embers trail upwards like a line of launching satellites.

Tammi observes Marc's discomfort, comprehends it, and waits for him to settle, "By the time he died, the knowledge he'd amassed about us was a considerable dossier…and it got passed on to James Chadwick."

Marc's face screws up in incomprehension, "What *is* it with Jim?! That French Inspector had a picture of him...and some gobbledegook made-up name...?"

Tammi struggles back to a sitting position, exhausted, but unable to temper her exasperation, "Marc, you know *nothing*! It maddens me you can only ever see one piece of a puzzle! You can never complete the whole damn jigsaw! Why is that? I'm possessed of exactly the same information as you. I can see it. You can't. It's...*infuriating*!"

Hurt, Marc shrugs sulkily, responding with a sarcastic, "Sorr-eeee."

"Geoffrey's childhood chum – good ol' friend-of-the-family Jim Chadwick – is a fucking *gangster*! He's one of the nastiest crooks South London's seen since the Kray twins!"

Marc stares, agog; disbelieving.

"Yes, Marc! Lovely, well-spoken, posh boy Jim – with his investment funds and his fancy yachts, all paid for from the proceeds of extortion, thuggery, and murder! He knew Ricky from way back when...and he ended up with Ricky's meticulously-compiled dossier on us, and what we know that the rest of the world doesn't. Who do you think sent Phillip to Antigua to coerce us into cooperating?"

She's got that look on her face again; the one that unsettles him to his core; the one that implies he doesn't know her at all. Hesitantly, he ventures, "But, Phil disappeared...?"

Tammi runs her tongue across her teeth, stares into the dancing flames, and replies lightly, "Lucky that, wasn't it?"

"So, who got the dossier after Phil?"

"The M I 5 agent whose job it is to follow me. The chap you shot in the back this afternoon."

She thinks if Marc's eyes get any wider, they'll pop right out of his head.

He squawks, "M I 5?!"

"Didn't you recognise him?"

"Eh?"

"You've seen him before."

"I have...?"

"He arrested you in Antigua. Is your memory really that bad?"

"That was *him*?"

"Yes!"

"Good Lord... He looks completely different. I'd never have recognised him."

"Yes, he's good at being instantly forgettable."

Marc shakes his head in frank amazement, as Tammi asks, "Do you know a man called Julian Franklin?"

"Uncle Jules? He's a chum of my Dad's."

Tammi smiles condescendingly, "Uncle Jules... They're not as matey as you might think. 'Unc' is after your Dad, Marc. He's been flinging shit at him for thirty years in the hope some of it'll stick...but it just slides right off. It sticks to you. It even sticks to shiny old Geoff, but Daddy somehow always stays squeaky clean."

"*Sticks* to me! I'm buried up to my *eyebrows* in it! What's the deal with Uncle Jules, then?"

"He wants to expose The Cabal's dodgy dealings."

"But he's *in* The Cabal!"

Tammi interlaces her hands above her head and arches her back, stretching her bruised, tired body, "It's done his career no harm, has it? Keep your friends close and your enemies closer? Why not make the most of the situation he finds himself in, until the time's right...?"

"So, he dispatched an agent to follow you and, what, wait for the right time to screw over my Dad and everyone associated with him? Why are we bothering with this – hideouts, campfires – when M I 5 already know everything?"

"No Marc. *One agent* knows everything...and dead men can't spill their secrets. I knew him as 'Nightingale'. I presume that's his operational name. He picked up our dossier in Antigua *four years* ago! Why do you think he's done nothing with it until now?"

"*Why* do you ask me questions like that when you know I haven't the foggiest?"

"It makes me feel infinitely superior to you."

"Delighted to be of use."

"*Think* about it! Why work damned hard for 'Her Maj' in a dangerous job for a measly few hundred grand, when you've just read a comprehensively-researched folder that tells you how to get forty million quid *for free*...? All you have to do is dispose of the only other three people in the world who know about it, once they've fulfilled their particular roles in helping you get your avaricious little mitts on it! Namely; you, me, and JC!"

"I don't believe it!"

"James Chadwick's been after me – us – since he acquired Ricky's folder of research and discovered we could easily make him forty million richer than he already was. I knew him by reputation, but I'd never met him. I got picked up by a suave Belgian in a Riviera bar, and I was enjoying myself, I can't deny it…right up until the point when Agent Nightingale informed me my exotic European boyfriend was actually a notorious South London gangster, killed him, and framed me for his murder."

"Why?"

"Keep up, Marc! To ensure my cooperation…and to make everyone back at M I 5 HQ believe *he* was dead! It was a piece of piss for a Government official with all the correct paperwork to remove you from Antigua and bring you here. He just had to keep the two of us alive long enough to release the funds…and then, literally, off he sails into the sunset on Jim's lovely yacht, the only person still alive who knows what happened, and *why*."

"And where's this dangerous dossier now?"

"Don't worry. I acquired it. I've dealt with it. It's completely destroyed."

"And Jim Chadwick is definitely dead?"

"Yep. Barbecued. I've seen the photos. Not a pretty sight."

"And I've shot a Government agent!" Marc's hands fly up in horror as if it's only just occurred to him.

Tammi's tone is surprisingly soothing, "A corrupt one. One who was already irreversibly committed to his own illegal career-exit strategy. Don't shed tears over him. Once he'd got what he wanted from us, we were next on his Hit List. We'd have lived another week, tops – until we'd released our money for him. Then he'd have sailed us into the middle of the Atlantic, shot us, and tipped us over the side. Fish food."

"What now?"

"For the first time in twenty years, we are once again the *only* people who know about our carefully-amassed little retirement fund. Ricky is dead. Phillip is...no longer a threat. James Chadwick is charcoal. Agent Nightingale has just dribbled out his last in the Mediterranean dirt. It's just you and me, mate – the way it was at the start of this; the way it always could have been if you weren't such a monumental prick."

Marc laughs. He can't help it. The one thing about Tammi is that you always know where you stand. Sugar-coating just isn't her style. He raises imploring eyes to hers, "I'm sorry. Really I am. About what I did. About the baby."

She drops her head. He feels a rush of guilt and protectiveness, and whispers, "Why didn't you *tell* me about the baby?"

Head bowed, she mumbles into her lap, "I was going to tell you on our wedding night. I wanted it to be a surprise. I never thought you'd get your surprise in first."

He stretches a long leg across the space between them, and nudges at her knee with his foot, making her jump, "If it's any consolation, my marriage wasn't happy. I made a mistake. I knew that almost as soon as we got home from the Honeymoon...but you weren't there to tell. You'd vanished."

She shakes her head in amazement, "Of course I had! What did you think – that I was just going to stick around while you flaunted her under my nose? You two made my position...um...what do the politicians say? Oh, that's it; *untenable...*"

Marc grins sheepishly, and swiftly changes the subject, "Well, I don't know where the money is. That's always been your job."

"Precisely. Fortunately, I *do* know where it is. I'm still *doing* my job, despite everything you bastards have tried to throw at me. I'm the best fucking employee your Dad's ever had, although I'm not sure he realises that. I've kept his reputation and his money safe from the double-dealing Sir Julian Franklin."

"Where are we going, then?"

"That depends on you."

"What do you mean?"

"I've stood by you, Marc, for all this time. I've protected you. I know you might not think it, but I have...and I've made sure not only that Daddy's money is safe, but that our little nest egg will provide us with a lifestyle for ever more. I've had enough. I want this to stop. You need to make a choice, Marc. You're either with me, or against me."

She reaches into the pocket of her hoodie and withdraws the passport, waggling the red leather booklet in front of him, "You see, I've got one of these. I can go anywhere...but you can't – not without my help. Not only are you required in Antigua to complete your fraud sentence, but now you're wanted in France for murder too. The fact you saved the lives of four policeman is neither here nor there...nor, indeed, is the undeniable fact that Nightingale deserved to die. You still shot him, and you're not *authorised* to dispense justice. I can make it all go away – new identities for both of us, a new life; a luxurious, wonderful life we could have been enjoying for twenty years! Better late than never, I suppose. I'm offering you my brain, my protection, my care…for as long as we both have left."

"It's never that simple with you, though. What do I have to do to get it?"

Before she can reply, their attention is monopolised by white arcs of light swinging through the dense forest directly beneath their hiding place. Marc leaps up and looks over the side of the rocky ledge, "What's that down there?"

Tammi scuttles rapidly to his side, shoving him aggressively, "Get the fire out!"

With nothing between his flesh and the flames but rubber flip-flops, Marc extinguishes the campfire with a clumsy combination of kicked dust, stamping, and the remains of his half-drunk milkshake, the hot embers fizzing as the liquid strikes them.

On her stomach at the lip of the ledge, Tammi peers down into the darkness, "Car headlights… Whaddya think? Something dodgy?"

Marc plonks down beside her, craning to see, "Too dark!"

"I know. What shall we do? Sit it out?"

Another vehicle approaches. They can hear the crunch of the tyres, the chug of the engine. As it slows, there's one brief revolution of blue flashing lights before they're shut off. Both gape at each other in the dimness. *Police!*

Tammi hisses, "That's Plod down there! How have they found us? It's too much of a coincidence!"

She's taking out her passport, feeling it, scrutinising it closely in what little light remains.

He prods her with urgent fingers, "What?"

Almost to herself, she mutters, "Maybe it's the guns…?"

"Tammi! What?"

"Something's telling them where we are… Wait a minute, did you get anything unusual today – before Masson's little excursion?"

"Unusual?" Marc can't remember a time when life last felt normal.

"Anything new? New shoes? New toothbrush? Did they suddenly give you your watch back?"

Marc waves his naked wrist, "My watch is in Antigua. I'll never see that again. Seven grand's worth of Rolex…"

"Marc! Focus! Anything new *today*?"

"No…well…only clean clothes…"

"What clothes?"

"This tracksuit."

"Shit! Take it off!"

"What?"

"Your jumper and trousers, take them off!"

"Are you out of your mind?"

"It's those or the guns!" Tammi's snatching up the weapons, running her fingers along their nooks and crannies, "Something is giving away our location. It could be a little beacon beaming a signal – something tiny we can't see! We might as well stand up and wave a flag!"

"Why does it have to be *my* tracksuit? Why can't it be *yours*?"

"Because *I* didn't get special new clothes today, you dollop! It's got to be that; something sewn in so we can't find it. Get 'em off!"

"Then I'll just be in my boxers!"

"Better that than back in prison. Hurry up!"

****

A drawn, white-faced, hard-eyed Masson squats in the open passenger door of the squad car, next to the seated officer with the tablet in his lap.

"Anything?"

"The signal's very strong, sir...and consistently in one position." The man tilts the device so Masson can see, "The beacon's within a few hundred yards' radius of this location. I'd say start up this side towards that rock ridge. It's the closest pinpoint I can get."

Masson stands, and turns to address the semicircle of expectant officers, "You heard him. Ok, between them, they've got a rifle and two handguns...and, something we didn't realise, Marcus Pickford can actually *use* them! Be bloody careful. I can't take anyone else getting hurt. If it's not safe, get the hell out – understood?"

"Yes, sir."

The officers group together, muttering strategy, then fan out across the clearing and advance up the densely-wooded hill towards the outcrop of jutting rock just visible in the gloom. Masson stands beside the open door of the police car, eyes flicking between the torch beams climbing steadily up the hillside and the pulsing red dot on the computerised map, tuning out the crackles of communication on the radios ranged around him...silently willing everything to be ok this time...

Suddenly, a louder burst of static penetrates his private prayers. He jumps, gasping, "What was that? What did they say?"

His eyes rake the hillside. Torch beams illuminate pink stripes across the rock, and flashes of bright green pines in the otherwise-monochrome night.

The officer in the driving seat of the car leans across his colleague, relaying the message, "Campfire, sir! On that ridge above. Embers still warm. Half-burnt fast food wrappers. And...oh..."

"Oh? Oh-what?"

The officer hesitates as more information crackles through. Masson almost jumps up and down with frustration, roaring, "*What*!?"

"And the tracksuit, sir."

"What do you *mean*?"

"*Just* the tracksuit, sir. No Pickford."

TWENTY-SEVEN

Sir Blair Stocker-Pickford sits at the grand desk in the considerable study of his palatial Sussex manor house. The French doors stand open to admit a light July breeze, the sounds of chirruping sparrows in the nearest lilac hedge, and the distant baa-ing of sheep from the grazing fields beyond the walled garden boundary. He chews on the end of a cigar he's supposed to have given up, and swills ice cubes around a glass of whisky he's meant to be cutting back on. Yesterday had gone like a dream. He'd never seen Julian go so pale. He'd never silenced a room so quickly. Imperceptibly, the balance had shifted; the body language altered. Like wind rippling through ears of corn, every head and torso had swayed gently from the waning of Julian's dying star to bask in the full, glowing light of Blair's restored power. He'd strutted out of there an hour later elated by his triumph.

Then, just as quickly, it had started to go wrong.

It transpired his Mole within M I 5 was already *in* France – better and better! But, the guy had no idea Marc was there, and informed Blair of exactly the same intelligence Julian had imparted – that Tammi Rivers was about to be exchanged for a French hostage! She was going to slip through his fingers yet again, and there was absolutely nothing his man-on-the-ground could do about it. Before his chap was in a position to step in, the French police operation spectacularly backfired, leaving Julian's pet agent – the duplicitious Nightingale – dead, and Marc and Tammi nowhere to be found. And Julian would know it all, just as he did. Blair could get information about what Julian was up to...but he couldn't necessarily get it *first*. How long before Julian used this latest débacle to label him a cavalier fraud, recklessly imperilling everyone's precious anonymity; no more able to recover The Cabal's missing funds from Tammi's clutches than Julian himself! Julian could afford to take such a risk. If The Cabal imploded, he had his legitimate government role to fall back on. He was a spy after all, permitted by law to say one thing and do another.

As far as his Mole could ascertain, Marc and Tammi were still in France...but France was a big country that bordered several more. As a lone fugitive, Blair would've been confident of Marc's recapture within hours...but he's not alone. He's with Tammi, and that's what's making Sir Blair reach for the alcohol and the nicotine, despite emphatic doctor's orders to abstain. If anyone can evade the most-determined hunters, it's that troublesome little bitch.

Blair violently stubs out the half-smoked cigar in the cut-glass ashtray, unaware his hand has curled into a white-knuckled fist on the polished walnut. The ice clinks in the glass as he takes a generous swig of expensive spirit, and swills it around his mouth before swallowing. The sparrows twitter, the sheep baa, and the warm wind rustles the established foliage around the study door. England basks in all its balmy, midsummer glory, but it fails to please or pacify embittered, ungrateful Sir Blair Stocker-Pickford. And then the telephone rings.

****

A dig in the ribs. She holds out a mobile 'phone.

"Where did you get that?"

"Off a bloke in the 'Maccy-D's' queue. It was sticking right out of his pocket. He should've taken better care of it."

Marc puts a hand over his eyes, "Oh Jesus... But...how did you unlock it?"

"Because muggins spent the whole time he was waiting for his lunch fiddling with the damn thing. It kept hibernating itself, so he did the finger-code pattern about five times, almost as if he *wanted* me to learn it...simply too peachy an opportunity to pass up. Unlike you, I pay attention to what's going on around me."

Shaking his head, still gaping at her, Marc nevertheless reaches out to take the 'phone, "What is this *for*?"

"Call off the dogs. Ring your Dad. Tell him I'll give him what he wants if he agrees to finish it right now. By tomorrow, he could have back control of his money. I'll give him enough to hoist 'Uncle Jules' by his own petard, if that's what he desires. The Cabal will be his personal fiefdom again, *if* he leaves it there. No pursuit. No revenge. Done. Dusted. If he doesn't agree, tell him I'm talking. I've had enough. I'll spill it all... I'll take them all down before they finally catch up with me...and you'll be the first. His boy, the murderer. You'll never get out, Marc. You shot a British Government Agent in cold blood."

"I did it to save you!"

"Show me you *mean* that. For the first time in your self-obsessed, privileged joke of a life, put me first."

He takes the 'phone from her, and sits looking down at the handset as if he's never seen one before.

She's on her feet, ferreting in her trouser pocket for the Euros they stole from Masson, counting what's left, shoving it carelessly back, "Ok, won't be long."

She's nearly out of their hiding place – an abandoned, ramshackle barn on a sylvan slope of lush meadow grass and gently nodding wildflowers – before Marc even realises she's leaving, "Where are you going?"

"Down there." She points to the small town a half-hour trudge beneath them in the picturesque river valley.

His stomach tightens in apprehension, "Why?"

"Aren't you hungry? I know I am."

He holds up the 'phone, "What about this?"

"You're a big boy, Marc. You can use a 'phone."

"You want me to just ring him? Without being here to supervise what I'm saying?"

Tammi smiles indulgently down at him, like a mother who's just watched her son successfully tie his shoelaces for the first time.

"You got on all right unsupervised day-before-yesterday, didn't you? You pegged it off into those woods, in handcuffs, with an armed copper after you…and came back five minutes' later with two guns and not a copper in sight! I'm starting to think leaving you without a babysitter brings out the best in you."

Marc chuckles, wheedling, "Give me a small steer, maybe…?"

"You can't do anything without your passport…so you need it. He must get it to you."

"It's in Antigua!"

"Then he's got to get you another, hasn't he?"

"What about a picture?"

"You're holding a camera in your hand, aren't you?"

"It's supposed to be against a plain white background!"

"Oh, Marc, a picture of Geoff'll do! It's only a formality for the border and the bank. No one ever really looks…especially if you pass it over with €200 folded up inside it. Makes their vision ever so blurry."

"Where are we going to get €200?"

"Daddy knows you're in France, right?"

"Yes…?"

"This is your father we're talking about! A man obsessed with power and control! He'd have dispatched a minion to that police station the minute you told him you were there. Too late…but that's not his fault. He didn't know Masson was going to start 'improvising'. Just tell him you need another passport and you need it now."

"How – ?"

"Make what you require a condition of our cooperation – like you promised me you would! *We* don't get what *we* want, and *he* doesn't get what *he* wants. He'll be mad, but he'll do it."

"I thought they didn't do border checks between France and Switzerland?"

"Get real, Marc – look at the state of us! Even if they don't pick us up at the border, a copper's guaranteed to stop us and ask for papers sooner or later! You need a clean, legit passport."

"What about the small matter of my criminal record?"

"Oh Marc, it's Switzerland! Half the people here are hiding from something. That's the lovely thing about the Swiss. They still respect people's privacy. If you've got the right paperwork and you don't cause any trouble, they don't waste their time turning over stones and disturbing all the creepy-crawlies. They just let 'em wriggle around in the dark, unmolested."

Marc's response is to screw up his face, and fidget in the dust. Tammi sighs, and squats beside him in the strong ray of morning sunlight shining through the propped-open door of their refuge.

"I'm tired of this. Aren't you? Constant ducking and diving, scrambling from one near-miss to the next by the skin of our teeth. It's getting old. *I'm* getting old! Do you want to go back to prison?"

"No…of course I don't."

"Forty million secret quid is a hair's breadth away from us, Marc; the closest we've been to it since the beginning, and you don't want to clear the final hurdle? You just want to keep sitting here, on fifty years of compacted cow-crap, hungry, thirsty, wearing clothes we nicked off some Frenchman's washing line?"

"Of course I don't!"

"And yet you won't do the one thing standing between us and Easy Street; the one thing that'll release us from this damn-near thirty-year nightmare! I can't understand you sometimes… All because you're scared of him."

"I'm *not*."

"You are…or you'd ring him, without a flicker."

Marc juts his jaw defiantly, grips the 'phone, and snaps loftily, "If you'd shut up, I could get on with it!"

Tammi smirks, and bounces back to her feet, "That's the spirit! I'm off. Wouldn't want to cramp your negotiating style. Consider everything you're going to say before you let it pass your lips, ok? And have a *proper* think about where we might want to collect passport and cash from…and how we might do it when we're not really suitable to be seen in public. Daddy'll dispatch his minion the moment he puts the 'phone down…and there's a distinct possibility 'Uncle Jules' might send someone hot on his tail. Consider all of that, won't you."

Marc shakes his head and rubs at his dusty eyes, making them prickle, "Can't *you* just – ?"

"No. You can do this. Just do the telephone equivalent of whatever you did in that woodland a couple of days ago."

"I rolled out of a tree and crushed the bloke!"

"Well, roll out of the blue and crush Daddy! He'll never see this coming, and he certainly won't be prepared for you calling the shots. Get in, get it done while he's still reeling, and get off the 'phone. Fast as you can. Once you're done with it; lob it. We won't need it anymore…and using it will make us easier to find."

"How long will you be?"

"As long as it takes."

His eyes betray fear. She relents, "As fast as I *can* be…ok?"

"Ok."

"Relish it, Marc! The first time in nearly fifty years on the planet that you've ever stood up to your arsehole of a father! He let you and Geoffrey go down to save his own neck. What kind of a parent does that to their child? He's supposed to put you before anything…yet he's used both of you your entire lives. Enjoy this opportunity to have one over the selfish old bastard. After all, you'll be giving him what he wants most in the whole world…"

****

A mobile number he doesn't recognise.

Blair snatches up the handset, and answers the call with a tentative, "Yes…?"

"Dad."

Thank God. Sir Blair's body sags like a scarecrow removed from its stake. The hand gripping his drink thuds onto the desk. Whisky leaps up the side of the glass, spilling over onto his trembling fingers, and spreading across the blotting pad. He barely notices.

"Marc! I sent someone to that police station – "

"Who?"

"It doesn't matter. A…representative… The point is, you're not there!"

"No, Dad, I'm not."

"Where are you?"

"Best if I don't say, Dad. I can't trust you not to make life difficult for me."

Blair's struck by how much this simple declaration stings him. His default response is aggression, "Now, you listen to me – "

Marc's voice is weary, but firm, "No, Dad. For once in your life, *you* listen to *me*…if you want your money back."

Irrationally terrified, Blair booms, "*You* presume to threaten *me*?"

"I do, actually…because I hold the whip hand on this occasion, and you know it. Do you want control of your money back, or not?"

No answer.

"Simple question, Dad."

Furious; frightened, Blair hisses, "Yes, of course I do!"

"Good. Ok. Listen, because I've got some conditions."

Unable to conceal his incredulity, Blair guffaws, *"You've* got 'conditions'?"

Marc's completely unflustered. That's what's shaking Blair to his core – the fact his youngest son sounds as if he truly doesn't care one way or the other, "Yes, Dad. Me."

Blair growls, "You'll suffer for your attitude."

Marc states, "You'll suffer more…for your *pride.*"

"What do you *think*, idiot boy; that *you'll* outsmart *me*?"

Marc simply sighs, and replies, "I never sought to fall out with you, Dad. I always just tried to do what you wanted…but I could never please you. I always wanted you and Mum to love me like you loved Geoff, but you never did. I couldn't understand what I'd done wrong."

"What you'd done *wrong*? What do you think, you clueless bloody fool!"

"Oh, I know *now*…I just couldn't ever work it out while I was younger. You were never as bothered about me as a kid because you had Geoff. You put all your energy into him, and then you didn't have any left over for me. No matter, I was only the spare…not worth as much effort, I daresay. I concede you only started *really despising* me later, when I married the wrong twin – "

Again, it's the utter unconcern in Marc's voice that pricks what's left of Sir Blair's conscience. He repudiates frantically, "I...I...*don't* despise you, Marc! You're my *son*."

Marc makes no further comment about this, as if nothing his father could say in mitigation would make a blind bit of difference to his own firmly-entrenched opinion, instead stating, "Dad, Julian Franklin's not to be trusted. He's not your friend."

Blair can't help the exasperation that washes over him. Why was the bloody kid always so slow on the uptake? He barks contemptuous laughter, "And it's taken you this long to work that out? Of course he isn't, idiot boy, he's a Secret Service snake! Why do you think I so readily let him into our...group...in the first place?"

"I – "

"Because it compromises him entirely! I'm not even sure *he* remembers which side he's supposed to be on any more. Who do you think shoved Rivers under my nose?"

Marc gasps aloud before he can stop himself. Sir Blair sniggers nastily, "Oh...she evidently neglected to tell you that part, eh? I believe she was intended as a little distraction for Geoffrey, but he wasn't remotely interested in her...too cheap. You, however, turned out not to be quite so fussy. I suppose Julian decided it didn't much matter which son she worked on, so long as he kept getting the inside track. However, I don't think he banked on little Rivers wanting to elevate her standing in the world. No matter how well she was likely to earn from playing each side off against the other, she didn't want to stay a worker-ant her whole life. She wanted to marry a Lord's son. She and I reached a little...understanding. I wouldn't stand in the way of her plans, if she used her very considerable acumen to assist me with advancing mine. She fed Julian enough to keep him on the hook, and devoted her loyalty to us...well, until you royally buggered it up, anyway. I presume you've had the error of your ways thoroughly explained to you by now?"

Marc tries, as he has so many times before, to fight his corner, "Dad, I'd argue, if you'd kept me in the loop...?"

"You were too stupid to be 'kept in the loop', Marcus. You could never keep your own 'loop' shut. The less you knew, the better."

"Until my lack of knowledge led to me marrying the 'wrong' twin?"

"If you'd just done as you were *told* – "

"And there's the problem, right there! I can't win. I *tried* to do as I was told, Dad...but no one ever *told* me anything!"

"If you'd simply married Tammi like you were supposed to, we could have got rid of the Julian Franklin problem decades ago. He wouldn't have been lording it over us all these years. We'd never have ended up so toothless! Geoffrey would still have his career. So would you, come to that. You'd never have needed to flee to the Caribbean to escape the scandal your stupid wife embroiled you in over here. You'd never have wound up in an Antiguan prison – "

It's always like this. Eventually, every conversation with his father turns into a catalogue of his failings. Tammi's voice echoes in his head, *'Get in, get it done while he's still reeling, and get off the 'phone. Fast as you can.'*

"Dad, do you want your money or not? Do you want to deal with Uncle Jules once and for all, or just keep haranguing me until the end of time?"

"Where are you, Marcus?"

"I need a new passport, do you hear me, Dad? Otherwise the bank won't accept my ID and release your funds. Your security requirement, by the way, not mine. I want it expedited to arrive at the following location in two days' time. I'm sure a man with your many contacts can organise that." Here, Marc reels off the address of the minor mountain town beneath his vantage point. He hears the scratch of the nib of his father's *Mont Blanc* as he scribbles it down.

"Your guy goes into the *Café Marco*. He buys an orange juice in a clear takeaway cup. He walks diagonally across the town square to the stone wall of the churchyard. He sits there facing the church, he drinks his orange juice, and he waits. Eleven am. French time. Two days from now. If he isn't there; if he doesn't do what's required, then no cooperation, Dad. You take your chances with Uncle Jules…and we take our chances with everyone. I fancy ours will be better than yours, somehow…and I think, deep down, you know I'm right. I want my passport, and I want €5000 in used notes."

"And my cooperation buys me…?"

"Twenty-four hours after I meet your representative, convene a Cabal meeting. Get everyone to bring their authorisation codes. Twelve midday French time, we'll call you, and the transfer will go ahead. Fail to help us now, and you won't hear from me again, Dad. You agree, and we do this…it's over. No pursuit. No revenge. You leave her alone, Dad. It's not negotiable."

His father is very quiet on the other end of the line.

"Do you need five minutes to think about it?"

"No. I don't. I'll do it."

"Good decision, Dad. You won't regret it."

Marc allows himself one controlled fist-pump of suppressed jubilation. He's won. The first time ever!

His father suddenly sounds old. The usual bluster is absent from the surprisingly-feeble voice that asks, "Can I call you on this number?"

It's satisfying to reply, "No, Dad. This is a one-time call. If things don't happen the way I've specified, the deal's off. You don't get back access to your fund. You're at the mercy of Uncle Jules. You made your bed, Dad."

"I've told you, I'm complying!"

"And I've told you what'll happen if you change your mind – just so we understand each other."

"We do." There's a note of wonder in the voice that states, "You know, Marcus, I think you might be more my son than Geoffrey's ever been."

Marc makes no effort to disguise the sarcasm in his reply, "What a revelation! Shame it's too late. I'll see your representative in two days' time, and I'll speak to you in three."

"Son, I – "

"Goodbye, Dad."

Marc cuts the call, levers the back off the 'phone with a grimy fingernail, extracts the battery, and tosses it over his shoulder into a cluster of brambles. He roots around near the tumbledown wall and finds a stone of pleasingly comfortable size within his gripping fist, using it to smash the 'phone into small pieces that he discards delightedly in all directions across the meadow like a boy skimming pebbles on a beach.

Then he settles down in the lee of the wall, enjoying the heat of the sun on his face and the warmed stones at his back, waiting impatiently for Tammi's return.

TWENTY-EIGHT

Tammi and Marc squat at the edge of the woodland that borders the cemetery between church and square. The town clock strikes eleven. A tall, slim, youngish man limps out of the door of *Café Marco* and progresses painfully across the cobbles. He's on crutches, and it's evident he can't put much weight through his left leg. With difficulty, he balances a cardboard cupholder containing a transparent beaker of orange juice. Slung across his body is a leather messenger bag. There's something familiar about him. As he gets closer, a dismayed Tammi realises what it is. The young man giving the correct signal at the specified time – Sir Blair Stocker-Pickford's 'French representative' – is none other than Agent Valentine! She stares at the hobbling figure in horror. What on earth can it *mean*? She's just about to turn to Marc, share this vital intelligence, and suggest they run for the hills with appropriate haste, when he begins to chuckle quietly, "Well I never!"

"What?"

"It's little Tris!"

Tammi gapes, "You *know* him?"

"Yeah! It's Tris Bradley!"

"Tris?"

"Tristan. I've known him since I was at school! He's quite a bit younger than me. His parents are friends with mine. He did a bit of political research for Dad…years back, while he was still a student. Internship, you know…summer job. Dad always said he had an excellent eye for detail."

It's Tammi's turn to laugh, "Don't tell me, your Dad suggested to Uncle Jules that, given his very particular skillset, young Tris might thrive in the SIS basement cracking codes?"

Marc shrugs, as usual missing the point completely, "I've no idea what he does. Haven't seen him in years!"

Tammi pats Marc's arm patronisingly, smiling grimly, "I think I've got a fairly good idea what he does. I detest your Dad, Marc. However, I can't deny a grudging admiration for the wily old bugger. He's *always* got an ace up his sleeve."

"I don't know what you're talking about."

"Never mind. Let's just get this done. You get into some deeper cover and keep that rifle trained on him, just in case. I'm going to go down to the wall and creep along it so I'm right below him by the time he sits down."

"Ok."

"Remember, you're only intended as a last-resort visual deterrent. *Don't* get overexcited and shoot him."

"I'm hardly going to shoot him, Tammi, I know his mother!"

"Yes, I'd imagine that *would* stilt the conversation at garden parties…"

"Very funny. Bugger off and get on with it. Clock's ticking."

"You were the one who went 'all *Hollywood'* and put such strict time constraints on everything!"

"And *you* were the one who sodded off to the Boulangerie and left it all to me."

To his amazement, instead of the cutting retort he's expecting, Tammi crows with delight and rubs his stubbled cheek affectionately with dirty fingers. Before he can react, she's scuttling out of the tree cover and sprinting at a crouch from headstone to headstone, making zigzag progress down the steep hillside to the encircling stone wall, dropping to hands and knees and crawling along until she's directly beneath the section of stonework Tris is gingerly approaching. She hears the grunt of effort as he sits as instructed, facing the church, sucking his orange juice up through the straw.

"Well, well, well. Detective Sergeant Vaseline."

He jumps, and turns with a wince of discomfort to face the direction of the voice. Uninjured leg straddling the wall, he scans the deserted cemetery.

"Down here, Valentine."

She's crouched in the mossy darkness beneath his swinging foot, "Hello, Tammi Rivers."

"You look in a bad way, Valentine. I thought you were suspiciously absent from recent proceedings. What happened to you?"

"Nightingale shot me."

"Oh, bad luck." Tammi volunteers chummily, "If it's any consolation, he was going to do that to us as well, but Marc beat him to it. He's very good at shooting. Did you know?"

"Yes, I did know. I've been grouse-shooting with him in Scotland. Cost me a fortune in lost wagers! The cocky sod never missed."

"Is that so? That's encouraging to hear, because he's in the trees about fifteen feet behind me, with a rifle pointed right between your eyes."

Despite vowing to betray neither curiosity nor disquiet, Valentine can't prevent his eyes raking the wooded slope.

Tammi beams expansively, and asks, "Got something for me?"

Valentine lifts the flap of the messenger bag, extracts an envelope, and drops it casually into her outstretched hands. She checks the contents, "Thanks awfully, Valentine. No hard feelings about me taking the piss in that interview room?"

Valentine grins, and sucks on his orange juice, "Couldn't care less. I've been paid twice."

"Once over the counter and once underneath, eh?"

"Something like that. Plus, I'll get compensation for being injured in the line of duty."

"Raking it in, aren't you, Valentine? *And* a macho scar to impress the girls."

"Yes…what was looking like a disastrous week has worked out surprisingly well, considering I had absolutely no idea Marc was even here until Blair rang me! Where are you off to now?"

"No firm plans, Valentine. None I'd share with you, anyway. I take it there'll be no onward restrictions to our travel; nothing to stop us crossing any border we choose?"

He winks, "I shouldn't think so."

"Good chap – appreciate your input. Off anywhere nice yourself?"

"First plane home. My mother's worried about me."

"Justifiably so, I'd say. A valuable tip, from one who knows – I'd do as little work for the Stocker-Pickfords as you can manage. They're a tricky bunch, and the old man's the trickiest of all."

"I'm not worried by Blair. He's not long for this world, apparently. Advanced liver trouble, so the rumours say."

"How interesting…"

"Geoffrey'll come into his peerage, leapfrog the Cabinet, and take up his seat in the Lords instead. The corruption scandal will be forgotten. I daresay there'll be an investment empire still to run, if Marc fancies it?"

"I'm not sure Marc's that interested any more."

"Tammi, what shit's going to hit Sir Julian's fan?"

"That's up to Blair. I'm not getting involved. I've had my fill of Sir Julian Franklin. Are you implicated?"

"Nope. I've kept my nose *very* clean on this job – you ask my French colleagues."

Tammi smiles wryly, "Poor old Masson. I almost feel sorry for him."

"Forget that! Seems he was keeping Marc a nice, juicy secret from me in one of his other cells – even though he'd had orders from above to cooperate with my investigation! All because I got under his skin a bit. They're emotional, the Europeans. They *care* too much."

Tammi giggles, "Yeah, they should be a bunch of cold-hearted, hard-nosed bastards like us English, eh?"

"It's stood us in reasonable stead up until now, hasn't it?"

Tammi wiggles her fingers in a cheeky wave, "Ta-ta Tristan Bradley. Stay out of our business, or life'll become very difficult for you."

"I get it, don't you worry. I've read your file – cover to cover. I'm not an idiot."

"No…but you play one spectacularly well. You had me fooled."

Bradley purrs, "Too kind…"

"Good job Marc recognised you just now, or we could have been in big trouble – legging it for all we were worth, and still no passport! Honestly, I *never* guessed you were playing Masson as hard as I was."

"I'm rather flattered. I find it staggering to believe a woman of your considerable abilities could've been duped by a mere beginner such as I…"

"Don't flirt with me, young man, I'm probably old enough to be your mother."

"By no means! Under normal circumstances, I'd consider you a very attractive, very accomplished catch – regardless of the age gap. Right now, though, you're not exactly my type. You're absolutely filthy from head to toe…and you stink."

Tammi, crouching in dank darkness at the base of the ancient wall, upturns a beatific smile and drawls dreamily at the grinning young man silhouetted against summer sky, "I may stink, Tristan Bradley, but I'm *free*… Well, almost…"

TWENTY-NINE

Masson's explanations are encouragingly met with a decreasing level of scepticism the higher he progresses up the chain of command within the small municipal police headquarters, but their collective confusion remains. Regardless of rank, as he talks, they all stare at him as if he's lost his mind. Perhaps he has?

Dispirited, but too dogged to give up, he persists until he's seated before their most senior Detective, "My commissioner's supposed to have already called and agreed my arrival with yours!"

His Swiss counterpart raises his eyebrows, and drawls laconically, "That'll be the reason we don't know a thing about it, then."

He prods himself proprietorially in the chest with a stubby forefinger, "Your boss should speak to the organ-grinder, not the monkey!" Smug chuckling from the massed ranks of Detectives squeezed curiously into their chief's office. Kommisar Rochat laps up his team's approbation, before noticing Masson's not joining in with the disrespectful sniggering as expected. Surely, it's accepted the world over that the best way to foster fellow-feeling with colleagues from another Force is to badmouth the bosses? He studies Masson thoughtfully. The Frenchman appears utterly defeated. He hasn't even got the energy to sit up straight in his chair. His shoulders slump. His head bows. The evidence of his extreme exhaustion is in red-rimmed, bloodshot eyes in sunken sockets; and hollow cheeks stubbled with several days' growth of unkempt beard. Whatever's brought him here *matters* to the careworn police officer sitting opposite. He's checked Masson's credentials. The Inspecteur is a law-enforcer of some note within his region. His division *performs*. If he's left the turf where he reigns supreme to come all the way from beach to mountains, he must have a good reason.

Kommisar Rochat signals one of his chaps closest to the door to fetch Masson a drink, reaches for a pad, and murmurs kindly, "Perhaps you'd better run us through it one more time, to make sure we've got all the pertinent details. If your fugitives went missing on the Riviera, how can you be so certain they're now here?"

Masson sighs, loathe to admit, "I'm *not* certain...but...something tells me they're close by, because of where they chose to cross the border. It seems to me they're making the most direct journey possible to their final destination."

"Which is?"

Wearily, Masson is again forced to confess, "I...don't know that either."

Rochat frowns, and jots on his pad.

"Ok...again...you tracked them to here because...?"

"Pure fluke...oh, thank you." Masson looks up gratefully as a junior detective places a coffee in front of him, taking a sip and exhaling in satisfaction, "Ahhhh...I needed that. Thanks. Where was I?"

"A fluke."

"Oh yeah. The trail had gone well and truly cold. My boss chewed my arse for the mess I'd made of it all, and then we got a 'phone call from a colleague in a mid-sized town a couple of hundred kilometres from us. The pickpocketing of a mobile 'phone in a fast-food place led him to look at their CCTV as part of his investigation…and there was our female fugitive, plain as day! We'd put an alert out – we were probably a bit slow to admit we'd lost them and we needed to cast the net wider – but fortunately he happened to see it. We obviously then had the mobile number of the stolen 'phone. The network provider had disabled it, so we got it reactivated – just on the off-chance – because we then knew who had it…and she doesn't commit petty theft; she does things for a reason. We didn't get the call data fast enough to prevent our fugitives crossing the Swiss border, but my hunch was on-the-money nevertheless. They *had* used the 'phone. Only once, but it was enough to roughly pinpoint their location – somewhere near a small town just the other side of the border here. We traced the call to verify, and it was to a number belonging to the male fugitive's father in England. Got a map of France and Switzerland here?"

"Hold on."

Kommisar Rochat brings up a map on his computer screen, swivelling the monitor round to show Masson, who leans forward and trails his finger across the image.

"A line directly from where we lost 'em on the Southern French coast up to where the mobile 'phone was stolen; then, an abrupt right turn. Thereafter, no other deviation. Continuing straight from that point, through the rough triangulation area near the Swiss border where the call was made, to the border crossing where we now know they passed from France to Switzerland…and, if you continue that line across…?"

Rochat's got the idea. He beams, "We're the next civilisation you hit!"

"Exactly!"

The Swiss detective chews the end of his pen ruminatively as he reads a computer print-out, "Records show they crossed the border yesterday. No problems with admission into Switzerland. Valid British passports. No additional comments from the guys at the border… Mostly, it's free passage, so they must have been reasonably conspicuous, to attract enough attention to get document-checked."

"I'd say they would be! She's black and blue from a previous encounter with British Intelligence, and he's a massive bloke. They'd stand out."

"But you don't know where they're going?"

Masson shakes his head regretfully, "No idea. Is there a station here? Or an airport?"

"Not close. Nearest station's in town. Are they not in a vehicle, then?"

"They weren't…but they could be now. It's unlikely – not really their style; they're white-collar criminals, fraudsters – but, any local car thefts reported in the last twelve hours?"

A voice behind him, one of Rochat's team, "I'll check it, sir."

"Good man, Benoit."

Masson turns to delay the detective, "Or, any hire car places around here that might have rented a vehicle to either of them. Also, any chance someone could look at the local station CCTV?"

"Yeah, we can do that, sir."

"Thanks." Masson turns back to his Swiss counterpart, "No airport close by?"

"There's a private airfield not far from here...light aircraft on mostly-local jaunts. The occasional larger jet lands...but it's a short runway, which limits the size of plane able to use it. The nearest international airport is, as you know, a reasonable drive away."

"Can we check whether anything's been chartered from this local airfield? Even a short-hop flight?"

Rochat signals another investigator to take on this task.

Masson feels re-energised, his case recovering its previous momentum with every syllable, "They had three guns on them when they left the Riviera...and yet nothing at the border?"

Another glance at the report, "No. They may have gone through the metal detector...or they could have been patted down if the Border guys thought their appearance warranted it. No guns. Inspecteur, if you didn't want them leaving France, why didn't you put out an all-borders alert?"

"I didn't think I needed to, what with the Interpol flag already on the female."

Rochat looks puzzled, "What Interpol flag?"

"Nothing came up?"

The Kommisar again scans his meagre paperwork, brows drawn together in confusion and concern, "No...?"

Almost to himself, Masson murmurs, "Wheels within wheels... Someone's taken that off. To let them get away...?"

Rochat's watching him keenly, unease on his face, "Not questioning your procedures, Inspecteur, but why has your Commissioner sent you all the way up here in person just to pursue a couple of fraudsters?"

"It's more complicated than that. The guy is an escaped convict – and he shot a British Secret Service agent dead in France earlier this week. The woman..." He shakes his head regretfully, "I wouldn't put anything past her! This is my investigation and I'm here to see it satisfactorily concluded."

"We're not a big outfit here, Masson. We're a small, municipal police force! We're not equipped to deal with trigger-happy international criminals!"

Sensing Rochat's discomfort, Masson counters, "You've just told me they entered Switzerland unarmed." He tries to keep it light, quipping, "Anyway, I'm sure it's not going to come down to a shoot-out in the town square!"

He crosses his fingers under the table where no one else can see them, and continues reassuringly, "I just need some manpower to help me check hotels and guesthouses, and circulate photographs of them around the bars and restaurants. Local knowledge could be the key here! I'm not asking your guys to put themselves in danger, just to back me up with some vital investigative resources, that's all. Someone will remember two Brits of distinctive appearance. If they're here, they'll stick out. They've followed such a direct and specific route for hundreds of miles. There's *got* to be a reason for that!"

****

Marc squirms, scowling, "These pants are too tight – they're right up my crack! The bloody trousers are too small as well! They flap around my ankles. I look ridiculous!"

Tammi snaps, "There are two clothes shops in this one-horse town, and neither of them caters for meatheads like you...so just be glad we've had some proper kip in a comfortable bed, a hot shower, some decent food, and we're on target to upkeep our end of Daddy's bargain. That's what's important here. The comfort of your arse-crack should be a considerable way down our list of priorities!"

"But – "

"Stop bleating, Marc! Seriously...or I'll give you something to bleat about! I just had to get what I could with the money we had from the choice on offer. An hour from now, you'll be rich enough to flay peasants and sew new trousers out of their impoverished skins, should your narcissistic heart desire it. Until then, stop dancing about like a toddler with a full nappy! It's not sophisticated."

They stop before a minor branch of a well-known Swiss bank, "Just trust me that everything is in place. We've only got your Dad and his cronies to deal with, and this crap is over...and if you did your bit properly the other day, it should be over *forever*."

"That's what he said."

"Let's hope he meant it."

Marc catches at her elbow, "You said something at breakfast about new identities...?"

Tammi smiles mysteriously, teasing, "Why, got a secret hankering to be someone foreign and exotic?"

Anxiously, Marc asks, "I won't have to do a funny accent all the time will I…only I genuinely don't think I can keep that up long-term…?"

Tammi snorts with laughter, yanks open the bank's heavy glass door, and shoves him in before her.

****

Masson lopes out of the police station's main entrance, and trips lightly down its stone steps to the pavement. As he does so, an unexpected light flashes, capturing his attention. His head jerks up, stomach tightening instinctively, subconsciously reminded of the flashing barrel of Nightingale's gun as he whirled in the dirt, aiming unerringly…but it's only the late-morning sunlight glancing off the closing glass door of the bank across the road. He wanders a few yards down the pavement, and tucks himself into the disused doorway of a ski apparel shop, shut for high summer. He lights a cigarette, and squints through the smoke with swimming eyes. Across the street – a pharmacy, tobacconists, the regional bank branch, a café with tables outside. But for the distinctive chocolate-box style of the architecture, and the mountains rearing up in every direction to provide the most-dramatic of backdrops, the street-level life in this alpine valley town seems every bit as French as Calais, Paris, or Cannes.

"Masson! Inspecteur Masson!"

He cranes out of the doorway, waving at Rochat, "Over here!"

The Kommisar beckons excitedly, pointing down the street, "Guest house, right here in town! Come on!"

Masson gapes, trotting towards him, "What, a hit?"

"Yep! Checked-in last night. British passports. Names and descriptions match. No credit card. Paid upfront cash for a three-night stay. We're going up there now. You coming?"

Masson smears his half-smoked cigarette across the spotless Swiss cobbles with the toe of his brogue, and crows, "You bloody *bet* I'm coming!"

THIRTY

Despite looking as if they've dressed in the dark at a jumble sale, Tammi nevertheless acts as if she owns the place, demanding the immediate presence of the bank's manager to assist her, and flatly refusing to deal with any lowlier members of staff. Marc sinks onto a plastic chair a few feet away, hoping to disassociate himself from this shamefully-arrogant display, smiling apologetically at anyone who glances in his direction, until the manager finally appears. Summoned from a back room, he approaches the counter wearing a sour expression, surveying them with predictable suspicion and distaste. Undeterred, Tammi presents her passport, and demands a private room with the necessary equipment to facilitate an immediate fund transfer. Upon identification of his customer, the manager's manner instantly switches from irritably superior to positively servile. It suddenly occurs to an amused Marc that the guy's on commission for this. He wonders what percentage the bank charges for providing a facility of this kind. He expects it's considerable, as they are rapidly shown into the manager's private office, seated before his own boardroom table, offered coffee, and presented with the sort of patisserie selection that would not disgrace a Parisian Salon. A monitor is fetched and connected to a laptop. The conference call speaker is moved the limit of its cable across the desk towards them.

Tammi divides her time between watching the clock on the wall above the door, and murmuring thorough instructions to the toadying manager. Despite having already consumed a comprehensive hotel breakfast, Marc largely ignores the preparations progressing around him, and begins working his way through the cake plate.

"You know all that weight you lost…?"

"If the last four years have taught me anything, it's never to pass up free food."

She glances compulsively back at the clock, "Five minutes."

"Yep."

Uncharacteristically hesitant, she suddenly blurts, "Marc…do you really think he meant it? Do you really think he'll stick by what he told you?"

Marc wipes a smear of crème patissiere off his cheek, and grunts, "You tell me. You seem to know him better than I do."

This sullen dismissiveness won't wash with Tammi, and he knows it. If she asks a question, she wants an answer. She persists, "You spoke to him. You made the bargain. So, I'm asking you – do you think he meant what he said?"

Something unusual in her voice makes him stop hoovering up the pastries and turn to her, "Honestly? Yeah, I do. It was different this time. I can't explain it, but… It went differently to every other conversation I've ever had with him. I can't say *why* it was different. It just *was*. If I didn't know better, I'd say he sounded scared; unnerved by something…although that's daft. If we know anything about my dear old Dad, it's that nothing frightens him."

Tammi wonders whether to share the illuminating intelligence gleaned from the smooth Tristan Bradley…and elects not to. One job at a time. Security before sentimentality.

She looks back at the clock, "Just on twelve. Ringing him?"

****

Masson leans against the hotel room doorframe and watches the small group of Swiss detectives pick the place apart, while Rochat works his lantern-jawed charm on the wide-eyed Receptionist in the corridor. The hotel room is basic, small, chintzy, and dated; with heavy mahogany furniture and a beige bathroom suite. The bed's been slept in, towels and toiletries used in the bathroom, but there are no personal possessions in evidence, and no luggage. Rooting in the bottom of the wardrobe under a spare blanket, one of Rochat's crew unearths a dirty bundle of clothes that he tosses over onto the bed. The troupe of detectives fall upon it like vultures round a carcass.

"Sir!" They're holding up one standard-issue tracksuit (small), a pair of muddy jeans (large), and two filthy t-shirts that also look as if they came from French police stock. The final confirmation is the dangling of two flip-flops on separate index fingers. Rubber split and cracked, one sandal's massive, the other minute.

Masson nods enthusiastically, and offers a double thumbs-up to the grinning guys around the bed. Rochat peers over his shoulder, "So, what do you think? They coming back?"

Masson shrugs, "I have no idea. I get the impression the woman doesn't like loose ends. If you were in her shoes, you'd dispose of that stuff somewhere no one would find it, right? You wouldn't leave it as a big ol' clue for the chambermaid to discover."

"Not if I could help it. That points to them coming back, then. They have paid for three nights…?"

"We need to watch the hotel…got someone spare to do that?"

"Sure."

"I want to talk to that Receptionist again. Where did she go?"

"I sent her back downstairs. Didn't need her watching us constantly."

"Come on – I need you to schmooze her a bit more."

Rochat laughs self-deprecatingly, but Masson notices he struts back down the narrow corridor with increased swagger.

At the main desk, the Receptionist gazes intently into Kommisar Rochat's piercing blue eyes and gushes volubly, delighted at the enlivening of her otherwise-tedious day by a procession of dishy detectives. No, she didn't know where the couple were going. However, she did know when they'd left, because it was on her return from morning coffee-break – a few minutes after 11.30. They'd handed in their room key, walked out of the door, and straight towards the town square. She knew this because she'd observed the man as he'd walked away down the street, idly thinking his trousers were an inch or two too short, and considering that it must be hard for such a big chap to get well-fitting clothes…

She prattles, and Masson and Rochat exchange amused glances. Rochat smiles engagingly, and doodles in his notebook as if everything she's saying is solid gold…allowing Masson to stroll surreptitiously to the door, peering out through a glass pane at the few pedestrians in sight, formulating his plan without distraction. Minutes later, outside, they divide their efforts. One guy at a café table with a good view of the hotel frontage, and a pair of detectives down each of the three principal streets leading from the hotel's environs to the main square. Photocopies of the passports at everyone's disposal – like something out of a movie – and the knowledge their quarries likely aren't far away, adds a spring to everyone's step. Masson can't wait to encounter Tammi Rivers again. He wants to see the expression on her face when their eyes meet. He craves the satisfaction of this victory.

****

The authorisations appear in the on-screen boxes as lines of anonymous dots. Tammi and Marc are last of all. A quick scan of their passports, a thumb print each on a little infra-red pad slid across the desk by the smiling bank manager, then their codes. Marc can't remember what day it is most of the time, but he'll recall these digits until the day he dies.

Tammi goes first. The passport. The press, hold, and bleeped confirmation of the thumb-print acceptance. The keying-in of the required code, with the bank manager politely averting his eyes as if she's revealing her nakedness. Marc proffers his new passport. It's already passed the ultimate test at the border, so he's quite confident of its validity here. The slight scrape of the fingerprint pad being pushed across the tabletop towards him makes him start, and hesitate. Tammi inclines her head minutely, eyes narrowing. It's been utterly silent in the room since Marc made the initial call to his father, ascertained all were present and prepared, and the bank manager had talked them through the procedure in precise, barely-accented English.

Now, Marc clears his throat and says, "Dad, with this transfer, our professional association terminates. As you assured me. Yes?"

His father's voice. Again, to Marc's ears, it's somehow smaller, weaker, more muted than he remembers it, "As agreed. At an end."

Marc looks at Tammi.

Tammi gazes steadily back at him.

His fingers hover over the keypad, "I have your word, Dad?"

Is it embarrassing to so clearly articulate ingrained mistrust of your own father before witnesses?

"Son – " Sir Blair pauses. Does he want to say something he's unable to in present company? "My word. Yes. It's over."

His father can't see him, but Marc nevertheless acknowledges the declaration with one decisive nod, and reaches for the keyboard. As he types the authorisation code, he feels Tammi's smooth, cool fingers slide over his free hand, where it rests on the arm of the chair between them.

****

Masson and the young detective called Benoit have got the street opposite the police station, with its pharmacy, tobacconists, café, and bank. Masson doesn't really expect them to be in any of those places, but he's hoping by progressively moving down all the major routes simultaneously, they'll flush them out into the main square like a blockage from a pipe. Blank stares and shaking heads meet presentation of the photographs in the pharmacy and tobacconists, where Masson stocks up on cigarettes and watches Benoit throw his weight around unnecessarily to impress the out-of-towner. The proprietors haven't seen the suspects, and don't remember overhearing anyone speaking English in their shop over the last couple of days. He can tell Benoit's disappointed, and grins encouragingly at him as they leave the *Tabac*.

"Never mind, mate. It's a team effort. The others might be having better luck, but we've still got to do our job properly, so let's just finish this street, eh? Then no one can say we didn't try."

Benoit nods despondently, so Masson gives him a friendly shove in the direction of the bank, "Come on, don't lose your mojo now. Do your suave, Swiss thing."

Benoit smirks, straightens his tie, and tugs at the heavy glass door.

****

"Your box, Mademoiselle."

"Merci, Herr Müller."

The man unlocks the stainless-steel safety deposit box with a flourish, and steps back a discreet distance from the table. Tammi goes to open the lid, then stops, as if a thought has just occurred to her, "Herr Müller, do you have any sort of opaque bag I might be able to put the contents of this box in, please?"

"Certainly, Mademoiselle. I will find you something."

He's gone in a flash.

Tammi's head whips around the room. One visible security camera on the wall near the door causes her to swivel the box, so its contents aren't on show, and lifts the lid.

Marc whistles, "That's a shedload of cash! What have you got so many Swiss Francs for?"

Tammi rolls her eyes as if the answer is obvious, "Bribes! We're in Switzerland. We need Swiss cooperation. There'd be no point having Yen, would there?"

"And when did you set up that Bank of Bermuda account?"

"What?"

"The one we've just moved our money into. When did you set it up?"

"When we got to Antigua. I told you, I thought we were finally close to realising our retirement fund…and then everything went wrong again, like it always bloody does. Fortunately," here, she extracts a padded envelope and discreetly checks the contents, "the passports I set up then are still valid."

"New passports?"

"Yeah."

"For new identities?"

"Exactly."

"Come on, then, who am I?"

Marc tries to snatch the envelope off her, but she whips it away, "Just wait! Let's get clear of here, and then you can go through all this stuff as much as you like." She winks, "You know…try out your new accent…"

Marc's eyes widen in alarm, and he makes another grab for the packet. She clutches it to her chest, "Hey! Let's not get fake passports out and start waving them around in front of a bank CCTV camera, eh?"

"Oh…oh yeah…ok. Is that where we're going though; Bermuda?"

"Not necessarily. It's just the time had come to move it on from here. I won't leave it all in one place indefinitely. It's more practical to spread it around a bit. I just haven't exactly been in a position the last few years to sit back and consider the health of our investment portfolio. Now, I should be able to devote more time to it."

Marc sniggers, "What are we waiting for? Shouldn't we be getting going?"

"I'm not walking down the high street with this little lot tucked under my arm. We stick out quite enough without visibly transporting more money than most of these locals'd earn in a year. We'll be mugged in twenty seconds! We're waiting for a bag to put it in, then we'll be off. I've instructed the revoltingly-obliging Herr Müller to arrange our onward transport. Might as well get our money's-worth out of the oily little tick."

****

Benoit's getting nowhere, and it's not just his lack of experience telling; the bank employee behind the counter is definitely being evasive. Masson's standing back, slightly aloof, allowing Benoit to take the lead, but missing nothing. He can't interfere; it's not his manor – he's here at the discretion of Kommisar Rochat and his commanding officer – but Masson's not sure Benoit possesses sufficient guile to get past the obstructive Teller. The Inspecteur doesn't like the way the guy's eyes are pinging from side to side like a pinball machine. All smiles and cooperation as they'd showed their police IDs, the atmosphere cooled upon presentation of the photographs. The man's dull eyes widened in horrified recognition. If they're not here now, then they've been here recently.

Benoit's had enough. Frustrated at every turn, embarrassed before the observing senior officer, his patience snaps and he demands the Manager. In emollient tone, the counter clerk's profuse apologies and obsequious excuses tumble over one another, preventing Benoit from getting a word in. 'Regretfully, the Manager's in a client meeting. He cannot be disturbed. Client confidentiality is paramount. The bank has security protocols which only the Manager can override...'

Masson studies the man intently. It *would* be a smooth performance...but for the sweat beading at his receding hairline...and his eyes compulsively darting back and forth between the immediate threat of the posturing Benoit, and the unspecified menace of the unreadable Frenchman lurking behind him.

****

The Bank Manager reappears with a heavy-duty canvas carrier sporting a supermarket logo on the side. He's probably just fetched it from his own car boot. It's always tickled Marc how the merest whiff of money can strip even the most exulted individuals of their dignity...before he's struck by the sudden, chastening realisation that he's *never* known what it's like not to be wealthy. Even in prison, he knew he had money – *everyone* knew he had money – and it not only kept him safe; it kept his hope alive. A four-year hiatus, and he could return to the comfort he'd always known, and eternally taken for granted. Perhaps Herr Müller, the fawning Bank Manager, couldn't get by on his salary? Maybe he had feckless kids, a spendthrift wife, or a dotty Mother in an expensive Nursing Home? Potentially, the commission from this afternoon's transactions would keep him afloat for vital months, or even years? Marc chomps his way thoughtfully through another custard tart, and ponders how he'd behave if he was teetering on the brink and a lifeline marched in off the street; concluding he might stoop to kiss a little arse as well.

As the Manager slides as unobtrusively as possible back into the room, he's murmuring, "Your onward taxi is waiting at the end of the street, Mademoiselle."

Tammi glances up to acknowledge this intelligence with a polite smile, when her eye is taken by movement over the Manager's left shoulder as he turns to close the office door. The vision makes her blood run cold. Pushing through the heavy glass entrance, and striding swiftly to the counter with purposeful tread, the unmistakeable, rangy physique of Inspecteur François Masson, preceded by a shiny-suited, slick-haired Swiss copper, who's already waving around an obvious warrant card, and clearly preparing to flex his officious little muscles!

Tammi shoots to her feet, making both Marc and Müller gape in unconcealed amazement. She snatches the bag rudely, frantically upending the safety deposit box into it, no longer caring whether the Bank Manager or the camera witness its contents. She reaches into the top of the bag, scoops out several wrapped bundles of Swiss Francs, shoves them hastily into the gawping Manager's fumbling hands, and demands, "A *back* exit, Herr Müller, if you would be so kind…"

Juggling his windfall, the man hesitates a beat too long for the agitated Tammi to tolerate. She lunges forward, grips the left lapel of his jacket in one tiny fist, and hisses, *"Right NOW!"*

****

Masson's got it; the reason why the bank clerk's eyes are revolving like marbles. The guy's not taking turns watching both policemen. Masson's just realised the clerk's vision is in fact flicking between the immediate problem of the blustering Benoit, and the bank of ceiling-mounted security monitors away to his right, whose transmissions rotate on a loop between back offices, the main front entrance and ATMs, and the single door sporting a gold nameplate bearing the legend: Herr D Müller, Branch Manager. The sweating, shifty little obstacle-to-their-investigation is compulsively watching the Manager's office, whilst valiantly keeping the local Law at bay. Now, why might a lowly bank clerk feel the need to do that, unless something illegal's going on inside it?

While Benoit continues to monopolise the clerk's attention by growling empty threats, Masson takes advantage of his own apparent invisibility to slide confidently through the gap in the privacy screen erected around the mortgage advisor's desk, and straight up to the Branch Manager's door.

The Teller's poise evaporates like mist in sunlight, "Monsieur, you cannot go in there! Monsieur, you must stay this side of the counter! You do not have clearance – "

Masson whips out his ID card and holds it so close to the man's face he almost hits his nose on it as he rushes to get between the Inspecteur and the office door. It brings him up short, gasping, giving Masson the chance to state with icy calm, "*This* is my clearance, Monsieur. Take a good look at it."

The man's practically cross-eyed attempting to comply.

"You are currently obstructing a *global* serious crime investigation; an offence which can carry a custodial sentence. Now, either you assist us with our enquiries, or my colleague here will be forced to arrest you!"

Benoit – clearly quick on the uptake – has slotted in two feet behind Masson as if they're on parade, and is already reaching illustratively into his jacket pocket to reveal his handcuffs, grinning nastily at the trembling clerk. The man bites his lip. His eyes dart again, calculating frantically. Eventually concluding he'd rather lose his job than his liberty, he swallows thickly, Adam's Apple bobbing visibly in his skinny neck. He opens his mouth once more, as if considering a final, futile protest...then closes it again without uttering a word.

"A superb decision," grunts Masson, sarcastically. Before anyone can stop him, he thumps down the door handle, and bursts into the private office of Herr D Müller.

THIRTY-ONE

To his credit, Müller maintains his composure. He doesn't recoil, or demand an instant explanation for Tammi's erratic behaviour. He merely reprises his ingratiating smile, clutches the providential performance-related bonus to his chest with one splayed palm, and peels Tammi's gripping hand from his lapel with the other, discarding her individual fingers as one might an unpleasant substance from one's skin. He backs across the office, Tammi's tense little form in close pursuit. He hurriedly slides open a waist-height drawer in the nearest filing cabinet, dropping the bundles of cash inside. They hit the metal bottom of the near-empty drawer with dull thuds. He closes it upon his grubby little secret with a ringing thump. Another two strides and he's at the rear door of his office. With an automatic gesture, he reaches for the security ID clipped to his belt, tugging its retractable cord to allow a quick swipe of the card through the door-release mechanism. The light on the card reader flashes from red to green as the door locks click and release. He tugs the door wide and marches through it, Tammi inches behind him, bulging canvas carrier held rigidly to her side under one elbow. Marc takes a swift look over his shoulder at the security camera above the office door, and follows.

They're in a bland, tiled corridor; smelling of stale coffee, and lit by fluorescent bulbs, one of which ticks and flickers irritatingly.

There's a small kitchen opposite. A little fridge hums noisily away in the silence. Several washed mugs stand upended on the draining board. The Bank Manager's already halfway down the corridor to the left, leading to a Fire Exit. One firm shove of the clanking release-bar, and the door swings open onto a street level alleyway lined with industrial dustbins and parked cars. Tammi cautiously pokes her head out. Low, Müller murmurs, "To the left. To the end of this street. Left again, and you will see your waiting taxi."

Tammi fixes him with gimlet eyes, and hisses, "And you've called ahead as I requested? The instruction is via the bank? No names? They're ready to go?"

Again, that repulsively-unctuous leer, "It is underway *exactly* as per your instructions, Mademoiselle."

At this reassuring utterance, Tammi delivers a toothy beam no less insincere than Müller's own, extends a hand, and purrs, "*Exemplary*, Herr Müller. I'll be recommending you to *all* my friends..."

Müller caresses her scratched and de-clawed paw as if it's diamond-encrusted, and there's a chance one or two might stick to his skin if he squeezes hard enough, simpering, "All part of the service, Mademoiselle..." inclining his upper body in a deferential bow, as Tammi eases her hand from his greasy grasp.

Marc regards the whole pantomime with the disdain it deserves, and mutters, "Enjoy your bonus, won't you."

Müller straightens at speed, fixes the giant with a wary stare, and perfunctorily shakes his hand nervously with a limp, clammy palm, "A very pleasant onward journey, sir."

Entertained to have elicited such a reaction, Marc grins engagingly, slaps Müller on the upper arm so hard that the man staggers sideways involuntarily, and chortles, "Must be off, Old Chap," He gestures towards Tammi, who's tugging desperately at his straining shirtsleeve, "Someone's in a rush."

****

A middle-aged man Masson presumes must be the Manager is just re-entering the office via a rear door as he barges in the front unannounced. Unruffled, the Manager absorbs the intruder's flushed cheeks and panting chest, and calmly asks, "May I help you?"

Masson glances around the tidy and functional office...and is perturbed to see the sort of room he'd *expect* the Manager of a small regional bank to occupy. Chipboard and veneered furniture. Gunmetal grey filing cabinets with box folders lined up on top of them. Walls with dinks out of the paintwork where they've been whacked numerous times by furniture moves since the last branch re-fit. If he's laundering millions for private clients, he's certainly not spending his commission on interior décor. Masson's utter conviction begins to waver. His frantic eyes do another circuit of the office. To the left is a small meeting table. On it, a tray of half-consumed refreshments, including two plates, and two coffee cups. If the Manager's 'in a meeting', where's the other attendee? There's also a monitor, a numerical key-pad, an outdated conference-call unit, and an empty stainless steel safety deposit box...on its side on the desk...as if it's been emptied in a hurry...?

Masson stares hard at the motionless Bank Manager. The man's expression is neutral, betraying nothing but mild concern at the unexplained intrusion. If there's nothing here upon which to hang a shred of conjecture, then the Inspecteur hasn't a leg to stand on. He's just about to show his ID and begin apologising for his mistake, when the Manager reaches behind him with such affected nonchalance it instantly reawakens every instinctive alarm in Masson's ringing head. The guy gropes for and grips the doorknob, giving it as firm a surreptitious yank as possible to ensure it's shut…and the Inspecteur's eagle-eyes observe the fingers trembling…

Does the man possess the perennially-sallow complexion of the office worker, or is he turning unnaturally pale for a reason?

"Do you have an appointment, sir?"

Masson strides into the centre of the room, which brings the Manager forward, fussily attempting to usher him back out into the bank's main foyer before he gets any closer to the rear door, "If you don't have an appointment, I'll have to ask you to wait outside. One of my staff will be happy to assist with your enquiry – "

"Police." The briefest flash of the ID, gone as quickly as it appeared – the French Tricolore having no jurisdiction here. Fortunately, Benoit's legitimate ID monopolises the Manager's horrified attention long enough for Masson to dart behind him and reach the security door, shoving it firmly with both hands. It doesn't budge.

Flabbergasted, the Manager scuttles back to Masson's side, yabbering, "That door leads to a restricted area! Security-cleared staff only! This is a *bank*! You can't just barge in here! I need to know what this is all about!"

Masson ignores him completely, casting about in desperation. He recalls the bank staff going in and out of a similar door behind the main counter. All wore ID cards at their belts, which they swiped through a reader to release the door.

Masson glances behind him, makes brief eye-contact with the delighted-looking Benoit, who's evidently enjoying himself immensely, and takes another long look at the safety deposit box on the table. The way it's sitting is completely out of place with everything else in this controlled and tidy room. It's just been emptied, and dumped.

Masson's made up his mind. That counter clerk had seen Rivers and Pickford before. He'd *reacted* to those photographs; Masson hadn't been imagining it. The Bank Manager's veneer of calm is similarly evaporating under gentle pressure. This is worth the knuckle-rapping he might have to endure later if he's got it all wrong...because he *hasn't*. Something's going on here, and it's going on behind this door.

Before the surprised Manager can either protest or react, Masson reaches out a long arm and snatches at the card on the man's belt. He yanks the retractable cord, and clumsily swipes the card through the mechanism. The light beeps from red to green, and the locks release with audible clunks. Masson lets go of the card, which snaps back onto the Manager's thigh like a pinged elastic band, making him yelp. Masson doesn't hesitate. He yanks open the unlocked door, and shoots out into the corridor beyond. There's a bitter smell of over-roasted coffee and inefficient town drainage. Opposite, a shoe-box sized kitchen. To his right, further security doors requiring swipe card entry. To his left, the murkier end of the corridor. The furthest two fluorescent strip-lights have blown, but the Fire Exit sign is clearly illuminated, bright green in the stuffy gloom. By law, if the bank's open, so must the Fire Exit be. Footsteps scrape on the tiles right behind him. He whirls. It's Benoit. He hisses, pointing aggressively, "Check that end of the corridor – and don't let that slimy bastard Müller out of your sight. Make him let you into all those rooms, and don't let anyone touch that safety deposit box on the table! I want it dusted for prints. There's something going on here, Benoit. Get some help. I'll be right back."

He sprints down to the end of the corridor, smacking the release-bar, and bursting out into a narrow alley. Commercial rubbish bins stand in lines behind the café to his right. Parked cars are squeezed nose-to-tail, with barely enough room to slide between them. A grubby bumper leaves a smear of dirt across the knees of his trousers as he edges past. To his left, he can see that the alley opens onto the town square; into the main flow of traffic perambulating around the war memorial like a miniature *Arc de Triomphe*. The right leads back the way they've come, towards the hotel – and there's already someone watching that.

Masson therefore pelts left as fast as his long legs will carry him. He slips on a squashed pastry mashed between the corner cobbles outside the bakers, and skids straight off the narrow pavement, shooting uncontrollably out onto the road in front of a cyclist; who swerves, swears, and is so busy waving his fist at the stumbling Inspecteur they're both almost hit by a lurching transit van, who speeds past with his hand on the hooter and his furious face filling the driver's window. Masson staggers backwards against the safety of the shop front, perching on the baker's windowsill, heart hammering, trying to catch his breath. Recovering somewhat, his head tracks busily from left to right. Lunchtime is approaching. The main square is filling up. There's no sign of them. Had he *really* expected there to be?

Masson rubs a hand across his hot face, and pushes wearily to his feet, schlepping back up the alley with his head down, mentally preparing himself for the barrage of ridicule to come.

Images crowd into his overwrought mind. The obstructive bank clerk, the shifty manager, the coffee for two on the meeting room table; that incongruous, suspicious safety-deposit box...

He stops short in the alley, fumbling in his jacket for his mobile 'phone, dialling swiftly, "Rochat? Masson. Anything? No...well, I think Benoit and I are onto something at the bank. It's all very fishy; I need you up here! I need sufficient clout to get a look at their CCTV for the last hour, and someone with the requisite authority to grill them 'til they wet themselves...and *please* tell me there are some traffic cameras in this town?"

THIRTY-TWO

Benoit's enjoying himself in the bank's tiny kitchen, exacting his revenge upon the obstructive clerk who'd made him look such a toothless fool.

The Bank Manager's in his office, watched closely by a uniformed policeman, apprehensively waiting his turn with the intense young interrogator. They've already viewed the last hour of camera footage; Benoit sliding open the incriminating drawer in the filing cabinet, scrutinising its contents, and raising reproachful eyes to the red-faced Müller. At this rate, the mortified Manager will be lucky to keep his job, and he knows it. His terror of disciplinary action is working wonders in loosening his tongue. Rochat's content to leave Benoit getting to grips with matters at the bank, while he hot foots it up to the Town Hall with Masson. The frantic Frenchman attacks the wide stairs at a gallop, beating the tubbier Rochat to the third-floor office where the town Traffic Management cameras are housed. In a stuffy, equipment-crammed room, the guy on duty wiggles a joystick like a teenage gamer, and the morning footage from the square reverses at speed, comical figures scuttling jerkily backwards as vehicles whizz the wrong way. Time stops just after 12pm as instructed, and runs forward again, while the two senior investigators lean in, holding their breath.

Nothing notable occurs.

Pedestrians pass.

Traffic rumbles by.

A taxi pulls up in a waiting area opposite the tram stop.

Rochat's just muttering to the controller to spool it on, when a movement to the right makes him pause. He glances at Masson, who hasn't taken his eyes off the opening to the narrow alleyway, "Is that – ?"

"Yep!"

A tiny woman, darting out, huge canvas bag over her shoulder and clutched tight to her body. She scuttles left up the street to the taxi, opening the door, leaning in, turning back to urgently beckon the giant who lumbers unhurriedly after her. The vehicle indicates, and pulls out into the flow of traffic circling the memorial like a merry-go-round. Masson grips the shoulder of the camera operator, making him jump, "We need to follow that taxi! Can you do that?"

The young man glances up nervously, "Only around the centre of town...?"

Masson exhales theatrically-Mediterranean exasperation, whirls to face Rochat, throws up his arms, and demands, "Then how are we supposed to tell where they've *gone*?"

Rochat shrugs apologetically, shaking his head. Masson's opening his mouth to vocally express his frustration, when Rochat's 'phone unexpectedly rings. He holds up a hand to pause Masson's outburst, walks a few paces away, clamps the handset to his head, and jams the opposite index finger into his uncovered ear, drowning out the noise of buzzing machinery, ringing telephones, and crackling radio communications.

Suddenly, he's waving the 'phone illustratively, and scurrying for the door, agitatedly beckoning Masson after him, "It's Benoit. The woman asked the Bank Manager to organise them a *flight*! She *specifically* instructed him to book it under the bank's authority, *not* to give names, and to request the pilots begin fuelling and pre-flight checks *immediately*, so they'd be well underway with preparations by the time she got there…"

"There…where?"

Benoit's on speaker, his tinny voice distorted by the echoing staircase as both men pelt down to the street again, "Local airfield, sir."

Masson's eyes narrow. He glares at Rochat, hissing, "Your boy said there'd been no bookings up there!"

Rochat admirably defends his man. Masson knows he'd do the same, and the Swiss goes up in his estimation as a result, "And there *hadn't* been – until about forty minutes ago – and not under the names you gave, either!"

Masson acknowledges this with a conciliatory nod, and calls to Benoit, "Why did he do it? He must've known it was dodgy!"

Benoit's voice crackles back, bubbling with glee, "Because she gave him thirty-thousand francs, sir! Straight out of her safety-deposit box! It's all on camera. He can't spill his guts fast enough!"

Rochat asks, "Destination of the flight, Benoit?"

"The guy says Northern France."

Masson shakes his head, "She *can't* be going back to France! That's against all reason, given what they've just been through to get out of there. He's got to be lying, Benoit. He might've been instructed to play for time; thirty-thousand francs upfront, and another thirty later for a job well done? Keep the pressure on him. We've *got* to discover the true destination."

Benoit's voice hesitates minutely on the other end of the line, "He's...nearly blubbing, sir! I think he's telling the truth...as he knows it, anyway. I'll keep on him, see if I can push him any further."

They burst out into the street, rapidly powering the few hundred yards towards the police station. Masson puffs, "How quickly can we get out to that airfield?" He glances at his watch, "By my reckoning, we could be as much as thirty minutes behind them by now!"

Rochat beams, and breaks into a clearly-unaccustomed jog, "With 'the blues' on...fifteen minutes...? Maybe less!"

Encouraged, Masson grins and begins to run too, long-legged stride easily catching and outstripping his Swiss counterpart, "If we get shifting, they might still be in the Departure Lounge! Come *on*!"

****

"Messieurs-Dames, Bonjour. Bienvenue à l'aéroport – "

Tammi cuts off the long-winded greeting with a brisk, British, "Yes, yes, very nice. Good afternoon. Do you speak English?"

"Of course, Madame."

"Splendid!" She peeks inside the padded envelope, withdraws two British passports, and hands them to the man seated behind the main desk in the small Terminal building, with its steel pillars and smoked-glass windows, "Mr and Mrs Lester. I believe Mr Müller,

Branch Manager of the bank in town, called ahead on our behalf to pre-book an *extremely* urgent flight?"

"Ah, yes Madame...Les-ter..."

Blue eyes flick from the identification pages in the back of their passports, to the two expectant faces before him, "He did not give me your names...but he was very specific that you would be flying immediately to Strasbourg. The payment he made has gone through. Here is your receipt."

He points out onto a tarmac pad adjacent to the building, "That is your plane there, Madame...Monsieur...the Cessna Citation. The crew have fuelling and pre-flight checks underway."

"Excellent! All paid. Plane ready. Can we just proceed then?"

"You must both pass through security, Madame, including the body scanner...and also your...er...luggage..." he gestures nervously to the canvas bag, "must be put through the x-ray machine."

He returns the passports, which immediately vanish back into the padded envelope clamped under Tammi's armpit. She stands on tiptoe to lean further across the chest-high counter, "There is just *one* alteration..."

"Madame?"

She whispers, "I need the flight plan changed as a matter of urgency."

"You need...what?"

"We won't be flying to France this afternoon after all. Our itinerary has unexpectedly changed. You'll be taking us to Austria. Innsbruck will be most satisfactory."

"Um...Madame...preparations are already underway as per Monsieur Müller's very precise instructions! It's most irregular to alter a flight plan moments before take-off – "

Tammi smiles sweetly, swings the canvas carrier off her shoulder, and dumps it onto the counter between them. She doesn't know where the cameras are, so doesn't open the bag wide. Instead, she directs her gaze very pointedly downward, inviting the check-in clerk to do the same. She subtley parts the straps. The Swiss Francs sit in tidily-stacked bundles of five thousand each. They fill the whole, bulging bag almost to the brim. The man inhales sharply at the sight of them.

Tammi purrs, "Irregular to change the flight plan, but not impossible, right? Particularly when *only* you, I, and the pilots are *ever* going to know about it...?"

The man's head lifts. They make eye-contact. Without missing a beat, he states politely, "If you can both kindly progress to your left, through passport check and security for your *Strasbourg* flight, I will personally confirm all...um...*relevant* details with the Captain."

Still smiling, Tammi releases the straps of the bag, allowing the man to lift it gently off the counter onto the floor, foot sliding it surreptitiously into the shadows beneath his side of the desk.

Transaction complete, Tammi murmurs, "Quick as you can, please. We're on a schedule I suspect is tightening by the minute."

****

"Doesn't this thing go any faster?"

The driver glances in the rearview mirror, catching the eye of the Kommisar sitting in the back, who minutely inclines his head towards the impatient French visitor, and winks conspiratorially.

The driver firmly replies, "Not on these narrow, winding roads, sir. I'm sorry."

Masson grunts powerless acceptance, but still sits as far forward in the seat as he's able, clenched fingers clamped over his own knees, feet pushing down as if he wants to force them through the floor pan to add his own long-legged momentum to the police car's speed. He can't criticise. The specially-trained cop demonstrably knows what he's doing. The vehicle makes swift, neat overtakes despite the snaking mountain roads – flashing lights and blaring siren clearing their path with suitable Swiss efficiency.

Rochat's 'phone rings. He answers, listens intently for a few seconds, expresses thanks, and cuts the call.

"Well?"

"Dubarron, back at base. He got the license plate of the taxi off the traffic camera. They called the company, who confirmed the pickup booked by the bank, and the drop-off at the airfield less than twenty minutes ago, 'cos the driver's just been in touch on the radio for his next booking. They're here...somewhere..."

Masson clenches his fists in triumph, unable to stop himself whining, "How much further?"

The other uniformed policeman in the passenger seat points, "We're here, sir."

They swing through the entrance. The second car they've mobilised is metres behind. The lead driver slows slightly, "Some direction, sir? Where are we going?"

Rochat's at a loss. This is Masson's scent to follow. The Frenchman unhesitatingly barks, "Terminal building!", and the vehicles leap forward again. As they speed down the approach road, other cars pull in to allow them past, amazed faces gaping from the windows as they shoot by. To the left are rows of hangars, and a huge concrete area lined with parked light aircraft, neatly angled nose-first, amongst which little service vehicles scud. The herringbone symmetry is occasionally broken by the larger bulk of an executive jet.

To the right is the runway, running parallel with the approach road, behind high chain-link fencing topped by three rows of razor wire. The other side of the fence, the stretch of mown grass is criss-crossed with lights and signs.

Rochat's 'phone rings again. Benoit this time; on speaker, rattling out facts almost faster than he can breathe, "Strasbourg! They're flying to Strasbourg! The bank paid! All within the commission charged to move – get this – *forty million* Sterling into a private account! He's not legally obliged to tell us where unless we have a court-approved warrant...and even then it has to go through his Head Office, have their confidentiality agreement rescinded, and he needs to be given written authorisation to release the information to us. 'Bank policy', apparently. It's a joke! All that could take forever, because the banks make too much money from commission on this kind of crap to scare off their minted customers with even the tiniest intimation their money might be traceable, and – "

"Yeah. By the time the court's granted the authorisation and the right people have put their signatures in the correct boxes, the cash has already gone somewhere else. Bounce, bounce, bounce, around the world, three steps ahead of you all the time. Offshore banking…" Masson shakes his head contemptuously, "Should be outlawed!"

Rochat whistles, "Forty million, eh? No wonder she was so keen to get here and claim it. Stolen, do you think?"

"I'm pretty certain, but I've got no proof. I think it's been pinched from the British Government. Inside job."

Rochat gapes at him, "No wonder your Commissioner sent you here! It's political dynamite!"

Masson smiles wanly, "Only if we can prove it…and I've got nothing concrete to hang a prosecution on. I need those two in custody. Without them, it's case closed. She's the key!"

"What about him?"

"He's the one with family connections to the British Government. He's the fast-track route to the money, but she's pulling the strings."

The police car's braking sharply, swinging up beside the main door to the Terminal, siren still wailing.

"I'll do it! I've got the right ID! You get searching!" Rochat's yelling over his shoulder, already out of the car and thundering into the building brandishing his warrant card. Masson instructs the driver, "Stay here! Turn around, keep the engine running and your eyes open. We might need to move at speed."

"Yes, sir."

Masson clambers from the back of the small car, all gangly limbs and the clumsiness of haste, rushing down to the second vehicle, fumbling the photographs of Rivers and Pickford from his jacket and shoving them at the passenger, "Whip around the site here – every parking area, inbetween all those little planes back there. Don't overlook anything! Those two aren't necessarily flying anywhere. They could be picking up a vehicle here, or meeting someone. The whole 'booking a flight' thing could be a massive decoy to keep us looking the wrong way while they sneak out right under our noses. Keep your eyes peeled!"

The car's already turning. The officer in the passenger seat gives a brief salute to Masson through his open window, "We've got it, sir." He holds up the photographs, "If they're hiding out here, we'll find them."

"Be careful. They're both dangerous."

The officer nods, and the car surges away down the access road to the hangars.

Masson's abruptly left alone beside the runway fence. With no jurisdiction to throw his weight around in a foreign country, he has to rely on Rochat. He feels useless, needing to *do* something; the urgency of the chase still surging within him...but he can't arrest anyone; can't question anyone. He flails restlessly, momentarily distracted by a smart, white Cessna jet taxiing to its runway position. A sharp cry turns his head. It's Rochat, crashing out of the Terminal no less chaotically than he tumbled in. He tugs a resisting airport employee after him by the elbow, the young man's face whiter than his neatly-pressed shirt. One of the police officers is instantly out of the car and at Rochat's side, grabbing his prisoner. Rochat's other fist holds a familiar-looking canvas bag aloft. By now, the Kommisar's leaping like the Fool in a Tudor masque, pointing frantically at the runway, and waving the bag like a madman.

Masson's guts thud into his boots as he realises he doesn't need to hear the words to understand what Rochat's saying.

"No, no, no, no, no...." He yells at Rochat, "Radio the Control Tower!" not realising the gusting wind is snatching the sound from his lips and blowing it over his shoulder. He sprints towards the police car, the driver anticipating his need and racing forward to meet him, braking sharply and allowing him to dive inside, "Get on that runway!"

The driver says nothing, but rams the car into gear and roars off towards the service road, Masson gripping the dashboard with one hand while he fumbles his seatbelt on with the other.

"What do you want me to do, sir?"

"Stop that fucking plane!"

Masson rolls down the passenger window and sticks his head out, screaming, "Police! Move the barrier! Move the barrier NOW!" to the astonished operative manning the security booth, who only just lifts the metal bar in time. Already, the whining roar of turbines is building as the Cessna throttles up powerfully for take-off.

The police car screams along, the little vehicle tiny on the wide expanse meant only for planes. Although the driver's got his foot to the floor as they squeal onto the runway, the aircraft's acceleration is phenomenal, shooting away from them down the tarmac as if they're standing still. The backdraft causes the car to sway alarmingly, the driver swearing under his breath; correcting, and powering on. Already, Masson can see the Cessna's nose lifting, and daylight appearing between landing gear and runway. They're not even halfway down the concrete strip before the jet is airborne, sunlight glinting off the bright, white fuselage as it climbs with effortless grace into the cloudless July sky.

THIRTY-THREE

Listless; unimpressed by anything, she moons about the house, dissatisfied with décor, weather, surroundings, food… It's been this way for months now. Evidently, all that glitters is not gold. There's something missing, and it's not material.

He watches her restless passage across the deck, unsure whether the primary emotion it evokes is amusement or concern, eventually asking a question he already knows the answer to.

"What's up?"

"I'm *bored*…"

He chuckles, stands, picks up his wallet, 'phone, keys, "I know you are."

She frowns, "Where are you going?"

"Fishing."

"What?"

****

Simon Fanshawe's in trouble. He needs to give his inconvenient mistress two hundred and fifty thousand by the end of next month, or she's going to tell Olivia about the baby. She's threatening to turn up at the house once it's born and *show* her!

Olivia desperately wants children – and has done for six years – but so far nothing's happened. In a twisted way, it's comforting to have his virility confirmed. Somehow, it's better if their barren union is her fault, rather than his. It improves his self-image. Unfortunately, proven potency aside, it's certainly not currently enhancing any other aspect of his complicated life.

Stacey – that poisonous little gold-digger – had started off asking for fifty thousand. When he'd laughed in her face, genuinely thinking she was joking, she'd stood her ground and doubled-down: one hundred thousand. He'd determinedly ignored that too; had her moved from his department to another floor – a 'lateral promotion'; prayed it would go away. Of course, this kind of problem never does. Now, with two months to go, she's demanding two hundred and fifty thousand to maintain her silence both at work, and – equally crucially – at home... He's damned if he's being blackmailed into paying a cheap little tart a quarter of a mill just to cover up a misguided fumble in the stationery cupboard! Anyway, he hasn't got it. Olivia's the money. He's spent the past fifteen years congratulating himself on the most astute of marriages...and now this! Providentially, his wizened old dragon of a mother-in-law mercifully expired during the most recent cold snap, leaving Olivia her substantial Suffolk lodge in several acres...but his wife's digging in her heels over a possible sale. She's harbouring some romantic notion of them leaving London for a bucolic East Anglian idyll – probably pinning her hopes on this stirring her unresponsive ovaries into life. Barmy! Especially when selling up would solve his most pressing problem in a heartbeat. That's why they're here, ostensibly to give Olivia a break from the year she's had – losing her mother (not a moment too soon in Simon's opinion), and the attendant stresses of tying the loose ends of the estate – but really so he's got time to work on her without distraction; persuading her the last thing they need is an expensive holiday home in a looming recession. When he'd announced they were going away, for three weeks, and to five-star Tahitian luxury, she'd almost popped with delight. She didn't know he'd put it on a credit card. If he could convince her to sell, paying for this holiday wouldn't matter. *None* of it would matter. But, now they're here, he's struggling to find the right words to broach the subject. Meanwhile, the due date ticks ever closer, and the pressure mounts.

Just when he's starting to consider possible defeat – that he just needs to come clean to Olivia and face the consequences – Simon Fanshawe has a spot of unaccountable luck. He gets chatting to a chap in the hotel bar. Broad, tall, tanned, affable...possessed of the charming attribute of always buying the drinks, he doesn't appear to be a hotel guest, but seems familiar to the bar staff, and quite a fixture of the late-evening drinking set. A couple of hours of light-hearted smalltalk on the stranger's side, and determined boasting on Simon's, leads to the throwaway suggestion of a 'low-stakes' poker game – 'just for fun'. Simon doesn't mind poker. He and some workmates play sometimes...but 'low stakes' to Simon Fanshawe means saving all his five-pence pieces, and tossing them carelessly onto the green tablecloth in Dave Wilton's stuffy conservatory. There's never more than twenty quid on the table at one time...but that's surburbia, and this is fantasia. 'Low stakes' for his ebullient new chum is a grand a call – and Simon has to play along, because he's spent the last two hours talking himself into this corner. Fortunately, though his new mate's terrible at cards, he's nevertheless possessed of an unquenchable enthusiasm for the excitement of the flutter, which the elated Simon calculates sees him about twelve thousand up for a week's acquaintance! Maintain it, and he could have half of what Stacey's demanding by the time this cripplingly-expensive holiday is over – *and* be able to clear the unwise credit card debt without Olivia ever finding out!

A few evenings in the raucous party-bar, a profitable game a night, a good dose of booze and banter…and, to Simon's surprise, it seems their newest acquaintance has also made an impression on his normally-reserved wife too. As Simon cleans his teeth in their water-bungalow bathroom, she's calling to him from the other room, "You know Robin Lester…?"

He pads to the door, toothbrush jammed in one corner of his mouth, "What about him?"

"He told me last night his wife's name is Marian. Don't you think that's rather funny?"

Uninterested in this pointless nugget, Simon wanders back to the basin. She trails after him to the bathroom doorway, untangling her long locks with languid strokes of the hairbrush. He spits minty foam into the basin, swills it away with a scoop of water, and rubs his mouth on the towel, "How so?"

"Robin and Marian. Quite sweet really, isn't it? Meant to be, I mean."

Simon squints at her in oafish incomprehension. She rolls her eyes, and explains testily, "Robin Hood and Maid Marian? You know, the outlaw! Take from the rich and give to the needy…?"

"I see…"

"He said they laughed about it when they first met."

"…Oh, did they…? Simon's barely listening, picking forensically through the fruit basket like a monkey on a nature documentary. Her words gradually sink in, prompting him to blurt, "I didn't know he *was* married! I haven't seen her. He's always in the bar on his own. Are they even *staying* in the hotel?"

"No…they live in a villa the other side of the headland."

"How do you know this?"

"He *told* me!"

"When?"

"Last night, when we were all talking! After dinner. Once you two had finished playing cards and come inside to join the rest of us."

"In the bar?"

"Yes!"

"I didn't notice you talking to him in the bar…?"

Olivia's expression is odd; prim and judgemental. She drawls drily, "No…doubtless you didn't. You were too busy stroking all the money you'd won."

His cheeks flush. He vaguely remembers them all sitting and chatting in the bar until late…although the nights are already beginning to merge into one long, debauched kaleidoscope of cocktails and cash. He *had* noticed Olivia doing that light, tinkly laugh she adopts at parties when she's getting squiffy and flirtatious. He can't recall Robin Lester even being there once their card game finished…but he does remember what he'd thought was mere seconds of staring down at the wadge of winnings as he pushed it into his wallet, trying to decide whether it was bad form to elevate the stakes obscenely high in subsequent games, to ensure he made the most he possibly could from his new best friend during their remaining fortnight here.

It strikes him as odd that you'd have a wife across the island, and spend every night of the week with a bunch of drunken holidaymakers you barely knew, "He's a permanent fixture at that bar. Mrs Lester must need escaping from, eh? More Friar Tuck than Maid Marian!"

Pleased with himself, Simon sniggers indulgently. Robin Lester may be brown, and butch, and the life and soul...but clearly possessed of the sort of empty existence that drives him out of his house and into the company of strangers every evening.

Olivia shakes her head authoritatively, confidently in possession of the facts, "No...she's a bit of a numbers genius, actually. Robin told me he'd been able to take early retirement because she'd made an absolute killing playing the money-markets from home! He said she makes so much money amateur-trading, he doesn't have to work *at all* any more...and he evidently doesn't care about money, given the amount he's lost to you over the last few evenings."

She tugs at the forest of hair caught in the bristles of the brush, discards the matted lump into the bin with delicate fingers, and murmurs, "I was thinking...perhaps she'd be the sort of person we might talk to about Mummy's money...? You know, what was in her ISAs and savings accounts?"

Simon pauses in peeling an overripe peach, the juice dripping over his knuckles and onto the plate beneath. What ISAs? What savings accounts? She's never mentioned them before... He can feel the sudden quickening of his heart. Maybe there's a way around this after all?

He feigns unconcern, and asks lightly, "What were you thinking?"

"I thought...perhaps...if we see Robin in the bar tonight...we might, you know...ask him if we could chat to her? Given she seems to have had some success...wouldn't you say?"

****

Lush foliage crowds in upon them as they advance up the stone path, making it impossible to see anything of the house at all beyond the grey-painted front door.

Robin Lester bounds up the shallow steps, and opens the door with his key, stepping inside, holding it open, and beckoning them enthusiastically, calling, "Marian? Marian! Visitors!"

Standing in the cavernous hallway, Olivia grips Simon's wrist in suppressed excitement the moment Lester turns his back. For his part, he's struggling not to pant with the rapid beating of his frantic heart. Their five-star over-water bungalow's got nothing on this palace. Understated luxury assaults the senses from every angle. Expensive furniture is placed with the subtle style you'd expect of a millionaire's island escape. Abstract carvings and immense vases of tropical flowers occupy alcoves with the artless confidence of an interiors photoshoot. Robin troops through the opulence as if he doesn't notice it. It's normal to him. That's a wonderful thing for the Fanshawes to comprehend. It bodes extremely well for this evening's encounter.

"Drinks, you two?"

The gleaming teak floorboards extend seamlessly across the vast expanse of one-level luxury to ultimately surround a long, slim infinity pool at the rear of the property. The lack of division between indoors and out is beguilingly exotic to the English couple, accustomed to their Surrey semi. It's titillating to imagine slipping off the sofa and sliding straight into the cool, still water. The dark-wood roof cantilevers out over the deck, providing shelter from heavy tropical downpours. Beyond the virtually-invisible lip of the pool, the volcanically lush landscape drops away dramatically towards the glittering sea, giving the impression the villa is a treehouse, set high in dense green canopy amongst which birds and insects call incessantly.

Robin doesn't wait for either of them to answer, already at the little outdoor bar in the corner, popping champagne, pressing a cool, fizzing glass into Olivia's trembling hand, and clinking it with his own, "To memorable holidays…and new friends!"

A sound behind them. Robin beams over their heads. The Fanshawes turn as one.

Mrs Marian Lester. Not what either of them expected. Simon had anticipated a plump geek in unflattering stretch-fabric, shovelling crisps and cola, glued to the ticking of stocks across a computer screen. Olivia had envisioned a librarian – all sensible shoes, white legs, and glasses like milk-bottle bottoms; the school swot cranked up to the max. She acknowledges the foolishness of this even as she absorbs the sight of Mrs Lester. Such a charismatic, jovial man as Robin would not remain purely for the money.

Maid Marian is neither a plump computer-nerd nor a stereotypical boffin. She's small and slight, with a mass of frizzy, sun-bleached ringlets tumbling carelessly over narrow shoulders. A deep golden tan contrasts attractively with the long, light blue sundress she wears. Diamonds on ears and fingers catch the setting sun, and reinforce the success that's already evident in her even, white smile, lightly-lined complexion, and effortless style. She's like her husband. With nothing to prove, they don't need to try. They've already made it. It's up to the rest of the world to catch up.

She reproaches Robin gently, "*Darling*! You didn't *say* you were bringing people over...and I look such a *fright*!"

She touches a hand to her hair, as if self-conscious...but nobody's fooled. Everyone here recognises it's a privilege to be in the presence of such greatness, including Marian Lester herself.

She's coming forward, beaming delightedly, shaking hands, "Hello...welcome. I'm Marian. Lovely to meet you..."

Impatient with the formalities, Robin gestures with his glass, and cuts to the chase, "Simon and Olivia Fanshawe. New chums of mine. They've got a little inheritance they want to invest. Told 'em they should absolutely talk to you...get some advice."

Mrs Lester smiles broadly, "How interesting! Have you all eaten? I was just making some dinner..." She winks at Olivia, "Don't know about yours, but mine always comes home when he's hungry."

Olivia's caught between hopeless enchantment with the lavish glamour of absolutely everything, and the conventional politeness of the English middle-class, "We don't want to intrude..."

"Nonsense! You *must* stay and spend the evening. We can organise you a cab back to the hotel later. That way, we can have a lovely, relaxing chat...and discuss what options are open to you for long-term investment."

Simon scoffs, "Long-term? There's a recession on the horizon, you know!"

Marian Lester cuts him off with a self-satisfied smirk, pointing out to sea, "Sit here...watch the clouds. Spend enough time doing it, and you'll learn what the sky looks like when it's about to rain. Wise investment is just the same as that. Learn the climate of your market, and keep an eye out for approaching storms. I'm not saying you'll never lose – life's a gamble, after all...but if you're vigilant, the wins will more than cancel those out." Here, she glances across at her grinning husband, "I'd say we're living proof of that."

She claps her hands together, "Anyway, enough shop-talk! Are you in Finance, Simon?"

Gruffly, "Recruitment."

"Aha...a psychologist, eh?" She nudges Simon playfully, a close physical encounter that makes him grin despite himself, "So *lovely* to have some evening company! You two sit here, polish off that champers, dangle your feet in the water...and I'll just go and check the dinner. Won't be a tick. Darling, can you carry some things through for me?"

In the kitchen, Tammi raises an eyebrow, and Marc fills in the gaps in a breathless whisper, "Ridiculous people, completely out of their depth. They live in *Staines*, for God's sake! Get the impression the cash is hers, not his. She's inherited a Suffolk farmhouse on seventeen acres, which she's adamant they're holding onto as a family home, and he's equally insistent he'll talk her into selling – "

"What do we want with a poxy cottage in Suffolk?"

"Nothing! It's not the property…although that might come into play if you can persuade her to sell it…but, it sounds like there's several hundred thou sloshing around in half-arsed, low-return tax relief accounts. I've had to lose a few grand to him at poker to get him to trust me. Don't you dare tell me I've wasted my time."

"*Had* to lose…?"

Marc smirks, "To get him thinking he was cleverer than me!"

"Everyone's cleverer than you, Marc."

He chuckles, "Maybe…but they're not cleverer than *you*, are they?"

Tammi cups his grey-stubbled cheeks in both her little hands, "What's brought this on?"

He sighs expressively, "You were fading away, Tam. The quiet life evidently doesn't suit you. Too many Sudokus, not enough *real* calculation."

Tammi smiles wide, stroking a gentle thumb around the curve of his ear, "'Fishing', eh?"

Marc Pickford slides his big hands around her waist, and draws her close to him, "Hook, line, and sinker."

Tammi giggles, wrapping her skinny arms around his neck, and pressing her lips to his ear, breathing, "Do you know, Mr Pickford, I think the old team's finally back in business…"

Printed in Great Britain
by Amazon